D0292063

BY KATE HOPE DAY

If, Then

In the Quick

IN
THE
QUICK

IN THE QUICK

A NOVEL

KATE HOPE DAY

RANDOM HOUSE
NEW YORK

Copyright © 2021 by Kate Hope Day

Published in the United States by Random House, an imprint and division of Penguin Random House LLC, New York.

RANDOM HOUSE and the HOUSE colophon are registered trademarks of Penguin Random House LLC.

Hardback ISBN 9780525511250
Ebook ISBN 9780525511267

Printed in Canada on acid-free paper

randomhousebooks.com

9 8 7 6 5 4 3 2 1

First Edition

Book design by Alexis Capitini

For Bennett and Sullivan

QUICK, ADJ.

1. Moving at a high speed: *as quick as lightning*
2. Fast in understanding, thinking, or learning. Mentally agile: *a quick mind*
3. Reacting to stimuli immediately and intensely: *quick-tempered*

QUICK, N.

1. Characterized by the presence of life. Living persons: *the quick and the dead*
2. The tender flesh of the living body, esp. under the nails: *nails bitten down to the quick*
3. Informally, as by astronauts: the final minutes of life before total oxygen deprivation: *in the quick*

1

Space is cruel to the human body. We aren't machines, rockets with metal skin and polymer bones, rovers with microchips for guts. Our bodies are full of fluid and soft tissue. We aren't built for space. Our thoughts, the things we know, are sturdier in zero gravity, but they originate in gray matter. They change shape, even disappear in the face of disorientation, dehydration, oxygen deprivation. Because ideas require bodies too, hands, lips, a tongue, ears. Otherwise they're about as useful as dust motes drifting in the air.

When I was twelve years old and watched test rockets spark through the sky outside my aunt Regina's house, I imagined their destinations—perfectly round planets colored red and pink and white. I pictured spacesuits, puffy and bright against a black expanse. It didn't occur to me to think about the bodies inside those suits, the brains inside those helmets.

Not until a frozen day in November when the news came that the *Inquiry* explorer was in trouble. It was on a six-year mission, the first of its kind, to travel farther in our solar system than any manned mission had gone before. *Inquiry* was special; more than a decade of research at the National Space Program had gone into building the explorer, and it was manned by four of the most talented astronauts in the world.

It was a Saturday, late morning. I sat in the window seat in the living room with a book on my lap: *New History of Energy*. A chapter was devoted to my uncle and his famous fuel cell. The book smelled like him—like metal shavings and pen ink. Since he'd died I'd read the chapter at least twenty times.

I turned a page. Outside, rockets launched from the NSP campus lit up the hard gray sky. The sound of the TV came from the living room; a man was talking about *Inquiry*. I went into the hallway to listen and my limbs went cold. The explorer had lost all propulsion control just as it was beginning its orbit around Saturn.

The newscaster lowered his voice and began talking about the minutes leading up to when the explorer lost power. He said its fuel cells were suspected. But that couldn't be right because my uncle had invented those cells. I moved closer, my stomach a heavy weight. He didn't say anything more about the cells. Instead he talked about the *Inquiry* crew, and I grew impatient because I already knew everything about them, where they grew up, how old they were, what they had studied in school. If they had siblings and how many. Their hobbies and what they liked to read—I could tell you every detail.

The newscaster began reading from a statement issued from NSP. They were in constant communication with *Inquiry,* it said, and were working around the clock to troubleshoot the suspected fuel cell malfunction. *Inquiry* had recently received an unmanned supply capsule, the second of twelve scheduled to reach it at six-month intervals, and had ample food and water and an open line of communication with Earth. NSP was confident a solution was imminent. The crew were not in any immediate danger and had been in contact with their families. Then the man stopped talking about *Inquiry* and the weather report came on.

I returned to my spot in the window and called the dogs, Reacher and Duster, to come sit with me, but neither came. I felt chilled and stiff, and pulled my sweater to my chin. The words in *New History of Energy* swam on the page. I got up, went into the kitchen, and opened the closet door.

Inside was my aunt's new vacuum, a sleek silver machine with a nozzle like a two-headed snake. I used a knife to disconnect the nozzle, take out the screws, and remove the plates and filters. When I lifted the motor's cover the smell of dust and paper filled my nose. The fan inside was a perfect plastic flower, with curved gray petals and a small red center that made a soft clicking sound when I turned it with my finger. Clockwise, and then counter-clockwise. I imagined that when the flower moved forward I was turning time, that night was falling around me. Everyone was asleep and there was no rush. I could look at all the parts of the vacuum and think about how they could be put together differ-ently, combined with other things and made into something new.

I imagined that when the flower moved backward time re-versed, to before the news about *Inquiry*. To before my uncle died, when he held me in his lap as he typed on his computer or pored over sheets of paper with faint blue pictures on them. I tried to imagine before that, further back than I could actually remem-ber, to before I came to live with my aunt and uncle. Back to when my parents were alive, but the flower didn't go that far.

I let go of the fan and began to untangle the wires coiled un-derneath. I wanted to understand how the suction mechanism worked, to see if it could be reversed. But I should have pulled the vacuum into my room because my cousin John found me before I had finished looking at everything. He called to my aunt, Look what June's done! And I had to push all the parts into the closet and shut the door.

I went back to the window seat, opened my book, and pre-tended I'd never left. But after only a few minutes my aunt Re-gina came into the room. She was wearing a red wool dress with sleeves like upside-down tulips, and her hair was dark and shin-ing.

June? Her voice was sharp.

She pulled the curtains back and saw *New History of Energy* in my lap. She'd told me to leave my uncle's books alone.

There's no point staying in here all day, she said. Go outside with your airplane—

It's too cold.

—or finish your Monopoly game.

John cheats.

Her brown eyes were flat, unyielding.

You know he does, I said.

She pressed her hair back. Well, it's hard to win against you, isn't it?

I didn't care about Monopoly. I wanted to ask her about *Inquiry*.

I'm going to have to pay to have that vacuum serviced, she said.

I can put it back together.

I tried, but—

It's easy.

No, June. It's not.

The window rattled; the spark of a rocket lit up the sky.

It would have been easy for him, I said.

She sighed. She came closer, sat down. Her shoulders bent in her red dress.

What's wrong with *Inquiry*? I tried to ask in an adult way so she would answer.

I don't know.

They say it's Uncle's fault.

But we know that's not true.

Yes.

Because he didn't make mistakes, did he? she said.

She was very close and I could see her charcoal-colored eyelashes, could smell her bright perfume. She studied me like she was looking for something. My eyes, nose, lips. She reached to tug at a knot in my hair, but I pulled my head away.

Your hair's tangled, she said, and stood up. Go get your brush.

2

When my uncle was alive I used to bring him pieces of things, screws and safety pins and button batteries, wires pulled from a broken stereo, tiny white tiles I loosened from the bathroom floor. He would look at them with a serious face and turn them over in his hands. Once I brought him the inside part of a doorknob and he asked me, What does it do? His voice was soft and precise.

I imagined turning a doorknob and then the door swinging open. It moves a small thing so you're able to move a large thing, I said.

Who moves it?

I do. With my hand.

You're providing the energy, and the doorknob the mechanism?

You have to have both, I said.

He smiled. Or it won't work.

Exactly.

Then he opened his desk drawer, brought out some papers, and said, I'll show you something now. The papers had pictures of a box with wires and tubes inside.

These are schematics for a new kind of fuel cell, he said. One that will power an explorer to the edge of our solar system. He spread them out and explained how to read them, how to understand the markings for the cell's dimensions and functions, and decipher the schematics' key.

As he talked the box with the wires and tubes transformed in my mind. It became something solid that worked. I could see its moving parts, could see how it turned one kind of energy into another. How it could power something small, like a light bulb or a fan, and also—with many cells working together—something large like an explorer.

There are only two people in the world who have seen these plans, he said, and winked. You're the third.

Inquiry was the start of NSP's Explorer program and the first of many missions that would travel to the farthest reaches of our solar system—and maybe even beyond it, my uncle said. This trip would take six years, and it would be powered by his fuel cells. But on the day of *Inquiry*'s launch he wasn't there to see it. He was lying in a cold white room on the sixth floor of the veterans' hospital. Everyone was crowded around him. My aunt, my cousin John, my aunt's sister. I stood near the window and craned my neck to the sky.

My aunt and cousin were talking but my uncle was silent and still. Then he said my name softly, June, and everyone drew back. I leaned over his broad, pale face.

His eyes drifted to the window and then to the clock on the wall. The launch is in forty minutes, he said.

I looked at my aunt. She was speaking to her sister.

If you go now you can make it, he said.

My aunt had already said no that morning when I'd asked to go to the launch. She had said, What's more important? Your uncle or a piece of metal?

But now she was occupied with her sister; she was digging in her purse for something to eat for John. I edged past her and looked back at my uncle. His face was white like the sheets but his eyes were dark and bright, and he winked as I ducked quietly into the hall.

I hurried to the elevator and jammed my thumb on the ground-floor button. In the lobby I pushed through the heavy front doors. Outside the air was icy and the ground hard with frost. I circled around the back of the building and cut across a field so my aunt wouldn't see.

The NSP campus was at least a mile away so I stuffed my hands in my coat pockets and ran. My boots crunched through a layer of day-old snow, and the air stung my eyes and nose. After only a few minutes my breath grew quick and tight; a sharp pain pressed against my left rib. My nose ran and the mucus froze on my upper lip. But my uncle's face hovered in my mind and I kept going, tripping more than running for the last quarter mile.

I had only a few minutes to spare when the campus came into view, a cluster of buildings and hangars, dark against the flat gray sky. The airfields were just beyond. I skirted a chain-link fence and ran through a hangar where my footsteps made an echo across its smooth floor. The launch pad was framed by the hangar's open bay door, *Inquiry* a tiny shining capsule atop its massive red-and-white rocket. Everything was so still I wondered for a second if I'd made a mistake. Then a rumble moved through my body; smoke billowed from the bottom of the rocket. I ran into the field—the snow was thicker here and my boots sank before they hit the shaking earth. My eyes were pinned to the small silver shape atop the rocket but I became aware that someone else was standing in the field too.

My uncle's student and protégé James Banovic. He was a few paces away; he wore a large coat but it wasn't buttoned and it flapped open in the cold wind. His dark curls twisted around his angular face.

He turned to look at me and a purple bruise marked his right eye like a half moon. Why are you here? he asked.

Same as you, I said, and he shook his head—he couldn't hear me over the sound. Same as you! I yelled.

He came closer. How is he? he asked.

I thought of my uncle's face against the white sheets of his hospital bed and said okay, even though it wasn't true.

He kicked the snow hard and it seemed like he was going to walk away, but then he didn't. The second-stage rockets fired and I saw his lips move slightly—I think he was counting. I counted too, down from one hundred, and when I reached thirty the air seemed to vibrate against my cheeks, to buffet my body forward and backward. There was the briefest pause, and James's lips stopped and his body went rigid. The rocket shot up and broke the horizon in half and the earth sprang back. I staggered and fell forward as the sky filled with fire and smoke and a beating roar.

He held out a hand and pulled me up—his fingers were freezing. Then he stalked away.

I walked back to the hospital fast with my burning hands pushed deep in my pockets. I wanted to get to a television, to hear what NSP was saying about the launch, and the rendezvous *Inquiry* would make with a supply station in orbit to stock it further for its six-year mission. I wanted to tell my uncle about the launch.

But when I got there his eyes were closed; he was asleep and by the end of that day the doctors said he wasn't going to wake up anymore.

I still collected pieces of things, even though my uncle wasn't there to show them to. For a while I would make little piles on his desk with the idea he might somehow know they were there. His study was the only room that stayed the same in the house. My aunt was always hanging new curtains, changing the light fixtures, rearranging her paintings and photographs on the walls. Even my bedroom had new pillows, a different rug. But my uncle's room didn't change. Its bookcases still bowed with the weight of books and journals. Stacks of paper still teetered on the shiny metal desk and on the floor. His computer still sat by the window, unplugged, its face blank.

Sometimes I would stand outside and worry it would be different when I opened the door. But it never was. The only thing that changed was that my piles of things would disappear. I assumed my aunt threw them out. A few times when I looked inside my aunt was in there, just sitting with her hands flat on my uncle's desk, doing nothing. When that happened I put my roll of twine or burned-out light bulb or handful of hinges back into my pocket and went away.

Eventually I stopped making piles on the desk. But I still collected stuff. I didn't care so much about the things themselves.
But when I picked something up—something that most people
would consider junk, not worth a notice—a crowd of other
things would appear in my mind. I'd sift through them until one
piece joined another in my imagination. Then the pieces would
do something together, some movement or action, and I would
hear my uncle's voice asking, What does it do?

Sometimes I never figured it out, what the movement did,
what it was for. And the idea would fade away. But other times an
answer surfaced and the idea would cohere into something
whole, an invention, so vivid it felt real.

3

I hadn't been in my uncle's study for months. It seemed like I was in trouble every day, and I didn't want my aunt to catch me and yell. But I kept hearing the man's voice on TV, saying the *Inquiry* explorer was in trouble. I kept seeing the faces of the crew.

So when my aunt was out I picked up one of the dogs, Duster, slipped inside the study, and shut the door behind me. I didn't believe the TV report that said the fuel cells were to blame. I'd find my uncle's schematics and study them, and then I'd know for sure.

Whenever I came in here I rarely touched anything. The room was so still, everything exactly as he left it, as if he had stepped out for only a minute and would be right back. It even smelled faintly of him.

I hesitated to move anything, so I walked around the room, just looking and thinking. Behind me the windows rattled as a test rocket streaked through the sky. On the walls were astronomical charts and pictures of planets. Opposite the desk was an artist's rendering of the Pink Planet, glowing pink and white in an expanse of black; it had hung there since I could remember. The Pink Planet wasn't really a planet but a moon, my uncle had taught me, and it wasn't actually pink. The reflection of its atmosphere against the silty haze of its surface only made it appear that way. NSP had established a satellite outpost there the year I was born, and because of that my uncle had always called it June's moon. He used to say it was a bit inscrutable, like me. And then he would laugh and say it was salty too, like me.

Duster whined at the door so I let him out. Then I sat at my uncle's desk and opened a drawer and found pads of paper and mechanical pencils. In the next, extra hard drives, a graphing calculator, and a large magnifying glass. The top-left drawer rattled when I opened it, and it took me a minute to recognize the things inside—my aunt hadn't thrown away my piles after all. Nearly a year had passed since I'd set these items on my uncle's desk. Now they looked old and broken, their magic gone.

I closed the drawer and moved to my uncle's filing cabinets and found indecipherable charts and spreadsheets inside. I opened drawers and riffled through folders. Time passed. The sun went down and the gray sky wrapped itself around the room. Test rockets vibrated behind the glass, and the room turned cold and my fingers stiff.

Then the windows went quiet. It was five o'clock, the silent pause between the day and night launches, when the sky stilled and it felt like the earth was holding its breath.

I kept looking, and finally I found something, a thick folder full of schematics like the one my uncle had shown me. Some of the schematics were more detailed than others, some in color and some not, with pages and pages of calculations attached. Some showed pictures of what the fuel cells looked like in real life, stacked fifty or sixty at a time inside the walls of *Inquiry* and NSP's second and identical explorer, *Endurance.* Encased in thick graphite, they were each about the size of a bread box, and together they generated all the energy *Inquiry* needed for its major systems—propulsion, life support, communication—and also produced an essential by-product, water, used for drinking and for watering the crops in the explorer's grow modules.

The schematics were numbered from one to thirty-two, and studying them in order I could follow the evolution of the cell from inception to completion. I laid them out on the floor in front of the window and read them page by page like a book. At first I focused on how the cell changed, in shape and size and complexity, from one page to the next. Each modification made sense to me, and the final design seemed perfect in every way.

Then I went back and read each sheet more carefully. There

were notes on every page, in my uncle's tidy hand and in other people's too. I could guess whose they were—the team of students who had helped my uncle develop the cell while at Peter Reed, the school named for him on the NSP campus. While most of the engineers at NSP worked with a team of adults, my uncle liked to work largely alone, with only his students as collaborators. When he died he had four research assistants assigned to his lab—and there were four hands in addition to his own on the schematics. One was a bold print that indented the paper, another a lovely loping cursive. Also a dashing script and a print so narrow and neat I had to squint to see it. I guessed the first was James Banovic's, the next Theresa's, and the last two Amelia's and Simon's.

They had come to the house a lot when my uncle was alive, and I saw them when he brought me to work. There was an eight-year age difference between us, but I wanted to be like them and would hang around my uncle's study when they visited for as long as my aunt would allow. James frowned a lot; he and my uncle were always deep in conversation. Theresa was beautiful and commanding. She had a clear, precise voice and a slight accent—she was born in South Africa—and everyone listened when she talked, including my uncle. Amelia was tall and strong and daring, and often impatient with the others. Simon was also tall and very thin. He was careful with his words and always had a book or notebook in his hand, and a pen. While the other three seemed to barely notice me when I hung in the doorway, Simon always nodded and said, Hello June.

Some of their notes on the schematics appeared routine, but others gave me pause. They had used the plans to dialogue about all the ways the cell could be better, how it could be fortified against possible failure once it was installed in *Inquiry* or *Endurance.* That's when it would face the challenges of actual space travel: stress from extreme heat and cold, damage from humidity, deterioration from vibration or air pressure fluctuation, contamination from the chemical components of the air, acidity, basicity . . . on and on until my head swam with the possibilities.

They all had different priorities, things they brought up again and again. But James and Theresa drove the conversation. James wanted the cell to be a closed system, powerful and contained. Theresa didn't agree. She thought the cell should be smart and adaptable—easy to modify on the fly. The dialogue circled back to this dispute on nearly every page. Amelia was usually on James's side. But Simon was more cautious; his comments were reminders that the cell would keep four crew members alive—would keep the four of *them* alive if they won the competition to be *Inquiry*'s first crew.

Threaded through their notes were my uncle's. He didn't take a particular stance one way or another but asked questions, played devil's advocate, suggested alternatives the others might have overlooked. He was optimistic and upbeat; he sounded confident they would come to the end of all their questions and the cell would be a success. Until the last few schematics, when Simon returned to the question of the cell's capacity to function at peak levels over time—not just over days, but months and years. Everyone chimed in, talking back and forth to one another, filling the page with ink. But then they seemed to get stuck. The last few lines were in my uncle's hand at the bottom of the page, where he started to pose a solution. But his answer stopped midthought. I looked through all the pages again but found no continuation.

The sun went down and the room grew dim. I turned on a lamp, got a pen from my uncle's desk, and read the notes again from the beginning. My uncle wrote something on page thirteen, about this question of how the cell might degrade over stretches of time, that could be interpreted two ways. At least that's what I thought. I brought my pen to the paper, hesitated, and listened for footsteps outside the door. All was quiet, inside the house and out. I added one comment, and then another, and my writing filled in the blank spaces between the other hands. Page after page. When I got to the end, to my uncle's unfinished sentence, I completed it. Then I wrote what I thought the others might say in response, and what I might say back.

Then I stopped. I looked hard at the last schematic, at the whole of the fuel cell and the shape of its combined parts. I closed my eyes, and in my mind I made it work. I slowed time down and watched all its parts in slow motion, and then I sped time up and watched it work over days, months, years. And when I did that I saw the problem the notes pointed to, the vulnerability. Every potential difficulty had been addressed by the modifications posed, discussed, and implemented in these pages—except one. Vibration.

When I used to watch the four of them in my uncle's lab in their blue uniforms—James, Theresa, Amelia, and Simon—I never had any doubt they would find all the answers they sought. That the fuel cell would ultimately succeed. But the unfinished dialogue created another story, and this story made me uneasy.

I remembered the last months my uncle was alive, when he was too weak to go to work and his students started showing up at the house. They camped out in his study with the door shut, and my aunt was tasked with keeping me and John away. At dinnertime my aunt would tell them all to leave, but James and Theresa never did. They stayed until late into the night. One morning I looked into my uncle's study and the two of them were asleep on the floor, curled against each other, pieces of paper spread out all around them. That day my uncle couldn't get out of bed—he was having trouble catching his breath—and my aunt yelled at James and Theresa. She told them to go home and not to come back.

Outside the window a test rocket fizzed through the sky. I got up and moved around the room. The fuel cell had gone through many iterations, had been refined and modified. At first this was a matter of making a cell that would function well in the lab. Later it was a process of arming it against the hypothetical scenarios spelled out in the schematics' notations. But maybe that conversation should have kept going—maybe it stopped too soon when my uncle died.

There was something else too. When James, Theresa, Amelia, and Simon wrote these notes they thought they would be the team chosen to be *Inquiry*'s crew. The decision was made between two teams and they had been the favorites. But in the end the team commanded by Anu Sharma had won. Anu's team had helped develop the explorer's communications system and hadn't worked on the fuel cell at all.

The front door opened, and footsteps sounded in the hall. I quickly picked up the schematics, careful to keep them in order, and stood near the door. My aunt was talking to John in the hallway, and I waited for her footsteps to pass. They didn't—they came closer. I ducked behind the desk just as the door opened and revealed the sleeve of my aunt's blue coat, her soft blue glove.

Why's the light on in here? she said and stepped into the room. I could see her shiny black boots, and the hem of her coat floating above the floor. The door closed, and for a second I thought she'd gone, but she hadn't.

Her cheeks were flushed from the cold outside, her hair tied in a complicated knot. She stood still for a minute. Then she walked slowly around the room and touched things. Papers, instruments, the silver handles on the filing cabinet. Her movements were slow, reverent even. She pulled a book from the case and pressed it to her nose.

I made a decision. I would come out from behind the desk and accept my punishment, and then I would ask her for help.

My aunt turned when I stood up. Her eyes were wet, smudged with black. She blinked at me.

I need to ask you something, I said. It's important.

She looked at the papers in my hands and frowned. What do you have—

It's about Uncle's fuel cell—

You went through his things. She pulled the papers from my hands and the pen dropped to the floor. Her mouth twisted. You wrote on his things.

It might help *Inquiry*. I can explain it—

You're twelve years old, she said. Do you know that?

I felt a surge of irritation but tried again. I described the prob-lem with the fuel cell carefully; I spoke slowly and used the right words.

But she held up her hand. Stop talking. She straightened the papers and put them carefully into their folder. She pressed the label on the folder flat once, twice, and tucked the folder under her arm.

You haven't brushed your hair, she said. I told you to do it, and you haven't. Then she put her hand firmly on my shoulder and steered me out of the room.

4

That night I woke at midnight and sat up in bed with a start, my head full of whirrings and scrapings. I had been running it in my mind as I slept, the cell. Slowly at first, it made a soft, familiar hum. Then quicker, moving through time at such a clip, at break-neck speed. Until the hum started to shudder and break.

One of my aunt's paintings on the opposite wall loomed, a white canvas with swaying black lines. In the dim light the lines seemed to tremble like the cell had in my dream. I jumped out of bed, wrapped a blanket around me, and went into the hallway.

My aunt's room was dark. I opened her door a crack and whispered, Aunt Regina? But she didn't answer. I went inside and got close to the bed. Her head was in her hands on the pillow, her forehead smooth. One of the dogs, Reacher, was at the foot of the bed. He stretched out long and grunted. I said my aunt's name again and her dark lashes fluttered but she didn't wake.

I leaned on the bed and looked at the cracks in the ceiling. A hook. An arch. The number fourteen.

My aunt sat straight up. What?

She saw me. Oh June. You scared the— What's the matter now?

Reacher lifted his head.

I can't sleep, I said.

Go back to bed. Sleep will come.

Can I stay?

No.

Just for five minutes.

Reacher shook himself and bits of silky hair momentarily filled the air. He turned once in a circle and lay back down.

She sighed. All right.

Can I sit on the bed?

She moved over and I settled between her and the dog on a white comforter that smelled like down feathers.

She reached to rub her feet and moaned softly. My feet hurt.

Mine do too, I said.

I'm watching the clock, she said, and closed her eyes again.

Did they say anything more about *Inquiry?* I asked.

No. She pulled the comforter around herself.

I don't know why anyone would want to be an astronaut, she said after a minute. They must always be hungry, or cold, or scared. Or all three at once.

I hadn't thought about whether the crew were scared or cold or hungry. I carried their faces around in my mind, but those pictures were smooth and flat. I knew the facts of their lives on Earth and their jobs on the explorer. I knew what they could do, their abilities. But that was just information. Now I thought of them floating inside the compartments of the explorer, with empty stomachs, with cold hands and feet.

Time's up, she said. Back to bed.

I didn't want to go.

If you can't sleep, read a book, she said. Or draw something.

For you?

All right. She laid her head on the pillow again. If you want to.

Back in my room I got some paper and a pen from my desk. In my mind I heard my aunt's soft moan and I drew an invention that would help her. The idea was a wire basket with legs that could climb stairs so she wouldn't have to run up and down them all the time. The drawing was detailed like my uncle's schematics. It showed the invention from different angles, different positions. I hoped it would work. Then my aunt would admire it and say, Thank you June.

Whirrings and scrapings woke me every night that week. But I didn't go back to my aunt's room; I worked on my invention. At night I roamed the house to collect things. Parts from a dryer that didn't work anymore, wiring from a broken remote control car, the telescoping neck of the lamp in my room. Bicycle spokes. Bolts and screws I'd hidden in my dresser drawers.

During the day at school, bored with math lessons I'd already taught myself a year or more ago, I filled sheets of paper with drawings of baskets and mechanical feet. At home I worked close to the TV, even though the reports on *Inquiry* said nothing new. I started to put the things I'd collected together, and then to take them apart and put them together in a different way. I wasn't systematic. I tried one thing and then another until I'd built something that roughly resembled my picture—a haphazard-looking wire basket with metal and silicone feet, and a battery pack screwed to its underside.

To test it I built a makeshift staircase in my room out of old boxes and duct tape and set my invention in front of it. Its articulated metal feet stood flat on the carpet, its basket level with the first step. I pressed the up button on the remote control, and the machine clicked twice and lifted its foot. But the foot only hit the step, *tuc, tuc, tuc,* like it was trying to get through it rather than over it.

Tuc, tuc, tuc.

Tuc, tuc, tuc.

I took it apart and put it back together again. Over and over until it started to look nothing like my drawing, and I didn't know if it was better or worse. I tried five toes instead of three. A high heel instead of a low one. The loops of wire like toenails were a problem, so I replaced them with plastic nobs unscrewed from the bottoms of the dining room chairs. The screws I'd used to fasten the basket to its legs were too short; I switched to bolts.

The basket started to do what it was supposed to do in a very ugly way. It hobbled up the stairs like a person who had half forgotten how to walk. It needed to be faster, smoother. I made it faster. That was easy. But I got stuck on smoother. There was something heavy about the way its metal feet hit the floor. It stomped when I wanted it to half walk, half fly. I drew hundreds of solutions but none of them satisfied me. My mind roamed the house to find better materials, into every room, closet, cupboard. Nothing was right. I was stuck, and I pushed the basket under my bed.

5

I spent the weekend sitting close to the TV. They didn't say anything new about *Inquiry*, just repeated things I'd already heard.
But late in the afternoon on Sunday they started showing old
video recordings of the crew. There was a clip of Anu Sharma,
Inquiry's commander, dismantling an oxygenator in a timed
training exercise. Another of the four of them floating in bright
white suits in a neutral buoyancy tank, part of the underwater
training facility that prepared astronauts for working in zero
gravity. They were secured to the side of a mock explorer, their
tethers like tails behind them. Anu held a wrench in her hand
and waved cheerfully to the camera.

The video made their training look simple. But I knew it
wasn't simple because I'd watched Anu and her crew in that tank
when my uncle was alive. A week before they announced which
team would crew *Inquiry*—James Banovic's or Anu Sharma's—
Anu's team was scheduled for a routine exercise at NSP. I asked
my uncle if we could go and watch, just for a few minutes, and he
agreed.

When we opened the doors to the observation theater, rows
of empty chairs stretched out before us and a deep blue glow
came from the center of the room where the tank stood. In it was
the mock explorer, a replica of *Inquiry*, complete with its arrays,
equipment panels, egress hatch.

Bubbles filled the water as four people in white suits descended into the tank, tether cords twirling behind them. We
watched as they crawled along the side of the station, moving

their harness clips from anchor point to anchor point, and my uncle explained they were practicing a manual rotation of one of the arrays. The exercise was timed—a light on the side of the tank went from blue to green to yellow based on the number of minutes they had left, and it turned red when their time was up.

Anu went first—I knew it was her because of the commander patch on her sleeve—and got into position at the farthest point on the array. Dimitri and Lee followed, tethering themselves at the base of the array, and Missy took up position at a set of controls near the egress hatch. Anu retrieved a tool velcroed to her suit and loosened the hardware on the underside of the array. The light switched from blue to green as Anu, Dimitri, and Lee slowly turned the array.

They're going to finish, no problem, I said to my uncle.

It looks that way.

They secured the array in its new position, replaced their tools, and began to move back to the egress hatch. But halfway there Dimitri's and Lee's tethers became tangled. Anu was behind them—her tether was fine—but she couldn't move past her current anchor point. Dimitri and Lee attempted to untangle themselves, an awkward slow-motion dance of limbs and torsos and helmets. Up, over, around. They seemed to be making the problem worse. Anu gestured. The light switched from green to yellow. She gestured again.

Why don't they just detach themselves? I asked.

Because in open space they would float away, my uncle said.

Dimitri and Lee finally managed to unravel the knot they'd created and they moved toward the hatch. When they reached it the light was still yellow. Anu was behind them, and she went from anchor point to anchor point swiftly and efficiently—but the light turned red before she got there.

She hovered for a moment at the hatch and I pressed my face against the cool glass, trying to discern her expression behind the dull shine of her visor. Then a harness descended into the tank to pull them up and the timer went back to zero.

Will they go again? I asked.

Another team was already descending into the tank.

No, my uncle said. They get their time and they have to make the most of it.

That day I stayed with my uncle in his lab through dinner, and when the sun went down I fell asleep with my head on his desk. I woke sometime close to midnight, my head full of images of the neutral buoyancy tank, its startlingly blue water, its shifting bubbles and glinting arrays.

My uncle was next door testing something in the vacuum chamber—I could see him through the glass. Across the room James and Theresa stood over a long table piled with needle drivers and circuit boards and tangles of cable and wiring. Their voices were low but intense; their heads were bent together.

That won't work, Theresa said.

It will, James said.

You said yourself it wouldn't an hour ago.

Maybe I was wrong—

You're admitting that? Theresa laughed and touched her lips to his.

I felt strange watching them and ducked out of the room—they didn't look up—and made my way to the observation theater. The hallways were dark and empty after the bustle of daytime, the sky a smudgy black as I walked across the catwalk between the research complex and the NSP training facility.

The theater was lit only with the blue glow from the tank. My eyes adjusted as I moved toward it. It was so quiet. The water was clear, the shape of the mock explorer distinct and still. It seemed to take up more of the tank than it had earlier in the day. Its hull made a long shadow; its arrays and antennae stretched and refracted light from above.

A plume of bubbles appeared and I jumped back from the glass. Three suits descended into the water. One of them had a commander's patch—it was Anu. She landed at the egress hatch and tethered herself to an anchor point. But the other suits were oddly buoyant. I squinted through the bubbles and tried to understand what I was seeing.

The suits were empty. Anu had ahold of their tethers and they floated free. She started to crawl along the explorer and repeat the exercise from earlier in the day. Not actually rotating the array—that was a job requiring more than one person—but replicating all the motions involved.

Step by step, slowly and methodically, she simulated the actions of the manual rotation, dragging the empty suits behind her, and as she went she adapted the placement of the tether anchors. She clipped them in place and then unclipped them. Looped them around an antenna, above an equipment panel. Clip, unclip, clip.

I saw what she was doing and followed along. I walked right and then left inside the theater. I even motioned when I saw the correct way to place the anchors at the base of the array—but then remembered the glass was only one-way.

Once she found the best positioning, the best order, she didn't stop. She repeated the motions involved, over and over. Three times, five. Ten. She kept going. Finally she stopped. I counted twelve times she'd gone through the full circuit before she unhooked herself and the empty suits and rose slowly to the surface.

6

When the last video clip of the *Inquiry* crew ended I got up from the floor and went to my bedroom. I pulled my invention out from under my bed, took it apart, and laid all the pieces on the carpet. Then I reconstructed it, slowly this time. I scrutinized each step, each choice. I changed the length of the toes slightly. The height of the heel by a quarter of an inch. The tilt of the basket by an eighth.

I thought of the loping hop of the dogs as they ran up the stairs, and of the abstract painting that hung in my room—the airy lift of the black lines. Their seeming weightlessness. That was what I wanted to create, how I wanted my basket to move, and it was uncomfortable, this gap between my idea and the thing I'd made.

Early the next morning before my aunt and John were awake I roamed the house opening closets and drawers and cabinets. I picked things up and considered them and then put them down. A wire whisk was too thin. A blade from a table fan was too wide. Then I remembered a toy my uncle had made for John, a helicopter kept in a glass case in his room. Its propeller was exactly right.

I went into John's bedroom and the work was done in minutes. I put the toy, now missing its elegant metal blades, back in the case and installed the propeller in my walking basket. When I was done my invention looked like a bird with two tails. I tried it on the cardboard stairs. Better. I tightened some screws. And again—the best yet. I went out into the hallway, to the bottom of the staircase, and set it carefully on the hardwood floor. I pressed the button on my remote control and the feet started to move, slowly at first, and then faster. It climbed one step, and then another. The propeller gained speed, and the basket bounded up the stairs not like a machine at all but like a living creature.

Then John's footsteps sounded in the hall. I heard my aunt telling him, Wipe your feet for heaven's sake.

John still had his coat on; his nose was red from the cold. What's that?

Something to help Aunt Regina.

My aunt came into the hallway carrying her heavy coat and John's backpack and violin.

I made something for you, I said, and set the basket on the stairs, put a book inside it, and closed its lid. I turned it on and the propeller began to whir. When I pressed the button it bounded up the stairs in five seconds flat.

I beamed, turned the basket around, watched it climb back down.

Very creative, my aunt said, and started hanging things on the coatrack.

It's to help your feet, I said.

But she'd picked up a magazine from the side table and wasn't listening.

John came closer and pointed at the propeller. That's from my helicopter.

It's not.

It is!

It's better like this, I said. It does something now.

John grabbed the basket and twisted hard to get the propeller loose. I tried to pull the basket back but he dropped it before I could. Its feet snapped off; its toes scattered. I blinked tears and grabbed at the pieces.

John looked surprised, and maybe sorry.

The metal dug into my palms, sharp and hot. I ran at him, my head down, my fists out.

June! My aunt dropped the magazine and grabbed me. She pulled me away. June, calm down. The metal in my hands scratched her cheek, but it was an accident. I lunged for John again and he pushed me back. My head hit the banister and pinpricks of light exploded behind my eyes.

7

My aunt told me to go to the bottom basement step and count to one hundred. I didn't want to go but her voice was high and tight. So I climbed down the stairs and didn't cry. The basement was dimly lit and full of shadows, but its damp air was cool against my hot cheeks. I sat on the bottom step; the back of my head throbbed. I pressed my hand to it and when I pulled my hand away there was bright blood.

I'm bleeding, I called upstairs, but no one answered.

Nearby stood an old boiler with a vent like a mouth and I tried not to look at it.

I called again, I'm hurt. I want to come up.

My aunt called back, Count to one hundred.

I started counting. At thirty-two a watery vibration sounded from a wall nearby, an eerie roar that rose and fell. My limbs were full of pins and needles and I had the childish thought that if I turned to run up the stairs the boiler would leap at me.

I looked at it. Wide as a car and taller than my aunt, it seemed to crouch in the shadows, its pipes reaching like arms. But it was only a machine. It was as old as the house, my uncle had told me, and used to heat its rooms with steam before the house was switched to electric and then to geothermal heat. I used to come down here with him—he had a workbench in the far corner that was gone now. The boiler was like a huge pot that simmered, he said, and he drew me a picture of how it worked. I remembered the scratch of his pencil on the paper and the smell of WD-40 and epoxy glue. The basement didn't smell like that anymore; it smelled only of wet concrete.

When he finished the drawing he wondered aloud if he could get the boiler working again, just for fun. It would make a mess and your aunt won't like it, he said. But I bet we could do it if we put our two minds together.

His tools were still down here, locked in a cabinet. I got up from the stair. My head had stopped bleeding. I found a wire hanger forgotten on the floor, twisted it into the shape I needed, and picked the cabinet's lock. The shelves were full of drills and sanders and pliers and screwdrivers, and it smelled like I remembered, like oil and glue and also a whisper of something burnt.

I imagined my uncle standing beside me, his broad face and wispy hair. His wool sweater. In my mind he said, A flashlight, a wrench, and a box of matches. With those things in my hands I turned back to the boiler.

The sun had gone down. The narrow windows at the top of the concrete walls were black and my flashlight made a small yellow circle in the darkness.

Only one way to find out how it works, my uncle's voice said.

Take it apart, I said, and I imagined him nodding and handing me the wrench.

I climbed onto a crate and loosened one of the pipes at the joint, then shined my light inside. There was insulation stuffed in there and I pulled it out. I blew air into the hole and it made a low, vibrating note.

I went from one pipe to the next until they were all clear. I studied the box's metal pressure gauge, unscrewed its cover, pulled out its wiring. Then I put it back the way I found it.

Not much to it, is there? my uncle's voice said.

Will it work?

Let's find out, he said, and I lit my way to a bag of charcoal sitting under the stairs. The boiler's heavy drawer groaned when I opened it. I tipped the charcoal inside, struck a match, and dropped it in. I struck more matches and let them fall into the pile of coal until the coal began to cinder and glow.

I shut the drawer, opened the pressure valves, and flipped the boiler's switch, but nothing happened. I stoked the coals and they glowed orange, but the pressure gauge showed no flicker of movement. I waited several minutes, watching the gauge the whole time; it didn't change.

My aunt called from above, They're talking about *Inquiry* on TV. I dropped the matches and ran upstairs.

In the living room she sat in the dark, the TV flickering blue and green on her face. It's the communications system, she said.

I sat down on the sofa. What about it?

It stopped working. Or the crew's not responding. They aren't sure which.

I watched the screen. What else did they say?

There's nothing we can do about it, she said. We should go to bed.

Outside the dark window flecks of snow were falling. I wanted to say something to make her feel better. But all I could think to say was, I'm sorry I scratched your cheek.

I know you are, she said. She stood, picked up one of the square sofa pillows, shook it out, and left the room.

That night I woke to a hollow clanging in the walls and a low hiss. I stayed very still under the covers as the sound rose, and rose. I thought of the boiler in the basement and exhilaration— and panic—twisted my stomach. I forced myself to sit up and the air was thick like smoke. But it wasn't smoke; it was steam. I felt its warm droplets on my face and hands.

A shout came from John's room. I went into the hallway as he emerged from his bedroom. Damp hair plastered his round face and his cheeks were flushed red. Steamy air billowed through his doorway.

My aunt came out of her room, her eyes unfocused, in a robe printed with blue and green parrots. What on earth? She waved her hand through the steam.

John's pajama pants sagged with moisture. He looked like he had wet himself.

She tried to burn me in my bed! he said.

I did not!

My aunt bent down, gripped my shoulders, lined her face up with mine. What did you do? One of the parrots on her robe had an orange-and-green wing and a beady eye in the center of its small head. I reached out to pinch the tiny black eye, but she grabbed my hand and held it fast. June? Her voice sounded like it might crack in two.

Then—a jolt of sound under our feet. A popping, sparking roar.

My aunt streaked past me to the top of the stairs, the parrots rippling. Get out, get out! She pulled John and me down the stairs, out the front door, and into the freezing night air.

8

We stood in a neighbor's drafty entryway for hours, watching fire trucks and flashing lights from the window. There was only one chair and my aunt sat in it with her arms wrapped around John.

When the firefighters left, we were allowed to go back inside. My aunt went first, and John and I followed, quiet and shivering. We walked through the house slowly, all together in a group. Everything seemed the same, except for the smell of singed wood and something else too, like the time John accidentally melted a plastic spoon in a pan. My aunt touched things, curtains and paintings and lamps and pillows. We kept going and everything seemed all right until we got to the kitchen. The door to the basement was a ragged hole. The walls all around were black, and my aunt cried.

In the morning there was no electricity—the fire had burned the fuse box in the basement. We went to school like normal, but we had to eat cold cereal with milk from a box in the pantry. That afternoon men in gray uniforms came with plastic sheeting and large vacuums with hoses that attached to their truck. They sucked up all the gray cinders in the basement, and the bad smell faded. My aunt sent all her paintings to be cleaned, and then she started washing every pot, plate, cup, and spoon in the house. The next day more people came and replaced the fuse box, rebuilt the basement steps, reframed the doorway, and hung a new door.

My aunt vacuumed every room, aired out all the pillows and blankets, and changed all the sheets. She didn't talk to me. She didn't yell or even tell me I had to stay in my room. She kept at it for three days, until the house smelled like it used to again, like toast and her orchid perfume.

A week after the fire my aunt called me into her bedroom. She sat at her desk with a stack of papers in front of her. She wore a dark blue dress and a gold necklace that hung down like a pendulum. Everything in her room was soft or shiny. A large canvas hung over the bed; it had gray lines that looked like a dancer touching her toes.

Do you like living here June? She looked at the papers on her desk instead of me.

I didn't answer.

She waited.

No, I said softly.

You don't like living with your cousin and having books and toys and nice clothes to wear? She gestured to my cotton tights and new sneakers. And good things to eat?

I said nothing because I didn't care about any of those things.

Do you want to go away to school?

I don't know.

If you went to school you wouldn't see me or your cousin more than three or four times a year. But maybe you wouldn't miss us.

My face turned hot. Would you miss me?

She frowned and shifted the papers on her desk, and her rings glittered in the light from the window. I'd stared at one of them before—an emerald shaped like a cushion that sat cradled in gold—and thought how perfectly the gemstone fit inside the gold prongs, like they were of one piece, like they were made to go together.

The truth is— She ruffled the papers. We needed him to make this family work, and now that he's gone, it doesn't.

I didn't say anything. Snow flecked the windows.

I've made some calls and you can begin at Peter Reed next week.

I'm not old enough.

They're going to make an exception.

I thought about this. A thin layer of snow grew in the window frame.

Why? I asked.

She paused. Because I asked them to.

Because of Uncle. Because I'm his niece.

Yes. She nodded. That too. So it's decided? she asked.

Yes, I said. I'll go.

9

We watched the road, my aunt and me. The bus to the NSP campus was late. It was just after eight o'clock in the morning and there was a hard frost in the air. Above our heads a rocket crackled through the sky and I felt a ripple of excitement because I was going to school where I would learn how they were made. I might even, someday, leave Earth inside a capsule powered by one.

Finally a yellow vehicle appeared at the top of the road. When it stopped my aunt didn't say anything. I was quiet too. She handed me my bag. Then she put her hand on my head. She pulled at the tangles in my hair and sighed. I worried the bus would leave, but I held my body still. I didn't pull away. She combed her fingers through, tugging at the biggest knots until they gave way.

When she let go I climbed the bus's tall steps, lugging my bag ahead of me. I chose a carpeted seat next to the window and pushed my duffel under my feet. Out of the corner of my eye I saw my aunt was still there. But I didn't turn my head. If I did I would cry.

The bus hissed and staggered away, belching exhaust. It moved down the long, straight road. I turned; my aunt was nearly to the door. I watched her, the carpeted seat shuddering against my back. When she reached the front steps, she let her hands loose, and they swung a little at her sides.

The house was gone now; out the window was only gray sky and frozen trees. Inside was just the driver and a sea of empty blue seats. But, no, a person sat a few rows ahead of me. I hadn't noticed him because his blue uniform matched the color of the seats.

The shaking of the bus was horrible, the noise of it worse. There didn't seem to be any heat, and my body felt cold and hot at the same time. My stomach rolled as we went around a bend.

The person stood up and held on to the back of a seat, and I was relieved to see it was my uncle's student Simon. I hadn't seen him in at least a year but he looked the same, tall and thin, with soft wavy hair and a book under his arm. On his sleeve was the insignia of the NSP Explorer program. June, he said. I'm glad to see you.

I'd always liked how he spoke to me, not like he was talking to a kid at all.

Are you going to campus? he asked.

I'm starting school, I said.

He sat down next to me. I didn't mind him being close—he smelled like shampoo and snow—but I wished he wasn't looking at me so intently. My stomach was bad. The smell of the exhaust and the rumbling under my seat made it churn.

Are you all right? he asked.

I nodded.

You're young to be going to Peter Reed.

I know.

We were on the highway now and the road was smoother. My stomach calmed a little.

Feel better?

Yes. Thank you.

We were quiet for a minute.

You'll have Theresa in class, he said. She teaches math—

I think he said this to make me feel better, but I'd always been a little afraid of Theresa so it didn't help.

—and I have shifts at the dive pool. So I'll see you too.

Really?

I'll look at my hours and make sure. Okay?

The heat finally switched on below our feet and blasted our

boots. I let my body soften a little in my seat. He opened his book, *Space Materials Science*. The pages were dense with small text, and bookmarked with a photograph of a woman with cropped dark hair.

Anu, I said. *Inquiry*'s commander.

Yes.

She'll figure it out, I said quickly. What's wrong with *Inquiry*. Right?

Yes. His voice was soft but certain. I think she will.

The bus exited the highway and slowed. I looked out the window at the frosty trees and thought about my uncle's fuel cell schematics. Early that morning I'd searched the house and found them in my aunt's desk drawer. Now they were in the duffel bag at my feet. I could get them out and ask Simon about the cell—

But we were already approaching a large compound and I recognized the familiar outline of the NSP campus. We stopped at a red gate that blocked the road, and the driver waved at a man in a small shed. We traveled down a curved street past sleek modern buildings and bright white hangars, and after an expanse of field dusted with snow we approached three gray buildings, blockish, octagonal.

As we slowed my eye was drawn to the path that ran beside the road. It was etched with something—names. Four or five of them per square of pavement. I tried to read them. Marcus Slinger. Jill Morales. Chris Chambers. Alexi Petrova—

Simon put his book away and stood up. He said, We're nearly there. He walked toward the front of the bus, holding on to the backs of seats as he went. We stopped in front of one of the squat buildings, and I rose and dragged my bag down the aisle and steps and over the names engraved in the pavement below my feet. Henry Feinstein, Lisa Church—

Who are these people? I asked Simon. I pointed a toe at a name, Susanne Waters. Famous astronauts?

No. Just ones that died.

The air was icy against my hands and face.

Simon turned to go but then he stopped and rummaged in his backpack. The food's terrible, he said. He threw a granola bar into the air and I caught it. In case you get hungry.

I pulled my bag to the metal-and-glass door, and when I looked back he was walking away over the frosty, name-covered path.

10

The girls' dormitory at Peter Reed wasn't a real dormitory but an old gymnasium; it smelled of damp concrete and dirty socks. There were rows of beds at one end, and the rest of the cold, echoing room was empty, except for the large photographs of planets and moons that lined the walls.

That first night I laid my suitcase on my bed and found my pajamas—their blue plaid was vivid against the worn gray blanket—and undressed as quickly as I could, shivering. I kept my eyes on the floor as girls changed around me. Their long legs and sock-covered feet shuffled; some hopped up and down. I raised my eyes only once, when I pulled my pajama top over my head. Everyone was older than me—I was twelve and the rest of the girls were at least fourteen. Some of them had breasts like my aunt. Some of them had hair under their arms. A girl nearby frowned at me and I looked away. I got under the thin covers. The lights above were bright and I turned onto my side.

On the wall opposite my bed was the same drawing of the Pink Planet that hung in my uncle's office. It was strange to see it in this unfamiliar place, the circle of rose-colored light that glowed in the midst of darkness. It had always made me feel better, looking at it. But this time it didn't. This time the inky black seemed more like the ocean than the sky, and the Pink Planet itself—June's moon—like a ship lost at sea.

A few girls pulled out books and started to read, and others sat together and played games. There was the snap of cards, whispering, laughter, someone blowing her nose. And then the repetition of these sounds, down and down and down the long room.

Someone called, Ten o'clock! And the lights went out at the end of the room. The girls around me quieted. There were still whispers, but the laughter and card sounds went away. Then the lights above my head went out.

At home my aunt and John would be in bed, the dogs curled up with them. The clock in the hallway would be making its gentle *tac tac tac*. I couldn't make out the drawing of the Pink Planet anymore. The room seemed to grow colder and my teeth chattered. I didn't mean to whimper.

A whisper from nearby: Hey you.

The beds were only a few inches from one another, but I had forgotten this as soon as the lights went out. It seemed I was in the middle of outer space, free floating in the deepest black.

Another whisper: I'll never be able to sleep with you going on like that. Come over here. It's warmer.

Okay.

My eyes had adjusted to the darkness. I could make out one of the lights, a gray cage high above, and the girl who whispered. She had a long face and loose silvery hair.

Come on. I'm Carla. She reached out between our two beds and I did too, and she squeezed my hand, her fingers smooth and warm.

I let one foot touch the icy ground and got into her bed. She had more blankets than I did. Her sheets were rough against my skin but warm; they smelled faintly of flowers. I lay perfectly straight and tried to quiet my trembling body, my tapping teeth. She turned her back to mine.

I'm June, I said.

Put your feet against mine, June.

I did and my shivers eased. I felt the rise and fall of Carla's breathing. Soon it slowed and became shallow. Minutes passed. But for me sleep didn't come. Now I heard the sounds of all the other girls around me. Snores, sniffles, coughs. The creak of someone rolling over. Sighs. I tried to differentiate each sound, to figure out what it was. Who had made it. How far away that girl was. What she looked like, how tall, how heavy. Was her hair tied up or loose? Did she have extra blankets or not?

Carla was very still; I tried not to move because I didn't want to wake her. I became conscious of the sounds my own body was making. The slight whistle of air from my nose, a rumble from my stomach. I'd never thought about the noises my body made. I'd never listened to them.

I wished I didn't have a body. That I was made of air or dust or light. Of nothing at all. To my left my bed was a rumple of gray and white. I wanted to stay with Carla but I'd never slept next to another person and I didn't seem to be able to do it. I crawled back to my bed, my covers freezing to the touch.

11

When I woke everyone was up and moving around. Carla stood at the foot of her bed. Her hair wasn't silvery in the daytime, but plain light brown. She was pulling a sweatshirt over her head, pushing her feet into sneakers and her hands into gloves. Other girls were grabbing running shoes and hats and scarves and gloves too, so I dug my sneakers out of my bag and put them on. I had gloves but no hat. I put my wool coat on.

A bell sounded and everyone hurried to line up at the other end of the long room. I stood behind Carla in line and said, I have to go to the bathroom.

There's no time to go now, she said.

Everyone was moving out the far door and onto a snowy path between two hangars. A woman's voice from the front said, Let's go! Three laps! The group started running all at once and the thumping crunch of fifty girls' feet filled the air. I was jostled and then shoved; I stumbled and ducked out of the way and was immediately left behind. Everyone headed for a track that circled the dormitory. I hurried in that direction, my hands held out in front of me as my feet slipped on the snowy ground. I tried to catch up but the mass of legs and feet and ponytails was already far away. Only a couple of kids straggled behind, one whose ankle was wrapped in a stretchy bandage and another large dark-haired girl with a red face.

A teacher with a puffy blue coat was waving to us from the side of the track—Let's go, let's go!—and I tried to propel my body forward. Ahead of me the horizon bumped and jerked. Beyond a narrow stretch of snowy field was another track, this one fully cleared of snow, with lanes marked in chalk. I slowed to watch a group of men and women in blue uniforms run past—like Simon they had the insignia of the NSP Explorer program on their sleeves. They were fast; I could barely make out their faces. In only a moment they were around the bend and gone, and I forced my legs to start moving again.

My breath came out in big clouds; my thick jacket rubbed against my neck and my underarms. My body turned from too cold to too hot. I took off my gloves and unbuttoned my coat. A sharp pain pressed at the underside of my rib cage, more insistent with each icy inhale. I still had to pee and the pressure in my bladder grew. I managed to pass the girl with the dark hair and red cheeks; the one with the ankle wrap was still ahead of me. Then I felt a trickle of wet down my leg. I stopped and stood perfectly still. I turned around—the teacher was waving at me. Go on! I backtracked slowly to where she stood.

I have to go to the bathroom, I said.

She frowned. All right.

I hurried to the toilets in the dormitory, and when I got back outside everyone was lining up again and moving into another building.

I found Carla in the middle of the line. It still hurt to breathe, and my stomach felt empty and raw. When's breakfast? I asked her.

After math.

I'm starving.

You won't be when you see the food.

Inside, girls split off in different directions and Carla pulled me along with her into a classroom that smelled like dust and dry-erase markers.

I was relieved to sit down at an empty desk, its surface cold under my hot hands. A teacher faced the board and wrote a math problem on a large whiteboard at the front of the room. She had a smooth brown ponytail and the kind of blue uniform Simon and the runners outside wore. She wrote fast with big loping numbers. Even still, girls started calling out before she was finished. None of them raised their hands—they just yelled things. A girl with red hair got up and started scribbling on the board below the equation.

The teacher faced the class—it was my uncle's former student Theresa. I hadn't seen her in at least a year and she was taller, her eyebrows sharper.

Another girl wearing a sports jersey got up from her desk: No, not like that. And she took the marker away from the girl at the board, erased what the first girl wrote, and started again.

I tried to follow what they wrote. I had thought all math was easy, but this was beyond anything I'd encountered at school. I tried to focus on each voice; they were talking over one another, and some of the words they used I didn't understand. A girl with yellow tights jumped up to the board a lot. What she wrote almost always got erased, but she didn't seem to care. The writing on the board grew. Carla drew a shape with numbers at each of its points and Theresa nodded, and it didn't get erased. The next girl worked from what Carla wrote.

Soon a quarter of the board was filled with numbers and symbols. I was able to extrapolate, to some degree, from the math I already knew. I concentrated hard and began to understand Carla's diagram. I even tried to call out an answer, but other girls shouted over me. My answer had been the right one, or one of the right ones, and it was exciting.

The board was nearly half full. The short equation had turned into a tumbling mass of branching lines, the numbers and symbols and diagrams reaching fast like limbs. The girls' voices rushed and stretched too. They pushed against and alongside one another, asserting, correcting, expanding, rephrasing.

I followed the lines of thought for several more minutes. Then my mind snagged on something that had been posed early on but abandoned. I wondered if there was a quicker way—

Theresa took the marker back. She gestured to the board and said, with her slight accent, What do you have to add?

She was asking me.

All the heads turned, and the room went quiet.

I—

My face turned hot. I'm not sure.

She said, A wrong answer's better than no answer at all. She waited, her eyebrows raised, expectant. Nothing?

All but one corner of the board was filled with numbers and diagrams. I could have said something ten minutes ago, even five minutes ago, but now they were past me. My throat tightened. Carla avoided my gaze. Finally she shook her head slightly as if to say, Do not cry.

Girls started calling out answers again, and the writing on the board blurred. I blinked; I looked straight ahead. In another minute the equation was complete. Everyone returned to her seat. Theresa wrote three problems on another board and gave the class directions to complete them on paper.

She approached my desk, put a blank piece of paper and a pencil in front of me. She said, not unkindly, Start at the beginning.

I touched my chest. I'm June, I said.

I know who you are. She tapped Carla on the shoulder and said, Check her work, and Carla shrugged. Okay. Then she walked to the board full of writing and erased everything below the first line.

I picked up the pencil, cold and smooth against my fingers. I wrote the equation at the top of the paper. Around the room everyone had her head down and was focused on her work. I put my head down too. I remembered a lot of what was on the board and started to write from memory. Then I stopped. There was more than one way to solve the problem. I'd solve it faster than the class had and would show Carla and Theresa, and they would be impressed.

I drew a diagram. Then I wrote the equation a different way. The next part came out of what I wrote, easily, and soon I had several lines of computations. But then I stopped. The way I was doing it would take too long and I erased it all. The bell sounded.

The girls brought their papers to the front of the room and made a pile on Theresa's desk. I stayed in my seat. Carla was supposed to check my work and my face burned because my page was blank. But she was talking to another girl, and she walked by me without saying a word.

12

That first day I moved from one class to another, following the schedule someone had pushed into my hands, a sheet of white paper with inky blue room numbers and abbreviations I had to decipher. I got lost twice and sat through half a lecture before I realized I was in the wrong room. Passing from one class to the next I often had to step briefly outside into the frosty air. Snow was falling, quickly and heavily, making thick drifts across the pathway.

I looked for Carla in every class but didn't see her again. In between classes I took out the equation I still hadn't solved, pressed the paper against a chilly wall, and wrote out computations, erased them, and tried again. By afternoon, when I walked into classroom 108, a well-lit space that smelled strongly of melted plastic, all I knew was that I was meant to be here for something called MAT YR 1–2.

In the doorway I waited for someone to tell me what to do. Framed drawings and schematics covered the room's walls. One was an intricate drawing of the agricultural research station on Mars, another a series of sketches of the original Lookout Probe. On the opposite wall I recognized the schematics for the solar fields that stretched in a spiderlike grid across the Pink Planet, fields powered by technology my uncle had developed.

Nearby a group of kids were winding tubing through some sort of plastic bubble; at another table the girl with the yellow tights was operating a whirring sewing machine. In the middle of the room Carla and two boys stood at a table with metal shapes on it. Carla had her hair tied back. She had taken off her shoes and was leaning against the table writing on a pad of paper.

Finally Theresa came into the room. She was still in her blue uniform but now wore a cardigan sweater over it. She asked me, Where are you supposed to be?

I don't have a group—

She waved at Carla. Did you check June's equation?

Carla was turning one of the metal shapes over in her hands. She didn't answer.

Carla, Theresa said again sharply.

I haven't yet.

Well that works out because she'll be joining your group.

I thought Carla would be pleased, but she wasn't.

To observe, Theresa said to me. Her eyebrows pointed. To watch and listen.

Why? I asked.

You've arrived in the middle of the year. She appraised me with her small eyes. It's going to be hard to catch up.

The snow on my shoes was melting. I twisted my cold toes.

So your job is to observe. Don't get in their way. If the group wants to hear from you, they'll ask.

I didn't like it, and she could tell.

Carla's group is working on something special, she said, and her eyebrows softened a little. Try to listen quietly. Try to learn. All right?

At the table Carla was writing again, and a tall boy with a halo of brown hair stood next to her. His long frame seemed to lean toward Carla like a tree. On the other side of the table a shorter kid crossed his arms over his chest and watched me.

There wasn't any room at the table and I waited for Carla to acknowledge me. The tall boy turned first.

I'm supposed to join your group, I said. I looked behind me, hoping Theresa was still there. But she had gone.

How old are you? the short boy asked.

I'm twelve.

You look like you're six.

The other boy reached out his hand and his touch was warm. I'm Lion. Don't mind Nico. He's always in a bad mood.

Lion had stepped away from the table to greet me, and now I could see what was on top of it. Hands—like human hands but not exactly. Six of them. They seemed, at first, to be the same, but upon closer look they had variations. One was simply Styrofoam, two were made of plastic, and three were metal. They differed in size, slightly, and in breadth of fingers. The metal ones were numbered four, five, six.

Lion made room for me at the table.

We have to redo the wrist joint, Nico said. It's catching. He plugged the number-six hand into a battery pack and propped it up on the table.

It was working yesterday, Carla said.

Not really, Lion said. Only for a minute.

Carla flipped a switch on the battery pack and with a soft metal clicking, the hand made a tight fist. Then it stretched its fingers long. But when she moved another switch and the hand rotated to the right, the clicking grew loud and the hand skipped and stuck. It jerked to the right and left but wouldn't rotate back.

We should go back to number five, change out the thumb, Nico said. It will work—

We're going to spend hours to find out it won't, Carla said.

They kept talking. The hands gleamed in the center of the table. I picked one up. It was smooth but not cool to the touch like I thought it would be, like other metal things were—a pair of scissors, a pot, a curtain ring. It was beautiful but seemed oddly weighted.

Why are the fingers so heavy? I asked.

That's the old prototype, number four, Carla said. We fixed that—

Maybe we should go back to number five, Lion said. Changing out the thumb might work.

Carla turned her head. How?

Lion picked up the number-five hand, plugged in the battery pack, flipped a switch. Its wrist rotated without clicking, without getting stuck, but its grip was weak. When he placed a wrench in its grasp, the tool slipped from its fingers and fell to the table with a thunk. He turned the hand off, picked it up, and worked the tip of its thumb backward and forward.

Tell us what you're thinking, Carla said.

Let's just try it, Nico said. See what happens.

Yes let's, I said.

Carla frowned at me and waited for Lion to answer.

Changing the thumb might not improve the grip strength, Lion said finally. But it will change the angle of the thumb relative to the fingers. And maybe that's enough.

Great, let's do it. Nico started to dismantle number five.

Carla pushed the paper and pencil to Lion. Show us what you're thinking— she looked at Nico —and then we can start.

Nico scowled but he stopped what he was doing. The whir of the sewing machine one table over filled the air.

Lion tapped the pencil to the paper and started to draw.

Nico leaned over him. We've been through all that. Skip ahead—

I'm thinking. Is that all right with you?

They argued. Their hands were busy, moving through the air.

My hands rested on the chilly metal table. I wanted to know something—

I have a question, I said.

But nobody was listening.

I grabbed Lion's pencil and gripped it so he would stop. What does it do? I asked.

We're able to get good rotation or good finger grip, Carla said. But not both. That's the problem. Didn't you see?

I let go of the pencil, even though that wasn't what I'd asked.

I'm going to take number five apart, Nico announced.

Fine, Carla said.

Lion went back to his drawing, and Carla and Nico began to

dismantle the hand. They separated the thumb from the palm, fingertips from fingers. Wrist from hand. There was something awful about it, watching the hand become a pile of plates and screws and wires. As they worked they rehashed number five, each step they had taken, each decision they had made.

I looked at their faces instead of the parts of the hand. I tried to follow their words and gestures, to keep ahold of the through line of their thought. I wanted to stay with them and most of me did. But— Part of my brain caught on something. Some bit of the argument that had already passed. My eyes drifted again to the pieces of metal on the table.

In my mind I turned the parts of the hand this way and that. I made some parts larger, some smaller. I blew them up like balloons and shrunk them down like pieces of desiccated fruit. Then I put the shapes back together again in a wrong way, and again in a slightly less wrong way. I moved the fingers in my mind. It was still wrong. But the wrong was close to right—

All the while Lion drew. He didn't join in with Carla and Nico's discussion, but he seemed in a way to be drawing it. Every time their dialogue shifted he added something or erased something or started again. When he was done he had created a hybrid of number five and number six.

Carla and Nico finished dismantling number five, and they pulled Lion's drawing close. They weren't happy about it. They picked up pencils of their own and started adding things and erasing things. Lion talked now, defending what he'd done, relenting on some points, holding firm on others. Watching them I felt part of something exciting and important. And yet my own picture wouldn't go away. My question—What does it do?—wouldn't go away.

You're never going to make a *hand,* I said, louder than I intended.

All three of their faces turned toward me. Carla looked like she had forgotten I was there. Lion's face was a blank, and Nico's brow was furrowed and sweaty.

No shit, Nico said.

You're trying to copy. I turned my wrist in the air. But we're not made of metal. We're made of skin and muscles and bones . . .

The wrong thing—the combined small and large shapes—moved in my mind. My imaginary hand rotated its wrist; it wiggled its fingers.

What would a metal hand do? I asked. It felt like the exact right question.

That's what we're trying to answer, Lion said gently.

No, what I mean is— I struggled. I looked to Carla but she shook her head. She wasn't following. What I mean is what would a *metal* hand do?

Nico threw up his arms.

I wanted them to understand. I wanted to say it again another way, but I couldn't think how. They turned their attention to hand number six; they were talking to one another again.

All around us kids were packing things up, putting tools away. It was the time of day when my aunt would be in the kitchen stirring pots of food. But Carla and Lion and Nico didn't seem aware that everyone else was leaving, that it must be close to dinnertime. I was hungry. Lunch in the cafeteria had been soup that smelled bad. I picked up some small screws that came out of number five's pinkie finger and felt their edges against my palm. Tears prickled at the corners of my eyes and I turned my head to the window so the others wouldn't see. The light was fading and the snow falling fast. I watched the snow; I wiped my eyes with my sleeve.

13

The school day started at six with laps around the track. At seven was subjects—mathematics, physics, chemistry, or biology, depending on the day. There was a short break for breakfast at eight, and then back to subjects. From eleven to twelve was free period, when we wandered around in a yard littered with the shells of discontinued shuttles and jets and even a rusted-out blimp. On Wednesdays and Fridays we had our allotted time at a murky indoor pool inside an echoing and indifferently heated building. That was where we learned the basics of scuba, which would prepare us for more complex training later on in the NSP neutral buoyancy tanks.

On my first day at the dive pool everyone began putting on gear to start the first dive, but I was directed to wait by the equipment cage. In the big pool kids sank quickly into the water. Carla and Lion sat on the edge of the pool; they talked for a minute and then jumped in. The minutes ticked by. I listened to the thrum of the vents overhead, the flapping splash of the divers in the pool. The air was humid and slightly dank.

A voice came from behind me: You ready June?

It was Simon. He pushed a pile of equipment into my arms and led me to a smaller pool. He laid all the equipment out on the pool deck and explained what each thing was and how to put it on.

We went through a series of safety check simulations. I had to repeat these back to him three times, and then I finally got to put my mask on. Once it was secure, its rubber strap tight against the back of my head and pulling slightly at my hair, I pushed my regulator into my mouth, held my breath, and sank into the water.

Hold up, he said. Practice breathing first.

I straightened up and inhaled and exhaled through the regulator for several minutes. It hurt my jaw to keep my mouth secured around the regulator, but other than that it was fine.

All right. Go for it.

I submerged my head, blinked my eyes, turned my face. My line of sight in my mask was narrow. Below me Simon's water shoes were brilliant blue and the bottom of the pool had a crack down the middle that looked like a fishhook. I let out the breath I was holding, bubbles surrounded me, and then I slowly inhaled. It was incredibly loud. Every inhale a rushing roar, every exhale a bubbling whoosh. My breath quickened and started to shake; my limbs were full of pinpricks. Something wasn't right. I was breathing but didn't seem to be getting oxygen. Panic tightened my chest and I pulled myself back up.

Too fast. Simon put his hand on my shoulder and pulled the regulator from my mouth. You're going to hyperventilate.

Breathe from here, he said, and tapped his hand high on his stomach. Low and slow.

I replaced the regulator and lowered my body back into the water. I forced myself to fill up my abdomen with each inhale and empty my lungs fully with each exhale. After ten breaths I came up, and Simon said, Better. But don't bite your regulator.

With each repetition my body calmed. I let my hands float in the water and relaxed my mouth. Then Simon handed me a pair of flippers and threw rings into the pool and I swam to retrieve them. My vision was distorted under water—the rings appeared closer than they actually were, and I kept grabbing for them and missing. But after a few minutes my eyes adapted and I stretched my hands farther and began to gauge the distance right.

There's just enough time to try a real dive before the buses come back to get us, Simon said. He asked me to repeat back to him what he'd taught me about controlled descent and then dug around in the equipment cage to find a wet suit in my size.

It was impossible to put on. I struggled to tug it up my legs but couldn't move the thick, stretchy fabric more than half an inch at a time. I twisted and pulled and began to sweat. I stopped and watched Simon, how he quickly and deftly folded the fabric of his own suit before pushing his limbs inside. I tried to copy him and when he saw me he laughed. Here, he said, and came closer and grabbed my sleeve. His soft hair was hidden under his diving hood and I noticed for the first time how long his eyelashes were. He worked his hand inside my sleeve and pulled my arm through.

We repeated the safety checks I'd learned earlier, and finally sat on the edge of the big pool and put our regulators into our mouths. A few kids stood on the pool deck, but most of them were still under the surface.

We don't need to stay down there long, Simon said, and stretched his arms in front of him. Just a few minutes, and then we'll come up slow. Okay?

We dropped into the water and sank an inch at a time. It was an odd feeling, being in a pool in a wet suit, weightless but with no sensation of the cool water against my skin. My breathing was still loud but I could hear other things too, the glug of Simon's bubbles near my head, the *flup* of a kid swimming past—and in the background, a swaying hum that was the pressure of the water itself against my ears.

Simon made sure he was right in front of me, always in my line of vision, framed by my mask. When I drifted he shifted his body in the water; when my body rotated, he nudged me back upright.

We kept going, down and down. When the pressure in my ears increased, I held my nose and blew like Simon had shown me. I kept my breath low and slow. The pool was surprisingly deep, at least twenty, twenty-five feet. The water grew darker and quieter. Every so often I saw the kick of a fin or bubbles moving upward. I knew there were other divers nearby but it almost felt as if we were alone.

Eventually my feet touched the bottom. Now I could see people clustered on the pool floor. One group was collecting plastic diving rings. Another was untying a heavy box secured to the floor. My breathing was fine; I was doing okay. I rotated my head to expand the narrow field of vision inside my mask. Left, right. But then I looked up; far above me fins splashed and dark bodies moved through the water. What was up seemed like it should be down, and the dimensions of the pool seemed to bend. My stomach turned and pressed against my skin. I clenched my regulator in my teeth and pulled my arms to my chest, and my body began to rotate.

Then Simon's hands were on my shoulders, turning me slowly but firmly upright. My feet touched the bottom again, and I had an overwhelming urge to push myself up, up, as fast as possible to the surface. But I didn't do it. I slowed my breath. All around me kids were still collecting rings; the group at the box had successfully untied it and were dragging it across the pool floor. One of the divers with the box was Nico.

Simon made a hand signal to ask me if I wanted to start our ascent, and I signaled no. Nico and everyone else had been down here for at least forty minutes, and I'd managed only five. I slackened my breath more, emptied my lungs, and slowly filled them. I watched Nico. I wouldn't start my ascent until he did. His group pushed and pulled the box to the other end of the pool and secured it with another set of ropes. Then they turned and swam back to the center. I waited until his group clustered together, dropped weight, and started their ascent. Then I signaled to Simon and we dropped weight too, and slowly—by fractions of an inch at a time—we began to rise.

14

Our cafeteria was in a building with gray concrete floors and long yellow tables. Sometimes there was decent food, and sometimes there wasn't. At lunchtime after my first session at the dive pool the grilled cheese sandwiches were burnt, and only the baked potatoes were edible. I stood in line. Water was trapped in my right ear; I shook my head to the right trying to dislodge it, and then to the left.

At least a hundred kids packed the room. Their voices were a great murmur behind me, and their clacking utensils echoed against the walls. After I got my potato I walked to the table where Carla and Lion and Nico were sitting, along with some other kids I didn't know. I hovered behind Lion. There weren't enough tables. Everyone was already squeezed together on the bench, and I hesitated, holding my tray tightly in my two hands. Then Lion pushed in and everyone groaned. But I was so grateful to sit down I didn't care.

People were complaining about the potatoes. I cut mine open and it steamed. At home my aunt put bits of bacon on top of our potatoes. I didn't have any bacon now, but there was butter. I put a small pat on top and watched it melt.

I wish this was a sandwich, Nico said.

Across the table Carla hadn't touched her food; she was writing on her notepad. Lion was trying to talk to her about going to the airfields on Saturday to watch the test rockets take off. It's an hour walk, tops, he said.

I'd like to go, I said.

I just want to get out of here for a few hours, Lion said. What's wrong with that?

It'll be freezing, Carla said. We should use that time to work on the hand.

A TV bolted to the wall played a news channel. The woman on the screen began talking about *Inquiry* and everyone at the table turned to the TV and went quiet, and the wind buffeted the walls of the building with a *tunk tunk, tunk tunk*. The explorer had been dark for three weeks, the woman said, with no communication from the crew and no definitive proof they were still alive. A task force had been formed by NSP to investigate what happened but they had not yet reported their findings. Then the screen split in half and James Banovic's face appeared. His hair was shorter, his angular face thinner, but other than that he looked the same.

Can you tell us now if a rescue mission is planned and who will crew it? the woman asked him.

A rescue mission would be led by four of NSP's most talented astronauts.

And this mission would utilize NSP's second explorer, *Endurance.*

Correct.

Which means launching not from Earth but from the Pink Planet—

All future explorer missions will take advantage of the optimal launch windows on the Pink Planet.

Is *Endurance* ready?

It is.

And when will the task force make their decision?

His eyes shifted slightly. Soon.

Isn't it true that you yourself were slated to lead the second explorer mission and would be the logical choice to command the rescue?

I can't comment beyond saying there are at least three teams qualified to man *Endurance* and that yes, one of the teams is mine—

Do you think they're still alive? a girl named Brianne asked.

Who knows, Nico said. He stabbed his potato with a fork.

Someone from Peter Reed is commander of that crew, another kid at the table said. He had hair that stuck up on one side and he was in Materials at the same time as us—his group was doing something with microscopes and adhesive tape.

Anu, I said.

A girl from math class, Netty, made a face. Not from the Trainee Group there isn't. It's a crew of four on *Inquiry*, she said. They clean their own toilets. They replace their own light bulbs.

I didn't understand what she meant.

Brianne had eaten her whole potato, skin and all. If they aren't dead already they will be soon, she said.

They're not! I said this loudly and Nico snorted.

They're stuck, Brianne said. They're going in circles—she rotated her spoon slowly through the air—until they either freeze or starve to death.

Carla's sister's going to be on the rescue crew, Lion interrupted. She's going to be its pilot—

We're not supposed to talk about it, Carla said.

Netty looked skeptical. Who's your sister?

Amelia Silva.

I turned in my seat. Amelia Silva was my uncle's student, one of the four who helped to develop the fuel cell. She's your sister? I asked.

You don't have the same last name, Netty prompted.

Half sister, Carla said.

Netty sat back in her chair. If they think they're dead already they're not going to send a rescue crew.

What do you know about it? Nico asked Netty. Your brother works on trash transport—

So does yours!

The bell rang and everyone got up from the table.

My potato was still in front of me. It had gone cold. Do you think they're going to die? I asked.

Only Nico was left at the table to answer. They're going to send *Endurance* after them.

What happens if they don't?

If they're smart enough to fix the problem, he said, they'll live. If they aren't they'll die.

They are smart enough.

He picked up his tray. His potato skin was in shreds. I guess we'll find out.

During study period I looked for Carla and found her on her bed, reading a large textbook. She was wearing a thin T-shirt despite the drafty room, and large headphones over her ears. I had been working on my math equation. I motioned to her, and she glanced at the paper without taking off the headphones.

This is the right answer. Did you copy it?

I figured it out.

You have to show your work.

I did.

She pulled her headphones off. There's ten lines here.

I found a faster way.

She looked at me and frowned. Then she shrugged. Okay.

Wind rattled the walls of the dormitory and little gusts of cold air came from the cracks and corners in the walls. I sat on my bed and wrapped my blanket around my shoulders.

That girl at lunch said we're being trained to clean toilets—

I'm not cleaning any toilets.

But what did she mean?

Carla glanced at my paper one more time and then handed it back. There are two tracks at Peter Reed, she said. Trainee Group and Candidate Group. Candidate is better.

And we're in Trainee?

I won't be for long. We're going to move up, the three of us. Lion and Nico and me. She held up her book, *Physics Today and Tomorrow.* I'm already auditing Candidate Group physics.

We're doing things I already know in physics, I said. Maybe I can switch too—

They only let me sit in because we won the Materials competition last year, she said.

Then I'm glad I'm on your team this year.

She laughed. Then she looked doubtful. You have to pass a fitness test to get into Candidate Group. Most people stay in Trainee.

What kind of fitness test?

You don't have anyone to talk to, do you?

I did. My uncle. But he died.

Her face softened a little. Your uncle who started this school.

I nodded.

My parents are dead too. But I have my brother—he's in year six—and my sister.

Amelia, I said. She used to come to my house. Does she teach here like Theresa?

No. She's in orbit.

Do you get to talk to her?

Sometimes. Not as much as I want.

Is it true she's going to pilot the rescue mission?

Lion shouldn't have said that—

But she is, right?

A strong buffet of wind hit the walls and I flinched.

She shook her head. You're too young to be here, you know. Who sent you?

My aunt.

Did she know what this place was like?

I think so.

Okay June, she said. I'm going back to my book. But you can sit with me if you want. If you stay quiet.

But I had one more thing I wanted to say. Carla, about the hand—

You've only just joined the group. No one expects anything.

I do have an idea.

And it will turn out to be an idea we've already had, she said.

It has to do with— I hesitated, then reached across the space between our two beds and opened my palm —what a hand *is*.

She looked at me.

Take it, I said.

She did and I squeezed. Do you know what I mean?

She turned her head to one side; there was a strange expression on her face. Then she laughed and reached for her headphones. Did you do the extra equations for math? If you haven't you should.

I got my equations out, but I didn't do them. I turned the piece of paper over and drew hands instead. I liked being close to Carla. I wanted to show her my drawings and to ask her what she thought. I wanted to try again to explain what was in my mind. But I didn't. I stayed quiet because she asked me to.

15

Now that I knew about Candidate Group it was all I could think about. Carla and Lion and Nico had already passed the fitness test, but a girl whose bed was near mine told me she had failed it the first time around. She was allowed to take the test again after the holidays, but she was worried about the push-ups and sit-ups. She said she could run the ten miles and do the sixty-minute dive at the pool, but the other things she wasn't so sure about.

I could take the test then too, since I had arrived after the school year began. But I couldn't do any of the things she mentioned. Maybe I could do the dive—I'd managed thirty minutes during my last session at the pool. But the ten miles? I could barely complete two at our morning fitness run.

During the next free period I sought out Lion, who I'd seen running extra laps around the track in the yard during free period. I stood where I could see him go past. The cold pinched my fingers and toes, and I stomped my feet. Rockets sparked and fizzed overhead. I wanted to look at my book, which was about robotics, but I didn't. I waited. Finally Lion appeared and I waved. He ran past me and then ran back.

He stopped in front of me and put his hands on his thighs; his breath made clouds in the air.

I said, I'm not going to pass the Candidate Group fitness test. I'm smaller than everyone else to begin with—

Size isn't what matters. It's strength and endurance.

We watched some kids run by, their sneakers crunching on

the gravel. Lion leaned against the building and stretched his legs. Did you exercise before you came here? Train your body?

I used to throw a stick for my dog Duster.

I don't think that counts.

Can you help me?

You'll have to eat more.

The food is bad—

Yeah. It sucks. You have to choke it down.

I said I'd try, and he said we could start in the morning but I'd have to get up before everyone else. That's what he did, and I should too.

The next day I woke before dawn. The huge room was hushed; all the other girls were still asleep, even Carla, with their blankets pulled up to their chins. The floor was freezing under my socked feet and I dressed quickly.

I met Lion outside the girls' dormitory under a sky that looked like snow. He laughed when he saw me. My coat was puffy with the layers I was wearing underneath—track pants (I'd traded for them with another girl the night before), a long-sleeved shirt, and a thick sweater.

He was wearing thermal underwear under shorts, a hooded sweatshirt with the outline of a shark on it, and a pair of very clean white sneakers. His hands were buried deep in the pocket of his sweatshirt. At least take off the sweater, he said.

I pulled off my sweater and he showed me how to stretch my legs, and I tried to move my body the way he did.

No, your left foot. His breath made a cloud in front of his face. Bend it like this, over your right knee.

I pushed my hair from my face and did what he said but it still wasn't right.

He showed me again.

We did many more stretches, and I saw him suppress a smile when I lost my balance as I reached my arms behind my back like he did.

Finally we were done. This early we can run on the Candidate track, Lion said, and started toward the second track I'd noticed my first morning at Peter Reed. We skirted the stretch of snowy field, and Lion sped up as soon as we reached the pavement—unlike our track it was fully cleared of snow.

My feet smacked the pavement while Lion's barely made any noise at all. Just a soft *sup sup, sup sup.* The cold air burned my throat. My feet felt heavy, irregular. I was already breathing hard.

Up ahead another pair of runners came toward us through the frosty air—Theresa and James. They were wearing blue track pants and sweatshirts with the Explorer program insignia on the sleeves. I drew myself up, tried to get my breathing under control.

Then they were right in front of us, the sound of their feet hitting the pavement steady and rhythmic. Theresa wore a blue fleece headband that covered her forehead and ears, and her ponytail streamed out behind her. The way she ran seemed to be all one fluid motion. James took up more space on the track than she did, and he had a long, lean, powerful stride. His cheeks were red from the cold and it reminded me of the day we stood in the field and watched *Inquiry*'s launch.

They didn't acknowledge us as they ran past. I tried to catch James's eye—I wanted him to remember me. I wanted to ask him about the rescue mission. Lion shifted to the right, off the track to let them go by, and at the last second James turned his head. He had an intense way of looking at people, almost like his gaze was pinning you in place. A memory rose up in my mind—of him standing at my uncle's door, a stack of handwritten computations in his hands. He'd looked at me the same way when I'd told him, My uncle's not here.

Then he had pushed the pages into my hands and said, Tell him I figured it out, okay?

I'd brought the papers inside, sat down on the steps, and tried to read them. I stayed there studying them until the hallway turned dusky and my aunt's paintings threw up strange shadows on the walls, until I managed to decipher the first half of the first page.

I started jogging after James and Theresa. I don't know exactly why, what I intended to do, but for about thirty seconds I matched their pace. My feet hit the ground hard and my arms pumped against my sides.

Lion yelled, What are you doing?

Stop, I called after them, panting, and they slowed and turned around.

I put my hands on my knees. I was breathing hard and my cheeks burned with embarrassment. But I forced myself to stand up straight.

Where are you supposed to be? Theresa asked.

There's a problem with the cell, I said. Isn't there? A degradation due to vibration.

Theresa frowned but James looked at me with interest.

Have you fixed it? I asked.

James seemed like he might answer but Theresa spoke first. You know we can't talk to you about that. You should head back to your dorm.

Endurance and *Inquiry* are identical, I said. If there's cell failure in one—

Lion caught up to me then and pulled me off the track and away from James and Theresa. What were you saying to them? he asked.

I know them.

They're in the middle of training. And we're technically not supposed to be on this track.

A few yards away Theresa bent down to stretch and when she stood up her headband slipped from her ears. James reached to push it back in place, leaning close, and for a moment he hugged her face with his two hands.

I don't want to run anymore, I said to Lion.

All right. We'll lift instead.

I watched James's and Theresa's blue figures become smaller and smaller as they jogged away. I don't want to do that either.

Come on, he said. It'll be fun.

We walked back toward the dormitories and Lion waved me into a building with old glass windows covered in frost. The only light came from two yellow bulbs in the ceiling, and the air was filled with dust motes and smelled like rust and old socks. Gradually my eyes adjusted. The room was full of complicated machines with black metal weights that looked like wheels and thick, taut wires.

Lion's skin was darker in here than it was outside, and his eyes brighter. He showed me the machines crowding the room. Only a few steps separated them and it was a twisting maze to move from one to the next. A few pieces of equipment appeared new and had complex digital displays, but most of them were old.

I wanted to look more closely at a machine that resembled a mechanical butterfly, but Lion said, Come on, let's get started. He waved me to a tall black metal frame with weights threaded onto cables that hung down to the floor. He removed all but one of the weights and showed me how to stand, face toward the metal frame, legs apart, and leaning like a stiff wind blew at my back. And how to hold the handles on the ends of the cables down by my sides.

My eyes strayed to the butterfly machine nearby; it had a panel at its back secured with a line of tiny screws, and I had a small screwdriver in my pocket. I pressed my thumb to its tip and thought of James and Theresa on the track, their cheeks flushed from the cold, and about NSP's two explorers, *Inquiry* and *Endurance*—

Are you paying attention? Lion was pulling the handles up and his arm muscles flexed.

I let go of the screwdriver. Yes.

His face was solemn. He looked like he was concentrating hard, but not in his mind. In his body. Like his brain had left his head, had migrated down his shoulder and into his biceps.

He switched positions, held the cables behind his back with very straight arms, and lifted them behind him up, up. The flex of the muscles in the backs of his arms was slight, but I could still see it. He repositioned himself, moving his feet slightly, tilting his chest an inch forward. He started the movement again, and I could see it more—the bunching up of the muscles under his skin.

It made me think about the hand we were building in Materials lab and how it needed to be like Lion's arm muscles. I saw it in my mind. It curved its fingers; it made a fist. But Lion's muscles were soft, and the hand was hard—

Lion, I've been thinking about the hand.

He stood aside and held out the handles for me. We're not doing that right now, he said. We're doing this.

I took the handles and slowly and shakily brought them to my chest. They had stayed perfectly still and smooth for Lion, as if the cables, his body, and the movement were all part of the same thing. But when I pulled them to my chest, they quivered. They seemed to have a life of their own, and the more I pulled, the more they shook.

Keep going, Lion said. Three more.

The vibrating inside my body got worse. My face was hot, my feet inside my sneakers hotter. I tried to quiet my limbs but I couldn't. I told my muscles to stop shaking, but they wouldn't.

That's what you want, he said. That shaking's good.

I stopped. You didn't shake.

With a heavier weight I would have. That's how you know it's working. The shaking tells you your muscles are learning.

I let the cables fall. My arms felt unsettlingly light. Wobbly, like the bones had turned soft inside them. Lion pointed at another machine, one that worked the leg muscles. He showed me how to sit reclined on its cracked padded seat and push a weighted bar out, out, out with flat feet. Finally we both did twenty squats and twenty lunges. By the time we were done my thighs and bottom ached and I felt unsteady all over. I asked if we were finished lifting, at least for now, and he said it would get easier and we would come back tomorrow.

16

It turned even colder, and the snowdrifts grew tall in the yard. Someone shoveled the walkway between the dormitory and the schoolrooms each day, and as the snow accumulated, the path became an icy tunnel with walls of snow on either side. One night the wind battered the metal walls of the dormitory so brutally it seemed it would knock them down. But I had more blankets now—I had traded my extra socks for them—and Carla beside me who always slept through the noise.

Most days before Materials, Lion and I lifted weights. I learned all the machines and got better. Every few days he added more weight. Most mornings before everyone was up Lion and I ran, sometimes on the track outside the dormitories, if the snow was cleared, and sometimes on the Candidate track. We usually saw one or two Explorer program trainees and sometimes caught a glimpse of Theresa and James and Simon.

I got better—slowly. Sometimes Lion would stop and watch me run.

That's skipping! Not running!

I knew what he meant but didn't know how to fix it.

Move your arms! he yelled the next time I came around. They should move with your legs.

I tried and it was a little better. Less of a shock, less of a PAM PAM every time. I moved my arms and moved my legs and moved my arms.

Better! But elbows in! he yelled. You look like a—

But I was too far away to hear what I looked like. I pulled my elbows in.

I look like a what? I asked, breathing hard, the next time around.

Like a chicken.

I pulled my elbows in more.

He got up and ran after me. He had his hood up and his puff of hair underneath made it look like he was even taller than he actually was. Hey, it's a joke. He smiled and pumped his arms. Just try to match your stride to mine.

But his legs were so long. I couldn't make my short legs go so far, but I tried. I made my stride as long as I could—so long it felt like leaping, so long my legs felt like they might come out of my hip sockets. My legs burned with the effort, and my nose ran, but it worked. My leaps fit just inside his stride.

There you go, Lion said. Now let's speed up!

I was doing well in my classes. In math I was able to follow everything written on the whiteboard. I even went up to the board when prompted by Theresa, and what I wrote didn't get erased. She started giving me extra problem sets so I could catch up on what I'd missed before I arrived at Peter Reed, and I brought the finished work to her office after classes were over. I liked her office. It was a small corner room she shared with James in the faculty building. There were two desks that faced each other and two chairs and a space heater on the floor. Notes and diagrams and schematics covered the walls.

Usually when I showed up Theresa was alone, and she would check my work while I sat in James's chair. She took her time, and afterward she would ask me questions in an exacting way. About why I chose the method I did and the different ways I could have gone about solving the problem. Sometimes I would talk to her about Materials lab and the improvements Carla and Lion and Nico and I were making with the hand. But if our conversation strayed beyond the topic of school—if I tried to ask her about the fuel cell or about *Inquiry* and *Endurance*—she'd gather up my work, hand it back, and tell me she had other things to do.

Sometimes when I arrived I heard two voices behind the door when I knocked. On those days Theresa opened the door by just a crack—through it I could see James leaning over his desk on his elbows, a mess of papers in front of him—and she would ask me to come back another time. One evening I showed up after Materials lab and heard them arguing. Theresa's voice was more insistent than James's, but her words were muddled by what sounded like tears. I was surprised and stepped back from the door. Then I heard my uncle's name, Peter.

We're never going to figure it out without Peter, Theresa said, and her voice cracked.

We'll just keep working, James said. Okay?

At lunch I stayed quiet. I watched Lion and Carla, how they talked to each other and to the other kids at the table. What they laughed at. They laughed at Nico, mostly, who was always doing something weird to his food or making faces or arguing with other kids. But he didn't seem to mind them laughing; he liked it. I tried laughing too, but it felt strange.

In Materials I did what Carla asked me to do. A long line always formed to use the 3D printers, and sometimes we had to wait until the very end of lab to get on a machine. Teams with four or five members would send someone to hold a place in line, and that became my job. I spent so much time in line I got to know the printers, and when they broke down I figured out how to fix them. Eventually, even when I wasn't waiting for a printer, I got called over when one broke down. At first this annoyed Carla, but then Lion figured out we could broker this for more time on the printers for our team, or for spare parts, and then she was pleased.

When I wasn't in line I stood with Carla and Lion and Nico at the table and listened. I was allowed to do small tasks, like searching through the hardware bin for tiny screws and washers or cutting down pieces of metal mesh.

Lion and Nico decided changing the thumb on number five

would improve its grip after all, and eventually they convinced Carla to let them try it. They left me at the table while they went to go trade with another team for the materials they needed, and I picked up the hand. The metal was warm from Carla and Lion and Nico moving its digits and rotating its thumb. I wrapped its fingers and thumb around my own wrist, squeezed, and felt the give of my skin against the hard metal.

What does a hand do? I thought.

I repeated the actions. Open, shut. Unsqueeze, squeeze. Hands are soft, I thought. They change shape based on what we want to do, from one moment to the next. But that kind of softness can't survive in space—

How do you make a metal hand soft?

Melt it. In my mind I softened an imaginary titanium hand. But it was too soft. The hand in my mind turned to liquid, became a puddle.

Cut it so thin it gives to pressure. No, too hard. My imagined hand bent and cracked down the middle.

What then? I said this out loud, and the group at the table next to mine stared.

I squeezed the fingers of the hand around my wrist again, tighter this time. Tight enough that it hurt. Again I saw the hand in my mind blown up large, like a balloon, and then shrunk down small, like a piece of desiccated fruit. Its shriveled fingers made a fist.

What if—

Everyone came back to the table, talking loudly, and Carla asked me to find the hardware they needed to redo the thumb. Go look in the bin, would you?

I still had number five wrapped around my wrist, and the desiccated fist hung in my mind.

Carla's face was impatient.

Lion put his hand on my shoulder. His fingers were warm and firm. June? Did you hear?

Right, I said, and I went to the hardware bin and began digging through it. I didn't know the answer to my question—how do you make a metal hand soft? But I knew there was one. And I knew changing the thumb on number five wasn't it.

I found two of the six washers we needed. Then I went to the supply closet and got a latex glove.

Back at the table Carla and Nico were arguing again.

We're going about it all wrong, I said, and I held up the rubber glove.

Carla raised her eyebrows. Lion cocked his head to one side.

This is the answer. I took the glove and blew air into it and tied it at the wrist. I held it out to Carla, as if to shake hands with her.

It looked silly. I knew that. But I was trying to show them about the blown-up and shrunk-down hand—

Nico started to laugh. And then Carla laughed, and Lion too.

Their laughter wasn't mean.

Lion shook hands with the glove. Nico actually had tears in his eyes. You are a weird one, you know that? he said. But you're all right June. He wiped his eyes.

Carla shook hands with the glove too. When she did that it felt good, like I was wrapped up in something warm. So good I pushed the imaginary hand from my mind.

Now we've had our fun, Carla said, where are my washers?

17

The season slowly changed. Our classrooms were slightly warmer now, and some days the sun shifted between the clouds outside the windows. The snow started to melt and turn to slush, and when Lion and I met during free period to run, it soaked our sneakers. I was able to jog around the track five times without getting winded now.

But I still wasn't very fast, and my stride was still awkward compared to Lion's. One day I said I wanted to watch him and I leaned against a wall. Rockets flared through the sky overhead as I waited for him to come back around the track. When he did there was a rhythm in his stride. *1, 2, 3, 4. 1, 2, 3, 4.* The rhythm seemed to match him—the length of his legs and arms, the bob of his head. I started running again and in my mind I tried to find a beat that matched my legs and arms. Lion's beat was steady like a clock. *1, 2, 3, 4.* Mine was quicker, a scurrying backbeat. *1, 2, 1, 2, 1, 2.* I moved my arms and legs to the numbers, and two of my strides fit inside Lion's one.

Lion turned his head and smiled. You don't look like a chicken anymore, he called.

That night in my dormitory bed, with the sounds of other girls' sighs and sniffles and snores surrounding me, I thought about the hand and my uncle's question, What does it do? I thought about how different things moved different ways and had certain natural rhythms to them. Lion did when he ran. I did too. The hand had a natural way of moving—or it ought to. The group was trying to make the hand move like our hands do, I thought. But it needs to move how it wants to move.

Carla turned over on her side in the bed next to me. Her breathing was soft and slow.

How can a chunk of metal *want?* I asked myself. I recalled my first night at Peter Reed. How Carla reached across our two beds and squeezed my hand. I remembered how I felt the small bones underneath the pads of her fingers, and I thought, It can.

The next morning I went to Theresa's office to talk to her about my idea for the hand. I knocked; the door was ajar and it swung open. James was asleep at his paper-strewn desk, his head in the crook of his arm.

He started and sat up. His curly hair was wild and there were dark circles under his eyes.

What do you want? His voice was gruff; the space heater was on and the room was warm and close.

I'm not here about homework, I said.

I had some sheets of paper I'd drawn on and I held them out.

He didn't take them, so I sat in Theresa's chair and spread them out on top of his desk. I'm trying to figure out how— I paused, but this time the words came easier. How to create adaptive grip in a robotic hand. I kept talking and pointed to my drawings and tried to describe what was in my mind.

He listened and looked at the sheets of paper. He asked me a question and I answered it. He drew on one of my drawings. Like this? he asked.

Yes but— I took the pen from him and drew again.

We went back and forth like this for a minute or two, and then he put the pen down and rubbed his eyes. It's an interesting idea, he said.

I beamed.

There's only one way to find out if it will actually work.

Build it.

Exactly.

I can't do that without permission.

Why not?

Because it's a group project. Because Theresa said I was supposed to watch and learn.

He snorted. It's your idea. Do what you want.

The next day I made a model. I did it alone after everyone from Materials lab had gone. It was a latex glove attached to a simple vacuum pump, and when you squeezed the pump the glove filled with water. The next night I cut up a bunch of silicone-coated gloves and sewed little open compartments inside the fingers. I found a better pump in the supply closet, with a dial that measured the amount of water in milligrams. I filled and emptied the glove, filled and emptied.

My next model was another silicone glove, constructed in the same way but filled with tiny plastic beads I'd found at the back of one of the supply cabinets. They were about the size of a poppy seed and kept spilling. But I managed to fill the pump with them and then watched the beads move into the glove, increasing its volume slowly, slowly. I put a ball into the palm of the glove and watched the glove gently hug it.

It felt good, like I was making the idea I had seen in my mind, turning the blown-up and shrunk-down hand into a solid thing. But the materials I was using wouldn't hold up in the vacuum of open space. And the glove couldn't actually hold the ball—it could only sort of squeeze it. Over the next few days I drew more pictures and dug through the parts bin in Materials lab; I thought about the hand every free second I had.

I went back to James and Theresa's office early in the morning hoping to see James alone. I brought my prototype wrapped carefully in paper under my arm. The door was open, but no one was there. The space heater was off and the room was chilly. I sat down in James's chair, unwrapped my model, and set it in the center of his desk.

That day we had a substitute in math class, a short man with a tie and a beard who wanted us to raise our hands before going up to the board. Theresa was absent the next day too, and Lion and I didn't see her on the Candidate track. We didn't see James or Simon running either. I checked James and Theresa's office again and this time it was locked. I wished I hadn't left my model inside. But I hoped their absence was a good sign and meant the task force had approved the *Inquiry* rescue mission.

I hadn't seen any of them—Theresa, James, or Simon—for two weeks when we got on the bus for our dive time at the pool on a rainy Wednesday. I sat next to Nico on the way and told him my theory about Theresa being gone from class. I wasn't the only one—lots of kids were talking about it, wondering what it meant and hoping it was good news. I asked him what he thought as rain flecked the window, and he actually smiled and said, Maybe.

At the pool I crowded with the other kids around the equipment cage, found a wet suit in my size, and began to pull it on, folding the fabric before pushing my limbs inside. Then I walked to the edge of the pool. Carla and Lion and Nico were already there, and we did our safety checks together, put our regulators in our mouths, and began our descent. Once we reached the bottom I joined a group that was performing the box exercise I'd seen Nico doing during my first dive. I worked with two other kids—a girl whose bed was near mine and a boy who sat next to me in physics—to untie the box from its first location, drag it across the pool floor, and resecure it in a new location. We had some trouble at first; the thick rope wouldn't come loose from the metal rings holding it to the pool floor. Finally we were able to unhook it and begin dragging the box across the slippery floor. We reached the second location and quickly figured out how to retie it. I secured the last restraint and felt a sense of satisfaction as I locked it in place.

When it was time to begin my ascent I paid attention to my depth gauge and timer as Simon had taught me to do and slowly rose from the bottom of the pool up, up, watching the shifting light and splash of flippers on the surface of the water above me.

When I emerged the air was full of noise and commotion.

Someone was screaming. A teacher was hauling something large and dark from the water onto the pool deck. My mask fogged—I pulled it off. The large and dark thing was a person. Whoever it was their limbs were limp and heavy. Kids were yelling, climbing out of the water fast; I got kicked in the stomach, splashed in the face. I swam hard for the edge of the pool. I scanned the pool deck for Carla and Lion and Nico. Nico was climbing out of the water, and Carla was pushing through the crowd. I pulled myself out of the water, my arms and legs humming with adrenaline.

The teacher was yelling, Stand back!

I ducked between two kids. The figure lying prone on the pool deck looked like Lion. It couldn't be him, but there were his long legs, his circle of hair, dark with water, his face. The teacher pulled off his mask and it was him and my limbs went cold.

The teacher blew air through his mouth and his torso expanded like a balloon. She thumped the heels of her hands on his chest. I crawled closer, around kids' bare feet and shower shoes and damp towels that had been dropped to the pool deck. Carla was down on her knees next to Lion, her eyes like dark hollows in her face. Time seemed to bend and stretch. The kids around me were shifting on their feet at a normal speed but the teacher's breaths and thumps seemed to slow. Lion's lips were flat and blue. Carla blinked her eyes once, twice, three times—

Then with a splutter and a start Lion's body seemed to fold in half. Time sped up and bubbles came from his mouth. The teacher pushed him on his side and slapped his back as he coughed and heaved. Spurts of water came out of his mouth, more water than I thought possible. They made puddles on the pool deck, and Carla reached her arms over his body even though the teacher tried to pull her off.

18

The next morning they wouldn't let me see Lion at the infirmary, but I sat so long in the waiting room one of the nurses came out and told me he was going to be okay. You can visit after he does another session in the hyperbaric chamber, she said, and held open the door for me to go.

I wandered the snowy yard and tried not to think about Lion's body lying still on the cold pool deck. His dark wet hair and blue lips. Carla and Nico were walking on the other side of the track, toward a building beyond the dormitories. I caught up to them; they were talking in low voices, their heads together.

I hadn't seen Carla since yesterday at the dive pool, but she barely said hello.

I relayed what the nurse told me about Lion, and Carla said they already knew.

Where are you going? I asked.

You don't need to come with us, she said.

Building 4, Nico said, and put his hood up and kicked a piece of melting snow.

I followed them through a creaking metal door. No one was inside. It was just a big room that smelled like old paint and was filled with computers that made a low hum.

Carla walked to the front of the room and sat down.

It felt colder in here than it did outside.

You know what's going to happen now, Nico said.

What?

Carla's going to wait for her sister Amelia to call, and she won't. Or if she does, she'll talk for two minutes and hang up.

I looked at Carla sitting in front of a computer's blank gray screen.

Maybe she's busy. She has an important job—

She doesn't care about Carla. He walked partway to the front of the room and stood there watching.

Does anyone come in here? I asked.

Not really. There's better equipment in Materials lab. But this is the only place they've got an NSP relay.

Does that mean we can listen to *Inquiry?*

He looked at me. There's nothing to hear.

I sat down at a computer and turned it on. I know. But still—

Well, move over.

He sat down and began typing, and his breath made clouds in front of the screen. After a minute, the sound of static. He turned it up loud.

This is the main communications feed, he said. But there are hundreds of channels I think.

A long list filled the screen. I could figure out the labels of some—SM, GALLEY, GROW MOD, STOWAGE. They linked to different parts of the explorer or to specific systems or equipment. Nico clicked through a few of the channels and they were the same. Nothing but static.

At the front of the room Carla was still waiting. She didn't have her notebook or anything. Her hands were in her lap.

Can we look at the communications log? I asked Nico.

He shrugged and rubbed his hands together. I guess. He pressed a couple of keys and the screen changed. How far back do you want to go?

A couple of weeks before it went dark I guess.

He pulled up the log and we started reading.

It wasn't a back-and-forth conversation but rather a series of questions and reports because there was almost an hour and a half delay between Earth and *Inquiry*'s location.

Up until the week before all communications ceased, there were just checks of vital systems in the morning and a systems update in the afternoon. No changes, no developments. In the evening, a list of duties completed that day, all typical. Until a report of an unusual sound coming from a bank of fuel cells at the starboard side of the explorer. The crew's investigation of the sound was inconclusive. A few days later, another communication; this time it was the cells in the Systems module. They were making the same sound. A humming that was out of the ordinary but didn't seem to indicate any specific problem.

Then a much more serious report: the explorer had lost propulsion control. This communication was followed by eight days of the crew scrambling to understand what was going on. The log showed over a hundred systems checks on the power supply, and three failed attempts to mitigate the problem.

At eight in the morning on the ninth day mission control sent a message about a scheduled test of the water reclaimers, followed by . . . nothing. After an hour and a half control asked for a status update and still got no reply. Two hours later, the same. We scrolled down the page. In between control's increasingly insistent questions there was only white space. No words, no signals, no proof of human beings on the other end of the line.

It's weird to read a one-way conversation, I said.

It is. Nico's voice was sad. I'd never heard him sound like that.

I have these cards with their faces on them, he said. The *Inquiry* crew. Do you have those?

I shook my head.

Everyone wanted to be them, he said. Now everyone's glad they're not.

I thought of Anu floating in the blue water of the NSP neutral buoyancy tank, the white tail of her tether twirling behind her.

They're going to go get them, I said. James and Theresa and Simon and Amelia—

Maybe, Nico said.

A woman's clear voice came from the front of the room and Nico got up and went to sit next to Carla. I stood up too. I hadn't seen Amelia in at least a year but her voice was the same, strong and slightly impatient. She was strapped into a jump seat, and behind her was a jumble of buttons and controls. Her hair was shorter and she seemed larger, but maybe that was the way her body filled up the screen.

Hey, Carla said at the front of the room. Can you see me?

Yeah I see you Carly. What's new? Wait, hold on a second—

Amelia unstrapped herself and turned the screen, showing a narrow compartment beyond. She floated back into view and started doing something. She was changing her clothes, pulling off her shirt and pants.

Amelia, Carla said. It's not just me. Nico's here.

Hi Nico. Amelia was wearing nothing but underwear and a tank top now. She started pumping water onto a washcloth, and beads of liquid sprang into the air, drifted up and sideways.

Where are you? Carla asked.

In orbit.

In orbit where?

Amelia ignored this question. The droplets of water circled her head like a halo. How's school?

Lion got hurt. Carla's voice wavered.

Hurt how?

He was doing a dive and his tank wasn't right. They say he can't come back to class for a week—

If they're not sending him home he'll be okay.

We all use those tanks Amelia—

If inhaling some nitrogen is the worst thing that happens to you in training you'll be lucky. A kid in my year died.

Carla didn't say anything. All the beads of water had drifted away now.

What else is going on?

There's another team in Materials lab. They're working on some kind of adhesive tape. I'm worried they're going to beat us.

So don't let them.

The picture distorted for a second and then went back to normal.

Lion won't be able to help for a while and we're stuck on the wrist—

Amelia scrubbed her face with the washcloth, and her body drifted in the air. I recognized the water pump behind her. My uncle had brought one home once and we'd taken it apart.

Is that a BREE pump? I asked.

Who's that?

Carla sighed. June.

Amelia's face broke into a smile. June Reed. You've gotten bigger. Not by much though.

I moved closer to the computer, leaned across Carla so I could see. That's the third-generation pump, right?

What do you know about it?

I know that if you don't change the filter every seven days, instead of every ten like the manual tells you to, it spits water.

Amelia laughed. Hey, that's true. She clipped her washcloth to the wall and pulled a shirt over her head. Then she floated out of the frame.

Amelia, I said quickly. Can you tell us about the rescue mission? About *Endurance*?

Her voice came from off-screen. Carly, I told you not to talk about that.

Carla glared at me. She shifted her chair so it blocked me from the screen. Amelia, she said. The wrist—

Amelia reappeared and loosely strapped herself into her seat. She still wasn't wearing any pants.

All right, tell me the problem—

A beeping alarm sounded. Someone in a blue uniform

blocked the screen. A man's voice said something I couldn't make out.

Sorry Carly. I've got to go.

You just got on—

Next time, okay? Listen, you might not hear from me for a while.

Why?

I'll call again. Amelia unstrapped herself from her chair, started floating away.

When?

We heard her voice and the man's voice, but all we saw was her empty chair, the restraints waving in the air.

Amelia, Carla called. You haven't hung up—

The voices continued.

Amelia, you're still on!

Her face appeared again. Oops. Then the screen went black.

Carla whipped around. What were you doing, interrupting like that? Her voice got higher. My sister doesn't want to talk about a stupid water pump—

Seemed like she did, Nico said.

Carla's face was furious.

You know your sister's kind of weird, he said.

I don't think she's weird, I said. I think she's—

No one cares what you think, Carla said.

She went outside, and Nico and I followed. A few wet snow-flakes were falling.

Carla walked fast up ahead and Nico caught up to her, leaving me alone on the slippery path. It looked like he was trying to make up with her, to make her laugh. He picked up a handful of snow, packed it into a ball, and gave it to her. He said, loud enough for me to hear, Go for it. Right here. He pointed to his chin.

She threw it right at his head, hard, and he made a big show of wiping the dripping snow from his face. There was a big red spot on his cheek, and Carla laughed. They walked toward the cafeteria together, and didn't look back. I stood still for a minute on the frozen walkway, and then I turned around and went back to Building 4. I sat down at a computer, opened up the *Inquiry* feed, chose a channel at random, and turned it up loud.

19

Every day I listened closely to the news reports about *Inquiry;* every morning I set my tray down on a chilly table in the cafeteria and felt certain today would be the day NSP would announce the rescue mission. But I was always wrong.

I kept returning to Building 4. I'd open up the *Inquiry* communications feed and click through all the recognizable channels, the SM or GALLEY or STOWAGE, and then through some with more inscrutable labels, listed as simply EXT or INT or AUX followed by a number. Occasionally there was a distinct crackle or blip on the line, but when I asked Nico about it he said it was just meaningless interference, caused by any number of things between Earth and NSP's deep-space satellites—a passing station, a random piece of space junk, a natural satellite.

I think I listened to every single channel for at least a few seconds. Each of them was different, and it was sort of fascinating, the contrasts in sound and volume. Some rushed like ocean water; another crunched like car tires on gravel. One sounded exactly like the steady patter of rain.

On the weekends I'd listen to the feed for hours, and certain channels became like old friends, their sounds familiar and comforting. I thought about how each was supposed to connect Earth and *Inquiry,* and a picture formed in my mind of threads that stretched deep into space, like a spacesuit's tether cord but millions of miles long.

Sometimes I listened so long I thought I heard patterns in the feed's seemingly random crackles. But when I told Nico about it, he said I was crazy.

You think you're going to hear something NSP hasn't? He laughed. Dream on.

But I kept listening and started plotting the crackles in a notebook of graph paper. Date, time, length. Pages and pages I filled in. But my system didn't take into account intensity, or sound quality of any kind. I began listening carefully to discern differences in the noises, and after a while I came up with a code for recording each crackle and blip. A letter to denote sound quality, a number to denote length.

On some channels a sound appeared once and then never again. But on others there were little blips I got to know. A high whine, a quick tick, a bubbling hum. A3, E2, F5. On one of the auxiliary channels I regularly heard G1 and H2, which were maybe not two sounds but one because they always came to- gether: a hum of low static and then seven snapping pops.

I kept asking Nico to come and listen, and he finally agreed. Once we were in front of the computer I pulled up the AUX27 channel and played back G1 and H2.

What do you think is causing those sounds? I asked.

It could be a million different things—

They come together every three days, I told him. Approxi- mately every seventy-two hours, give or take a few hours.

His mouth turned up on one side, a slightly crooked smile. I'd only ever seen him smile that way at Carla. Whatever you think you're doing, mission control has already done it, he said. And they found nothing or it would be on the news.

Nico, wait, I said. Can I ask you something?

I've listened to enough static for one day, he said.

The wind rattled the walls of the building. It's about the hand.

What about it—

It's not good enough, is it? Number five.

The thumb helped, he said.

A little.

Yeah. He shrugged. Only a little.

What can we do?

Not much unless you've got a better idea. He grabbed his bag. Then he paused. Do you?

I thought of the blown-up and shrunk-down hand that hung in my mind in Materials lab, and the hand prototype I'd left on James's desk. But I shook my head no. Nico got up and told me he'd see me at dinner, and I stayed and listened to the hums and crackles of the AUX27 channel for a long time.

20

Lion was at breakfast the next morning; he walked slowly and his eyes were tired. I asked him how he was feeling and he said he'd woken up with a bad headache but it was better now. When we all sat down at a table with our cereal and toast I said I wanted to talk about the hand. I started to explain what was in my mind, slowly. I took out the notes I'd made when I was building my hand prototype. But Carla and Lion and Nico weren't paying attention—they were looking at the television. On the screen a woman was talking about *Inquiry.* She said there was going to be an announcement momentarily, and the clank of utensils and the clatter of trays went silent.

The screen cut to a man standing in front of an NSP research building, where my uncle's lab used to be. He said the rescue mission wouldn't be going forward. It was too risky to send another crew after Inquiry when there was no definitive proof the crew were still alive, and when there were serious unanswered questions about the integrity of the fuel cells that powered both *Inquiry* and *Endurance.* He went on, saying that after long and careful consideration NSP was suspending the Explorer program, effective immediately.

I felt a cold sweat on my palms and heard a low buzzing in my ears. All around us, kids were talking loudly.

Lion leaned forward on the bench. June? he said. June are you all right?

I nodded. My head felt oddly separate from my torso. Heavy and unwieldy. Like it was full of sand.

The rest of the day the hallways were oddly subdued. Our teachers gave us work to do at our desks instead of at the white-board. Kids showed up at class late or not at all. When I arrived at Materials lab no one from my group was there. I sat with a girl from the adhesive tape group and two boys who had been work-ing on a flotation device. The girl read a book and the two boys played a computer game, and after a while I got out my math book and did equations.

The next day was strange too. Everyone seemed sad or an-noyed, even the teachers and the women who served us our food. A few girls from my dormitory went home. Carla showed up late to Materials lab, and then she and Nico left early. The short time we were all at the table wasn't the same. Carla, Lion, and Nico didn't talk like they used to. Lion didn't draw and Carla didn't boss us around. Nico didn't argue like he did before.

The next day in the yard I saw Carla walking with Netty and Bri-anne. They passed by the cafeteria and moved into the field.

I caught up to them. The temperature had dropped again and my boots crunched through ice-covered snow. Aren't you sup-posed to be in physics? I asked Carla.

She shrugged and didn't look me in the eye. Netty and Bri-anne walked ahead.

We're going to watch the test launches, Carla said.

The other girls reached a wire fence and climbed over it. Carla hurried after them, and when she got to the fence she started to climb it too.

Can I come? I called after her.

The girls were already several paces away on the other side.

Can you get over the fence? Carla looked doubtful.

I wasn't sure either. But I got over it easily. I hopped down.

We walked for a long time across a field deep with uneven drifts of snow. Our feet punched through to knee height in some places and hit the ground hard in others. The sun came out from behind the clouds for a minute and I blinked. Netty and Brianne were laughing about a boy I didn't know, and Carla laughed too.

The sound of the rockets got louder as we walked and soon the air seemed to vibrate with noise. It wasn't one sound now but a group of different sounds crashing against one another all at once.

We reached another fence. On the other side was more snowy field, but beyond that I could see a group of gray structures. I knew them well—one of them was my uncle's old building. But the other girls stopped once we were over the fence. Netty pulled a blanket from her backpack and spread it on the snow. The sound was tremendous, as if the air itself were being cracked open, over and over. We sat down and looked up, our fingers in our ears. The rockets were so close it felt as if they might fall out of the sky and onto our heads. It was impossible to talk; we screamed a few things at one another and then gave up and just watched.

Then all at once, the sky emptied. A single rocket burned through the sky, its crackling roar fading like a lone firecracker. It was five o'clock, when the launches stopped for an hour. I hadn't realized how much time had passed.

We're late for Materials, I said to Carla.

Netty and Brianne got up from the blanket and started wandering toward the buildings in the distance.

Lion will be wondering where we are, I said. And Nico.

Carla got up from the blanket slowly. She watched the other girls move farther away. All right, let's go, she said.

We walked back. The sky was big and blank above us. The crunch of our boots in the snow was loud.

I asked Carla about physics and about Candidate Group. Didn't she want to move up anymore?

She walked stiffly, hugging her arms to her chest, and told me she'd failed her last physics test. I'm not going to be a Candidate, she said. I don't think I want to be.

But the hand, I said. We could still win—

We won't.

I wanted to say something to make her feel better, but I couldn't think what. They're going to change their minds about the Inquiry rescue mission, I said after a minute. When they find proof the crew are still alive.

You don't understand. Her voice was sharp but her eyes were wet. I'm glad the mission was called off.

Why?

Because I don't want Amelia to die June.

Ahead of us ice-coated snow reflected the blue-gray sky. Beyond that was the dark outline of our school buildings.

I'm not going to be a Candidate either, I said.

Maybe not this year. Only because you're younger than everyone else. But you will next year.

We reached the dormitory and went inside. We took off our coats and gloves, rubbed our hands together.

I don't want to be a Candidate if you aren't, I said.

That's stupid.

It's how I feel.

Carla lay down on her bed and put her headphones on. It's a stupid way to feel.

21

That night I went to the faculty building, my pockets full of tools, and in the silent and dark hallway I picked the lock of James and Theresa's office door and retrieved my hand prototype. The next night I went to the Materials lab and made more durable metal beads with one of the 3D printers.

I sorted through the parts bins for hours until I found some scraps of a thin Kevlar fabric, and the night after that I painstakingly sewed them in the same manner as the silicone glove. Now my hand could survive in space. I had the right materials; I had the ability to expand the volume of my hand with the pump and the metal beads. But the pneumatic hand couldn't make a fist. It couldn't turn its wrist.

I tried different things but none of them worked. I thought and drew and spent half of every night alone in the chilly Materials lab. Until it was the night before our team was going to be judged. I stood in front of the empty table, its metal surface cool against my palms, and asked myself what my uncle would say as the wind gusted against the room's walls.

My prototype was too soft. A hand is soft, and hard.

I got number five out of the locker and set it on the table.

Number five was too hard.

I put my prototype next to it. I knew what I needed to do, but was it right?

I thought of Lion's slower gait around the track since his accident at the dive pool. Nico goofing off in Materials lab instead of working. Carla's wet eyes as we walked back from the airfields.

I took a breath and began to dismantle number five, not the way I'd seen Carla and Nico do it, but all the way. I had to break the wrist where three pieces had been soldered together; I cut open the newly reshaped thumb. When I was done all that was left were the thin metal rods that powered the hand, and the silicone and wire joints that connected the rods. Then I set to work, combining my prototype with the stripped-down number five. I had already combined them in my mind, and it went fast. Then I put a ball into the hand's palm to see if I was right.

When I arrived at Materials lab the next morning, Carla, Lion, and Nico were all standing around the table. They had the hand—my hand—in front of them.

Where is number five? Carla asked.

That is number five.

Nico shook his head. Oh man.

What did you do? Lion asked.

Rain fell outside and it tapped against the windows.

I fixed it, I said. I didn't think it was going to work, but then it did.

Carla picked up the pump and put it back down. Work how?

I'll show you.

I plugged it in and as the hand grasped the ball Carla's face changed. Her brow smoothed.

Why didn't you tell us? Lion asked. We could have helped you.

I tried. But I couldn't explain it even to myself. I just had to *do it.*

She didn't need our help, Carla said evenly. She was better off on her own.

Now we can all be Candidates, I said. I looked at each of them and waited for them to smile.

My sister's like that, Carla said. She says other people's ideas crowd her own.

Did you hear what I said Carla? Now we can all move up—

A teacher approached our table. Theresa's substitute.

What's this? He was surprised. You've made a big change.

The rain grew louder outside. No one said anything.

He asked Carla to demonstrate the hand.

Carla hesitated, but Lion nodded, and she did.

The teacher asked several questions, about the material inside the glove and about the pump.

Whose idea was it to use the beads?

June's, Carla said.

Really? The teacher looked at me for the first time. It's very inventive. He asked us to show him the glove, and Carla did.

Who designed this? the teacher asked.

June, Carla said.

Who sewed all these compartments into the inside?

June, Lion said.

What did the rest of you do?

It's got the internal structure and wiring of one of our prototypes, Lion said. Number five.

I see. He picked the hand up and moved its fingers and thumb. And who combined the two models?

We all did, I said quickly. As a team.

Lion looked at the table, and Carla's cheeks turned pink. The rain had stopped but the wind rattled the walls.

The teacher wrote on his pad for a minute.

Thank you. I'm impressed, he said. You'll know the results in a week. Then he turned from the table to move to another group.

But Carla called out after him, It's not true. June did that too.

22

The day of my first launch was a month after I turned eighteen, in early spring. It was cold and damp, and melting snow covered the ground. When I got to the launch pad I was given my papers and told to wait. I was assigned to be an engineer on the *Sundew*, a cargo station orbiting Earth that distributed supplies to the moon, Mars, and the Pink Planet. As good a post as I could hope for. NSP maintained several cargo stations in orbit, as well as small satellite and research outposts on the moon, Mars, and the Pink Planet, but that was it. The Explorer program had never been revived.

The rest of my crew were already in orbit. Three times I'd requested a post with the only woman station commander in orbit, Carla's sister and my uncle's former student, Amelia Silva. And three times I'd been slated to serve at another post. Then at the last minute my assignment was changed, and not only Amelia's name but also Simon's was listed at the top of my paperwork.

I suited up for the trip to the *Sundew* in a mobile office. Up until that moment I felt fine. Candidate Group had made me stronger. The physical training hardened my body, built me up in some places, and whittled me down in others. My arm and leg muscles grew round; I lost the soft spots on my stomach and thighs. I knew how to do things now—run a mile in seven minutes, do five pull-ups without stopping, hold my breath under water longer than anyone else in my year—and I could count on my body to do them. I also knew things, lots of things. About advanced astrophysics, space materials science, robotics. I'd been trained in survival skills and basic emergency medicine. I knew how to tread water for hours, set a broken bone, stitch up a wound.

But when I saw my suit on the wall—small and shrunken looking on its hook—I hung back. In my uncle's books astronauts wore suits that glowed white against the flat black of open space; they were the brightest things on the page. In the videos I'd watched of astronauts floating in zero gravity, they took up the whole screen, and their arms and legs drifted like leaves on the surface of water. This was what I'd been waiting for my whole life, but now that it was here, I wasn't thinking of the astronauts themselves, strong and full of all the things they knew. I was thinking of the deep and endless expanse they floated in. My hands shook as I took the suit from the wall. I steadied myself, stepped backward into the suit, pulled the neck ring down over my head, and worked my hands through the arms. Then I straightened my ponytail and put my helmet on. I didn't need to be wearing my helmet, not yet, but I wanted to check the pop and suck of its seal.

It was just me, the pilot, and his second-in-command, and we walked, bowlegged and slow, the few yards to an open cage elevator. There was a partitioned area for relatives and friends to say goodbye to crew members who were going into orbit for months at a time. I barely glanced at it. But Lion was there; he was waving at me. He stood wearing a puffy blue coat (he was a trainer in the NSP neutral buoyancy tanks now). I hadn't seen him in months. I swallowed hard and waved back.

When I moved up to Candidate Group I didn't see Carla and Lion and Nico as much. We would talk when we ran into one another in the yard or at the dive pool. For a while Lion and I lifted weights on Saturday mornings. But we didn't have classes together, or Materials lab, and it wasn't the same.

The elevator went up. I held my helmet in my hands and the wind whipped and pulled at my hair. Lion was still standing in the same spot. He put his hood up against the wind. He smiled and kept waving. The elevator rose higher and soon I couldn't see his face anymore, just the spot of blue that was his coat.

At the top the wind was terrific and I held on to the platform as it buffeted my body. The pilot secured the Velcro on my suit, tightening it at my back, elbows, ankles, and wrists, and we crossed a swing arm toward the open hatch of the capsule. The pilot and second-in-command entered first and I followed. Dark and cramped and crammed with supplies, there was only enough space for the three of us to wedge ourselves into our molded plastic seats. I had an advantage being so small, but even still it was a tight squeeze in my suit. I strapped myself in and felt the walls above my head and against my left elbow; I could move only my right arm freely.

The hatch door closed. Minus fifty-four minutes was announced. I grabbed at my checklist but couldn't reach it. I strained against my chest belt and was just able to pull the checklist free. The pilot and his second went through their own lists and called things out to each other in a mix of English and Japanese. The compartment began to warm and I started to sweat. Oxygen was flowing but it didn't feel like it. The air was hot and still. I tried to concentrate on my tasks, but I was intensely aware of the walls pressing against my arms and legs, the lack of air. My eyes strayed to the low ceiling, to the sealed hatch door.

When the high-pitched whine of the fuel and oxidizer turbo pumps filled the small space I felt relief. Ten minutes to launch. I completed the tasks on my list, put on my helmet, locked it, and checked its seal. At two minutes to launch the whine grew. Even with my helmet to dampen the sound. I felt it vibrating through my chest, my jaw.

One minute to launch. Then, ignition. The capsule began to shake; my breath grew hot inside my helmet. Then a thundering came from below, a pent-up roar. The rocket swayed to the left, to the right, as if it would tip over. But it was all right. I'd read about it. My breath got hotter and hotter. We were tipping more and more.

Then—a lift, the loss of supports. A two-second delay—and a terrible spring into the air, like a crouching animal unchained. My body slammed against my seat, my visor fogged, and we were airborne. The second-stage rockets fired, and I was lifted up, my stomach and breasts straining against my harness as we separated from the rocket.

And then—a sudden quiet. The compartment cooled. My body was light. Out the porthole was an expanse of deep velvety black. The rocket's white body slowly fell away, and it was the most singular thing I'd ever seen. We began our first orbit and the pilot deployed the solar arrays and antennae. Things floated through the compartment—dust, slips of fabric, a few bolts. I watched their uneven trajectories, the unexpected arcs they made. My head felt full, my eyeballs huge. But my limbs were like air, like dust.

The pilot floated by. He'd taken off his helmet and he gestured for me to do the same. His face was red—zero gravity had pushed all the blood into his head. He started calling out systems checks to mission control. I took off my helmet and the air was cold on my face. I unstrapped myself, held on to my seat with my hands, and hovered just above it. Then I let go and propelled myself like a fish across the compartment.

The Earth's curved edge was hard and deep blue through the porthole. I remembered my uncle's globe, a plaster sphere painted blue and brown and written all over with small script, held by an arc of metal engraved with the sun and moon and planets. One time he set the globe on the floor and spun it, and we climbed on top of his desk to watch. Its oceans and continents blurred, turning from hard to soft before our eyes.

This is what it's like when you're in orbit, my uncle said. All the world moves fast underneath you, and you feel like you're a thousand feet tall.

Standing there with him, imagining myself in the kind of spacesuit I now wore, I did feel a thousand feet tall. But this wasn't like that at all. There was nothing soft about the ball of blue and white in the porthole, no matter how quickly its stretches of land and sea raced past. I felt the planet's size and force. It seemed to press against the darkness around it, against the porthole itself. Like it would keep pressing until it pushed the capsule out of orbit and sent us flying through open space.

I turned away from the porthole and my hands floated, my body drifted. The entry hatch was near my feet now, the seats at my head. I was upside down but felt I was right side up. My eyes swam around the room. I couldn't seem to find a place for them to rest. Nausea moved over me, a hot and cold wave.

I climbed back to my seat and strapped myself in. My stomach calmed a little, but I still felt . . . what? Untethered. Adrift. More like a speck of dust than a person. I thought of my uncle and all the things he knew about the history of our universe, the history of space travel. About the machines that made living in space possible. But he'd never left Earth. As of this moment I'd gone farther into space than he had.

23

I blinked inside the dazzlingly white airlock outside the *Sundew*, the cargo station where I was posted for the next six months. My breath was loud inside my helmet; I held on to a handrail with one hand and my feet waved around below me. There was a long scrape and a pop as the capsule that had brought me disengaged from the *Sundew* and began to inch away. Some numbers on a screen counted down from one hundred, and when they hit zero, I took off my helmet and gloves. A hot metal smell—like my uncle's soldering iron—filled my nose.

Out the porthole the capsule became smaller and smaller, and I had a strange feeling of being left behind. But three other people were on the other side of the interior hatch door, and I only had to press the button beside the door and it would open. I angled myself in that direction and pushed it, but nothing happened. I waited. My limbs drifted, my organs shifted inside my body. I tried to right myself, taking hold of a handrail with one hand and hugging my helmet to my chest with the other. I pedaled my feet.

A voice came from above, a woman's. Hold on in there. There was static. Got a faulty seal. Give us a minute—

The airlock shifted to the left. I thought it was in my mind, because surely they weren't going to rotate the airlock with me in it. But it really was moving, turning under my feet. A low whine filled the air.

Hey, I yelled. Hey!

I strained to keep my grip on the handrail and my helmet slipped from my hand and spiraled away. My hip hit the porthole, harder than I thought possible in zero gravity; my wrist twisted and I cried out and let go of the handrail. I bounced against one wall, and another. My helmet spun back at me, fast, and I batted it away.

Then all at once the rotation ceased. My helmet stopped too and hovered in the air like a balloon. I got hold of the handrail again, breathing hard. I rotated my wrist, felt tears at the corners of my eyes, and blinked them away.

All done, the voice said. And then the hatch door slid open.

Beyond it was a minimally lit gray module. The door slid shut behind me and my eyes adjusted to the dim. I smelled stale air, plastic, urine. Every surface was covered in panels and equipment, labeled in at least three languages; there was no ceiling, no floor. No differentiation between up, down, left, right.

I rubbed my twisted wrist. The air was warmer than I'd expected, slightly balmy even, and full of a low buzzing hum.

The woman's voice returned, near my feet. Sorry about that.

There was a video intercom just under my left foot. But the screen showed only an empty seat, its restraints loose in the air.

It's okay, I said. But it wasn't okay. Focusing on the screen below made my stomach press against my skin. The buzzing in the air seemed to get louder, or nearer, or something. I tasted sour, and I clamped my mouth shut.

Compression seat's to your left, the voice said, and I pulled myself in that direction as fast as I could, my teeth clenched against the rising vomit. By the time I got myself into the right module I was sweating. I struggled out of my suit, a torturous task without gravity, convinced I'd throw up inside it. The neck ring scraped my skin and pulled my hair; my wrist and hip smarted with every movement, and I was nearly weeping when I finally got free.

In my underclothes and socks I grabbed a bottle tethered to the wall and took a drink. When the liquid moved in the right direction, downward, I was grateful. I wiped my face with a wet towel from a box stuck to the wall, and it was cool against my throbbing head. I took another. I scrubbed my lips and found brown blood. In a square mirror next to the wipes my eyes were red like a rabbit's. I opened my mouth. During liftoff I must have bit the tip of my tongue.

I strapped myself into the compression seat, secured its one-piece with elastic and Velcro, and pressed a button I thought was right. It filled with water, squeezing each of my limbs, starting at the top and working its way down. It pushed the blood from my head into my shoulders, and my ears cleared. The throbbing behind my eyes ceased. Then it pushed the blood from my shoulders into my torso, and my stomach calmed. Once it reached my legs I felt almost normal.

Now the seat was in the center of the floor, not the ceiling. Now the portholes were high up, like they were supposed to be. I strapped on the ocular instrument—giant black goggles—and did my eye exercises. When I was done I really was better. The door was in the right place, and the mirror too. On the wall were my crew members' hanging suits. But I'd improperly tethered my own suit and its white arms and legs waved at me with animation, with a seeming sense of urgency. It gestured at the farthest porthole and I saw the edge of the Earth. It didn't press against the porthole like it had in the capsule. It was only round and still and impossibly blue. I stared at it for a long time.

Then I realized it was in the wrong place. It ought to be under my feet. If the chair was under me, then the Earth ought to be under it, but it wasn't. It was above my head. The room bent; I held on to the seat and bent with it. My skin slid upward. My feet were on the sky and my head in the Earth, and my skin slid up, up.

A movement at the other end of the module. A tall figure in a gray jumpsuit floated toward me, a woman, upside down. Her hand hovered. She turned clockwise, and the room bent again. An oval face appeared behind the hand.

I tasted vomit and didn't shut my mouth in time.

Something rustled. The woman had a plastic bag in her hand; she swam through the air to catch the bubbles of sick. I held my hand to my mouth and my cheeks burned.

The woman had short hair and long ears. Amelia, I said.

Sorry about the bumps, she said, and kicked a panel on the wall. This station's a piece of junk.

What's wrong with it? My tongue was thick and the words came out slow.

Oh it's all right. Better than nothing. She lightly hooked one socked foot under a panel and pushed the plastic bag into a trash compartment.

I'm glad to see you, I said. It's been a long time.

Has it?

We haven't seen each other in—I swallowed and tried to focus on a specific spot on the wall—six years.

Right. She released her foot from the panel and began moving back the way she came.

What should I be doing? I called after her.

Getting your space legs.

But I didn't want to be alone with my waving spacesuit, the smell of vomit, and the porthole with the Earth in the wrong place. I unstrapped myself and followed.

24

She called out the names of the modules as she swam past them, navigating around equipment and through airlocks with ease. I tried to orient myself based on the plans I'd studied before the launch, to take note of what equipment was where, but my limbs kept floating away and hitting things. It took all my concentration to keep them close, to hold my legs together and to press my arms against my sides. But I knew we must be getting close to the module with the toilets, because I could smell them, and I felt a dry heave rise up as we went past. I swallowed hard.

Amelia stopped in a compartment packed with large fabric storage bags that looked like they might have once been white but were now dingy gray. The air was full of whirring and blowing and beeping, and we had to raise our voices to be heard.

Storage and Systems, Amelia said, and opened a cabinet with tools velcroed inside. A small screwdriver floated out and I tried to catch it. I missed.

She grabbed for it behind her head and returned it to the cabinet. She tied a wrench and a pair of scissors to her jumpsuit, grabbed a roll of duct tape, put her hand through it, and pulled it up her sleeve. We got here late, she said. We're still doing systems checks.

I'll help.

She shook her head and drifted slightly in the air. Not if you're going to puke on the equipment—

I won't.

She looked at me. We've only got four hours before the first supply packet arrives. I can't babysit you.

You won't have to.

Then let's move.

We reached the Service Module—the SM—where a man was squeezed behind an equipment panel. All I could see was one long leg, one long arm.

Simon, Amelia said.

They still haven't replaced this thing, he called from the panel. I can't believe it.

Just fix it like you did last time. Amelia pulled the roll of duct tape from her arm and tapped his shoulder with it. Remember June? she said.

Simon stuck his head out from behind the panel. He was so different—his shoulders were broader and his soft wavy hair was gone, buzzed close to the skin.

Of course I do. He reached out his hand and I pushed my body forward in the air. He caught my hand and squeezed it firmly and smiled, but the smile didn't quite reach his eyes. All grown up, he said.

He ducked back behind the panel and we swam on, going in a circle (the station was a hexagon of modules, arranged around the SM). In another module a woman with waving dark hair was cleaning debris out of a vent. She floated horizontally in the air, a cloud of dust and fibers around her head.

Nine down, she said. Sixty-six more to go—

Rachel's second-in-command, Amelia said to me. She'll save the rest of you if this piece of crap station kills me—

Hey. Rachel turned her shoulders and rotated her body in the air so she was facing me. She had large bright eyes. Her hair billowed. Do you snore?

I looked at Amelia. No. Or, I don't think so—

Then we'll get along great.

Very funny, Amelia said. I don't snore.

I brought you a nose clip this time, Rachel said and she reached out as if to pinch Amelia's nose.

No you didn't, Amelia said, and ducked her head away.

I really did, Rachel said to me as Amelia propelled herself

into the next module. I followed her into the Storage and Systems module from the other side.

Amelia hung above a piece of equipment. Can you deal with this?

I was pretty sure it was a water reclaimer, although I'd never seen one exactly like it on Earth.

The tubing's shot, and it needs to be flushed, she said. She pulled a piece of plastic hose from a cabinet and handed it to me but didn't let go. Her face was serious. This is our only spare, so we've got to make it last.

Sure, I said. But she still held on to the hose.

I get it, I said.

She let go. All right. I'll be back. She swam away, her feet kicking at the air.

I opened cabinets and found the tools I needed. The water reclaimer had a series of small screws on its back panel, and when I removed the first it quickly floated away. I twisted my body and caught it; then I got a roll of duct tape from the tool cabinet, tore a piece off, and made a circle of tape around my upper arm. Then I proceeded, making sure each screw stuck to the tape so it wouldn't float away.

As I worked I tried to keep my limbs close—my legs, my left arm—but as soon as I turned my attention to something else, they drifted away. The air was stuffy and I began to sweat. But it felt good to have a tool in my hands. My body had no weight, but it could still create force like it did on Earth.

The video intercom on the wall showed the interior of the SM. Two figures took up the screen, Amelia and Rachel. But only Rachel's bottom half was visible; she must have been cleaning a vent just above. Amelia held a clipboard that was tethered to the wall and wrote something in pencil.

Amelia looked up. Rachel's feet hovered near her head. The expression on Amelia's face reminded me of someone—Carla.

She caught hold of Rachel's legs and pulled her body downward until they were face-to-face. She said something I couldn't hear, and Rachel laughed. Then Amelia reached out and tugged a piece of Rachel's waving hair.

I looked away.

I removed the last screw, got the panel open, and began to unclip the coiled tubing inside. There were over twenty clips and each had to be stuck—like the screws—to my circle of duct tape. When they were all out I straightened the tube, pushed out the remaining water into a sponge, and then coiled it up again.

A pinging alarm sounded. Amelia and Rachel weren't on the screen anymore. I straightened my body in the air.

Amelia reappeared and began rummaging in one of the tool compartments.

What's happening?

The first packet. Two hours early. She closed the compartment and secured it with its Velcro strip. Stay here, she said. Finish this. She pushed herself back through the airlock.

I waited a minute to see if the alarm would stop. It didn't and Amelia didn't come back, so I returned to the tubing. I got the hose in and flushed the system and waited while it filled. The bubbles in the tank didn't behave like bubbles on Earth, didn't rise to the top. They changed shape, from round to oblong to pear shaped, but they didn't merge with one another or pop. They hovered like jellyfish.

My eyes felt heavy watching them. I'd been awake for . . . I attempted the math but my brain moved slowly. I blinked. I tried to rouse my body, to move deliberately. But my hands and feet were sluggish. My eyes kept migrating to the bubbles as they stretched and fattened in the tank.

I let my limbs float. My eyelids lowered.

You're leaking, someone said near my ear.

I opened my eyes. It was Simon. The bubbles weren't in the tank anymore—they were in the air. A constellation of droplets swam around my head.

Oh shit. I waved my hands, lamely attempting to catch the beads of water swiftly floating away, shiny and globular.

You forgot to reconnect the intake tube, he said.

I scrambled to correct my mistake. I stopped the leak, grabbed a towel, and started chasing the water droplets.

When you're done head that way. He pointed to the next module. The packet's about to dock.

Water was moving toward an instrument panel, and I swam fast to catch it.

25

They were all in the airlock outside Cargo 2 when I got there, Amelia, Rachel, and Simon. There was a slight bump, and then a scraping suck, and the supply capsule docked.

I held on to a handrail and forced my eyes to stay open.

Rachel eyed me. Maybe you should head to your bunk, she said.

Don't you need me? My voice was hoarse.

Take thirty minutes.

They're only giving us three hours to unload. Amelia tapped my cheeks with her two hands. Wake up! You'll be fine.

The empty hold was huge in comparison to the station's tight modules and airlocks, and even more dimly lit. It was a different sensation being weightless in such a large space. There was no equipment in here, no wires and tubes waving. Nothing to bump into. Just scraped-up gray walls marked with faint yellow text—indicating loading zones in three different languages, English, Russian, and Japanese—and cargo restraints secured flat.

Simon moved ahead to the exterior door and began checking the seals, and Rachel handed me a pair of gloves.

Amelia swam toward us with two crowbars tucked under her arm.

Damn, Simon said from the other end of the hold. He'd opened the exterior door, but the supply capsule's hold was so packed you could barely see inside. Runner lights glowed dimly from the deck, but a huge crate, wider than the exterior hold door, blocked our view.

They do this every time, Amelia said. They forget we unload back to front.

Simon prodded the giant crate with a crowbar and it creaked but didn't budge. Someone's going to have to crawl through, he said.

The crate was secured to the deck with restraints and there was only a narrow space between its top and the hold door.

June will do it, Amelia said. Won't you—

Are you sure? Rachel frowned at me.

I'm okay. I swam to the top of the crate and my mind focused and my limbs woke up. I can do it.

Good, Amelia said.

Once you get on the other side, watch your feet, Simon said. Don't step on any of the restraints.

I pulled on my gloves, hovered for a second, and then began inching through the dark opening.

I felt the heat of my breath in the narrow space as I crawled my hands along the top of the crate. I smelled glue and metal and foam rubber. Eventually my fingers reached an edge and open air. Another crate was secured to the deck just beyond and I tried to judge the width of the gap between them, from my middle finger to my elbow.

You can shift it forward, I called. I looked over the side of the crate. And to the left. There's enough room to angle it out I think. It's wider than it is long—

You've got to undo the restraint, Amelia called. We can't get to it—

I was going to have to dive between the two crates. Would I fit?

I've got it secured on our end, Simon called. It's not going anywhere.

I put my arms in front of me, tucked my head, and wriggled into the gap. The sound of my breath and the creak of the boxes surrounded me. I groped for the restraints, the runner lights bright in my eyes. My hand found the cold metal of the release. A single dried bean floated past my face. Then another.

What's happening? Amelia called.

I loosened the release, and the crate wobbled in the air and bumped against my back.

June, stop moving, Simon called. I heard his crowbar. The crate moved away from me, and then back. All the air seemed to rush out of my lungs as it pinned me flat. I reached to protect my head.

Through a crack I could see Simon struggling. His crowbar crunched between the crate and the hold door. A space opened up by my head and I took a breath. But the crate was only half-way out. It tipped toward my legs and pinned me by my calves.

Simon's face was pink. Our eyes met. The crate squeezed my legs hard. I got you, he said. He torqued the crowbar sideways and yelled, Now!

The pressure on my legs loosened; I scrambled my body backward through the gap.

Things went more smoothly once we got that first crate out. Amelia had a manifest that said what parts of the shipment needed to be opened and their contents organized by final destination: the moon, Mars, or the Pink Planet; which should be moved as is; and which few were for us, containing food and other supplies to maintain the *Sundew* itself. Each crate, box, and container was marked with a zone (one through four) and a location (deck, starboard, port, and overhead).

Amelia and Simon and Rachel used crowbars to wrench the crates open. Bolts flew through the air and they didn't bother to catch them. They had a sort of shorthand that involved yelling Left! Right! Got it! and Hell no! at one another over the tops of crates and boxes. They worked fast and I tried to help despite my aching calves.

Mostly I seemed to get in the way until I figured out I should stay in the hold and direct where they placed the cargo. They were strapping it into any open spot in each zone without being strategic. But doing it that way created awkward configurations that would make it harder when we had to reload the cargo in a few days. So instead of getting in between them as they yanked off the lids of crates and broke down boxes, I floated up and through the middle of the hold to look into the gaps in each stowage zone.

At first when I started calling out directions—Flip that crate! Rotate that container! Turn those bins!—Amelia argued with me. But she quickly saw I was right. We were done faster than anyone expected, with fifteen minutes to spare.

26

In the sleeping module the bunks were arranged in a cloverleaf, with one each on the deck, port, starboard, and overhead. When I got there Rachel and Simon were already in bed, their eyes closed. Simon's long legs were tucked to his chest and his buzzed head turned to the wall. Rachel's sleeping bag was pulled to her chin but her hair floated free. I pulled myself into my bunk, which was long and narrow, with just enough room for me to stretch out, and zipped my sleeping bag around me. Rachel and Simon were very close. I could reach out and touch either of them without any effort at all.

I heard them breathing. I smelled toothpaste and dirty socks. I wanted to close my eyes, but they felt huge. My body hummed. The backs of my calves ached. My scalp itched where my helmet had pressed against my head, and when I reached to touch my face it was full of fluid and squishy under my fingers. I shifted left and then right in my sleeping bag. My thoughts roamed through the empty station, into all its modules and compartments and holds. Images shuttled through my mind—of water droplets spinning through the air, of massive crates creaking against their restraints.

Sleep didn't come. And didn't come. The thought that it might never come again entered my mind and my throat tightened. I felt a twist of panic low in my stomach. I shifted to my side, my back. I thought of my first night at Peter Reed, how impossible it felt to sleep in that big room full of other girls. How it seemed like I'd stay awake forever under my icy sheets listening to everyone around me breathe and cough and sneeze.

Amelia came into the module and I watched her through half-closed eyes. I heard the *rrrrp* of her sleeping bag, a cough, and then silence. I closed my eyes. I would be all right; I wouldn't be awake forever. Sleep would come.

And then—a low, guttural snore. And another. And another.

I pulled my sleeping bag to my chin, and then over my ears; I pressed my face to its slippery fabric and squeezed my eyes shut. Amelia's snores seemed to lengthen and amplify, to fill every inch of the small room.

I unzipped my bag and swam out of the sleeping module and the twist in my stomach loosened. I pulled myself into the next module and the sound of the snores faded and the twist disappeared.

I floated to Storage and Systems and checked the water reclaimer. It was running fine. On the intercom was the empty SM, its panel of monitors blank. I pressed a button and the image changed to the sleeping module I'd just left. Simon was still turned toward the wall. His long legs were tucked into his body making him appear small. Amelia and Rachel faced each other, and one of Rachel's arms was loose. It reached toward Amelia, as if they'd been holding hands and had just let go. I pressed the button again and looked into each empty module, into each of the three holds, including Cargo 2, the one we'd just loaded, which was full of dark and irregular shapes.

I pressed some more buttons and an exterior image of the station appeared: the dark shine of a solar array turned away from the sun, the long pole of a robotic arm tethered tightly to the starboard of the station. A series of vents on the station's underside, and below them, a dark expanse broken only by the tiny pinpricks of stars.

It seemed impossible that such a sprawling jumble of modules and airlocks and equipment and arrays could be so silent and still. But it was.

I kept clicking and was surprised to find I could access satellite feeds from other stations in orbit, as well as the outposts on the moon, Mars, and the Pink Planet. I skipped past all of them but the last, and a hazy pink grid filled the screen—a view of the solar fields on the Pink Planet. The visibility was poor, and the image seemed to change in waves. I pulled myself closer to the screen and remembered my uncle's soft, precise voice telling me about the power grid he helped develop and the challenge of generating solar power on a moon where frequent windstorms clouded the air with silt.

I watched the undulating image for several minutes, and finally began to feel sleepy. I quit the satellite feeds and returned to the interior view of the *Sundew*. The Service Module was still empty. Simon and Amelia and Rachel were exactly as they were except now Amelia was turned toward the wall.

I paused at Cargo 2. My eyes were heavier now. They began to close. Then a flicker of movement came from deep in the hold, a shadow that flitted past the runner lights. I kept watching and it came again.

I grabbed a flashlight and floated to Cargo 2, opened the airlock.

The hold was dark and dense with cargo and colder than it had been. I hovered just inside and moved my beam across boxes and crates and bags, and shadows sprang up and shifted. I floated through the rows and pointed my light into the spaces between the tethered shapes, catching the scents of glue and motor oil and pepper (a sack of spices had split when we were unloading). I saw nothing.

Then there was a sound, a scrabbling, living sound. I rose above a sack of linens bigger than me, twisted my body around a crate marked NO CROWBAR in three languages, swam deeper into the hold. Bits of reflective tape flashed when my light hit them; containers and bundles shifted and creaked as I swam past. I listened hard, heard a scrabble and a squeak, and turned my flashlight in time to catch a glimpse of a rat as it floated between two crates, its tail hovering and its hair standing on end.

I shivered; there was a strange feeling at the base of my neck.

A tingling ache. The shadow of a wide crate seemed to loom, to move toward me of its own volition, and I pedaled my feet. I didn't feel right. Something wasn't right. The tingling ache began to crawl up the back of my skull. I turned back to the airlock and something flashed from behind a large sack. I swam toward it. It was the loss-of-pressure alarm, but it wasn't sounding. Why wasn't it sounding? I rolled my body in the air and the pain in my head roared. I felt along the wall for the emergency pull. It wasn't there—

My fingers found it and I tugged and the air filled with sound. A bleating alarm, a staticky voice warning me of something; I couldn't make out what. I rolled again and pushed off a crate toward the open airlock, the flashing light beating time out of the corner of my eye. The lock was two meters away. One. It slid shut with a swift *thnnk*.

I hung suspended in the air and stared at it dumbly.

I pressed the button to open the lock and nothing happened. I pressed it again. The lock didn't budge. Through the porthole the corridor was empty. The alarm wailed on and on but no one was coming. The shadows around me changed; they distorted and bent. They doubled and joined. They became large and rose up like spirits.

They weren't coming. Why weren't they coming?

Amelia's oval face appeared in the porthole in the airlock door. June. What the hell.

I blinked. The air was colder. Pain gripped my head and squeezed and squeezed. My rapid breath made clouds in the air.

Amelia's face was replaced by Simon's. Behind him Rachel was talking. We've got a seal leak but no alarm—

June. Simon talked to me through the porthole. His voice was loud and deliberate over the alarm. I need you to do something for me. I want you to take low, slow breaths. Just like in the dive pool, remember? Low and slow.

I nodded but my lungs kept pumping.

June. Low and slow.

I swallowed. I forced my throat to release its grip on my breath, forced my chest to relax. I remembered my first dive at Peter Reed, the feeling of my teeth against my rubbery mouthpiece. It had felt impossible to ignore the impulse to blow air out fast and draw it in even faster. To ignore the quick beat of my pulse in my throat. But I did it. I did it then and I could do it now. I made my breaths low, and the clouds they made slowed. I focused on the clouds; I counted them and let each one dissipate before I made the next.

Simon's face was gone but I heard Rachel's voice. She was talking about a manual override. Amelia said, We need two suits.

I counted breaths. Counted clouds. Low and slow.

Rachel's face was in the porthole now. We're going to open the door. But there's a pressure difference. Things are going to shift. I want you to crouch down between two of the biggest, most secure crates—on the starboard side. And I want you to protect your head.

My vision blurred, and a peculiar fizzing sensation bloomed on my tongue. The pain in my head had become a single needle point behind my right eye. Okay.

Repeat back to me.

I'm going to— I squeezed my right eye shut and ignored a shadow that seemed to creep, and then recede, along the wall. I'm going to crouch somewhere secure. I'm going to protect my head.

In five, Rachel said.

I scanned the area where I was floating and chose my spot.

In four.

I tucked my head to my chest, put my arms over my head, and squeezed my eyes shut.

In three.

In two.

In one—

There was a slow suck and a terrific howl of air. A jetlike thrust against my chest. My shoulders smacked the wall behind me and my head bounced. My eyes jolted open and the air was full of things. Beans, salt, feathers. Flashing bits of metal. A twist of clear tubing, a spray of bolts.

White arms grabbed me. Amelia and Rachel in their suits, their faces pink and flat behind their visors. My limbs unfolded and I shut my eyes and oh! They were full of glass and I swallowed a scream.

Then we were inside the lock. The exterior and interior doors shut, and the alarm ceased. I held on to a handrail. My body was strange, my lungs rigid, my face like a stone. As if all my soft parts had turned hard. I held my eyes open—if I blinked it was much, much worse.

My eyes, I said. There's something in them. Rachel was pulling off her suit; she floated near my face. Okay. I see.

Amelia took off her suit too.

There's something in them, I said again and my chest shook and my eyes ran.

One thing at a time, Rachel said, and the two of them pulled off my track pants, my socks. Amelia cut off my overshirt. Their hands were warm and firm as they brushed bits of debris from my face and hair. They steered me to the galley, where they wiped more debris from my body with a sponge and I shivered.

Amelia opened a table and laid my body flat. Simon's face appeared over my own, his long eyelashes dark against his face. He secured my arms and legs to the table with Velcro straps. He moved quickly but was careful not to jostle my head. We're good, he said.

I lay flat on the table in my tank top and underwear, my eyes stinging and tearing. A long moment passed while they opened drawers and retrieved things. Eyewash and tweezers and gauze. I blinked once and yelped, and then Simon pressed his fingers above and below my eyelids to hold them open. Rachel washed the cuts on my face with antiseptic and then readied the eyewash and leaned in close. My eyes teared and I tried to blink but Simon's fingers were steady.

She's got at least one shard in her right eye, Rachel said. I think two in the left.

My body tensed as she lowered the tweezers. I squirmed. I had been cold but now I felt sweat on my forehead under Simon's thumb.

Still, Rachel said. I need you to be still.

She took aim and again I wriggled.

Don't look at the tweezers, Rachel said. Look at Amelia. Talk to Amelia.

I did what she said. I looked at Amelia's oval face and long ears. Her cheeks were red and her hair wet at the temples.

Say something Amelia, Rachel said.

What were you doing in that hold? Amelia asked.

Not about that, Rachel said.

You said talk.

Rachel lowered the tweezers and I felt her breath on my cheek and the pressure of Simon's fingers on my skin. I kept my eyes on Amelia's face.

Got it. Rachel held something tiny and glinting in the light and then carefully stuck it to a loop of surgical tape on the medical tray. Then she lowered the tweezers again and hummed between her teeth. She held up another shard. Two down, one to go.

She squinted into my right eye. Wider, she said. Simon pulled my eyelid taut and tears wet my cheek.

I watched Amelia.

The tweezers grew large again.

Done, Rachel said.

Simon irrigated my eye and droplets danced around us. He released his fingers. Rachel handed me some gauze and I blinked and dabbed at my cheeks. I coughed. I shut my eyes and felt them all watching.

Damn, I said.

Does it hurt? Simon asked.

I coughed again and opened my eyes halfway. Not really. I feel okay.

Simon unstrapped me from the table and I floated.

So why were you in that hold? he asked.

I saw something. A rat.

Amelia laughed, and Simon did too.

I guess we should be thankful for that rat, Rachel said.

I listed to one side. Outside the porthole was a dark blank. Exhaustion stole over my body and I moved my limbs to try to wake them up. I said I would help investigate the leak but Amelia shook her head and said, Straight to bed.

My eyes were already closing as I floated to the sleeping module. I felt my way into my bunk and hugged my sleeping bag to my chest. My tongue was tender; I ran it over the roof of my mouth once, twice, and then I fell immediately into a doze.

When I woke my crewmates were in their bunks, their eyes closed. Simon was on his back, his eyelashes long and dark, his forehead smooth, and Rachel was turned toward the wall, her sleeping bag tucked around her chin. Amelia floated just above her bunk, her mouth open. Her eyelids trembled and her feet waved gently in the air.

The sound of everyone's breathing filled up the small space. Up, down, sideways. Simon's breathing was soft and rhythmic. Rachel's was a nasal sigh. Amelia's was a loud inhale followed by an airy exhale. The noises kept me awake but this time I didn't mind. I listened to them for a long time until eventually sleep came again.

27

In the morning two packets arrived within hours of each other. Simon was still testing the seal in Cargo 2 so we had to fill every other space. The airlocks, Storage and Systems, even the galley. The interior of the station transformed. We could barely move through the tight spaces, and for two days it felt like we were moles crawling through a narrow burrow. I'd push my way into the opening of a tunnel into darkness only to bump heads with Simon or Amelia or Rachel in the middle, laugh, and have to slowly crawl out feetfirst.

I ate nothing but nut bars and squeezable milk packets for a full forty-eight hours. My arms ached from pushing crates and sacks through the station and pulling them out again. But I didn't care. My head was clear, my body light. My nausea had dissipated; my eyes were sore but as soon as I was out of my bunk and working it was easy to ignore the discomfort. The tasks I was assigned were challenging, and it felt good to do them well.

Then there was a sudden lull in our schedule—an unexpected twenty-four hours when we had nothing to do. We'd moved the last packet out. We'd cleaned and done systems checks, and Simon had fixed the seal leak in Cargo 2 to his satisfaction. Both holds were empty and ready, and the next packet wasn't due for a full day.

We could move freely through the station again and the space felt vast. We swam through the modules with our arms out, did somersaults in the air, and whooped. After a while we all drifted in different directions. Amelia and Rachel played a game with a ball and a storage bin only they seemed to fully understand. Simon ran on the treadmill in our tiny gym.

I floated through the station and looked out portholes that had been obstructed by cargo. I hovered outside the largest porthole—in the SM, port side—and watched the Earth's expanse of ocean and clouds move past like a massive ball rolling in slow motion. My stomach didn't lurch anymore looking at it. I didn't feel out of control. It felt less like I was teetering on a precipice and more like I was standing, firm footed and secure, at the edge of an ocean cliff.

That night we all slept for as long as we wanted, and by late morning everyone ended up in the galley hovering around the food compartments. We should eat something real, Rachel said. Eggs maybe. With what? Mushrooms and hot sauce? In a tortilla? She began rummaging through the dry goods compartment.

We hovered while Rachel assembled the food. You couldn't really call it cooking; it was more like compiling different things from different drawers. But it was good, what she put together. The eggs were crumbly but actually tasted eggy. The hot sauce burned pleasantly on my tongue.

We should eat the apples too, Rachel said when everyone was done. Before they go bad—

Real apples? I asked.

Our lockers came in the last packet, Amelia said. Rachel's dad sent apples.

Rachel floated out of the galley and came back with her locker, and mine and Simon's too.

She tossed us each an apple; it was smooth and warm in my hand. I bit into it and it was wet and tart and firm. I ate it quickly, taking one bite after the other without stopping, until all that was left was the thinnest core. Rachel threw another in my direction and I reached in the air and caught it. I ate that one fast too, and so did everyone else, and the small room filled with the crunching of our teeth.

I wiped my mouth. My locker hovered near the ceiling. I'd

packed it so long ago. Or, it felt that way. But it had been no more than a week. I tried to remember if I'd put anything in there I could share—

I undid the latch and the lid popped open and items began to float out. A pocket atlas, a container of iced tea mix, my favorite Candidate Group sweatshirt—red with white lettering across its front. Books and papers of my uncle's I'd been carrying around since I left home. As I pushed the atlas and tea back in, *New History of Energy* bumped out, and sheets of paper with faded blue schematics dislodged from their folder. They separated and dispersed in the air. I pulled my sweatshirt from underneath the spray of papers and pushed everything else back inside.

But Amelia grabbed one sheet, held it up to the light, and frowned. It was a fuel cell schematic covered in writing—my uncle's, Simon's, James's, Theresa's, and her own. Reflected light from outside the porthole shined through the paper and made the writing appear darker than it really was.

Why do you have these? Her voice was strange.

I felt silly; I had only a five-kilogram allowance for personal items and I'd used it to carry my uncle's old things.

I like having something of his with me, I said.

She slid the paper into the box.

I should have brought food or extra tools, I said. I shut the lid and slid the latch closed. Something useful.

It's your locker. She looked at Simon; he was pushing apples from Rachel's locker into one of the refrigerator bins. You can bring what you want.

28

Everything has a different weight and shape in space. Objects don't behave the way you expect them to: an enormous container of supplies that appears impossible to haul is in fact easy, but a small sack of hardware is unwieldy, potentially dangerous. Things move in unpredictable ways, change shape, even disappear. Food floats away or disintegrates before you can eat it; tools you gripped tightly in your hand just seconds ago seem to vanish into thin air.

My body itself was different on the *Sundew*, the contours of my face almost unrecognizable in the mirror. My cheeks were wider, my eyes rounder. My shoulders took up more room than they did on Earth, my legs less. I didn't move the same. Like everyone else on the station I developed my own unique way of getting from module to module, half swim, half climb. I didn't even sound the same. When someone asked me a question and I answered, my voice—lower and raspier than on Earth—seemed to belong to someone else.

It wasn't just tangible things that were different, things I could point to and say, That's not the same as on Earth. Time and physical space were different. The span of a minute, an hour, a day. The directions, up and down, left and right. The perceived dimensions of something as large as a module or as small as a bolt. My senses were different. Sight, smell, taste, touch, sound. They could distort and change shape; they could be one thing at one moment and quite another thing the next.

I had to reorient myself to my surroundings constantly, be

alert at all times. Even when I was tired, hungry, or hurting. Even when I slept.

I learned to distrust my sense of sight, to discount my sense of taste and smell (they were so dulled by the effects of zero gravity on my sinuses they were nearly useless). I relied more on my fingers, on my ears; instead of turning on lights when I needed to go to the toilet in the night I just felt my way there, listening instead of looking for anything amiss as I moved through silent and shadowy modules and locks.

I started to listen to the equipment and systems I was charged with maintaining and fixing. I got the idea from Simon who I found in Storage and Systems one morning, his ear pressed against the oxygenator. He was wearing a jumpsuit unbuttoned to his waist, a clean white T-shirt underneath. Rachel had just used the clippers on his hair and his scalp was pink.

I asked him what he was doing and he frowned and held up a hand. Hold on—

When he was done I pressed him to explain.

Every system has two sounds, he said. One when it's working properly, one when it's not. If you get to know them, you can stop a problem before it happens.

How do you know which is good and which is bad?

He drummed his thumb on the side of the oxygenator. Listen every day and you'll learn.

At first I didn't hear anything but a hum. Then I drew my limbs into my body and pressed my ear closer, the metal of the panel cold against my ear, and was able to differentiate three different noises: a dragging hum, a whoosh of air, and—every few seconds—a faint *tick, tick.*

I started listening to the electronics assembly, the heat rejection radiator, the space-to-ground antenna system. The water reclaimer and the thermal control system. At any odd moment, when I didn't have anything else to do, I pressed my ear to things— panels, vents, equipment. I floated from one machine to the next.

It got to the point where my dreams weren't about people

anymore, or places, or things. They didn't have pictures in them at all—only the sounds of the station. Hums and drips and scrapes; gentle scuffles and creaking rasps; jangling squeaks. Long stints of vibrating static. Rhythmic stretches of thumps.

One morning I woke with a full bladder and the swishing pops of the galley water pump in my ears. I wiggled out of my sleeping bag and swam to the toilet. It hadn't been cleaned in a while and it smelled bad. I sat down gingerly, pressed the suction button, and felt the toilet pull hard on my bottom. My body tightened. I took a breath and relaxed my thighs, bladder, stomach. Finally I was able to go, and the urine was whisked out of my body in an instant.

A red light warned me the waste tanks were full and I groaned. The urine processing unit had broken three days ago and there hadn't been time to fix it. I'd have to manually empty the tank before I could go back to bed. I got the tools I needed from Storage and Systems and powered everything down. Then I hovered over the unit to detach the electrical connectors, tape them temporarily to the wall with duct tape, and remove the tank, all while trying to avoid breathing through my nose. I started the pump and figured since I'd already taken the unit apart I might as well try to fix it.

I began to undo all the bolts on the broken part—a big metal drum that distilled water from urine through evaporation—and Amelia's voice came from behind me. You're up early. She floated into the module. She was eating a shriveled apple.

I hope you don't have to go, I said.

I can wait.

How long have you been up?

Awhile. I had to check the gyroscopes.

I looked at her. She was pale and thinner than she'd been when I first arrived; the skin under her eyes was dark purple in the dim light.

I don't need a lot of sleep, she said, as if she could read my mind.

She finished the apple, pulled her body closer, and grabbed the wrench I'd velcroed to my jumpsuit.

Did Simon show you how to do this?

No.

You didn't learn how to do it at Peter Reed—

I figured it out just now.

I didn't learn a whole lot that was useful there either, she said.

Together we disconnected and capped all the fluid lines, including the one that filtered into the brine reservoir, pulled out the broken assembly unit, and began installing the new one. It was hot in the small compartment with the two of us wedged inside and I started to sweat, but we worked efficiently and fast.

I learned a lot from your sister, I said.

Carla? You weren't in the same group.

We were my first year. Our beds were next to each other.

We reconnected the fluid lines, careful not to mix up gray water and brine.

I haven't seen her in a long time, I said. How is she?

She works at one of the private labs. She's got a boyfriend, or she did the last time we talked.

You must be glad to see her in between rotations.

There was an empty pause. The vent overhead whirred.

I'm better with machines than people, she said.

The metal wrench was cold against my palm. Me too.

She stretched her body in the air. You're like your uncle. She looked at my face and seemed to appraise it. My nose, my chin. A lot like him.

I felt warmth and a sense of solidness despite my floating limbs.

He understood me, Amelia said. Maybe better than anyone.

I nodded.

She folded her body in the air. Everything went to shit when he died. She shut the urine processor's cabinet, bolted it closed, and powered it up. You go first, she said.

I wiped my forehead with my sleeve and pressed my ear to the tank. One second—

But she was already pressing the button to vent the brine reservoir. I heard a rush of air, then seven high pops, and something about it tugged at my memory. I knew it. I knew that sound—

29

I hit the vent button over and over. Every time: a rush of air and seven pops.

Why are you doing that? Amelia asked. The processor's good to go—

I just— I put my tools away quickly. I need to check something. I left her and pulled myself into the next module. I bumped into things; I caught my elbow on an open panel, knocked my head as I swung my body through the airlock between the SM and the galley.

When I reached the sleeping module I grabbed my locker, crawled into my bunk, and pulled the partition closed. My breath was warm and loud in the tiny space as I rummaged through the locker. I had it somewhere, the static log I'd begun five years ago after *Inquiry* went dark. I knew I did because I'd nearly thrown it out when I was cleaning out my dorm room after Candidate Group graduation. I'd found it at the bottom of an old duffel bag and laughed when I pulled it out.

I did have it, a dented green notebook with my name written inside the cover. I turned on the tiny reading light attached to the side of my bunk compartment, opened the book, and began to read. I scanned every page, squinting at my twelve-year-old handwriting in the lamp's small spotlight, until I found my notes on G1 and H2. They included the dates I heard the static, the channel's letter and number designation, AUX27, and the interval between the sounds, between seventy and seventy-four hours.

I stayed in my bunk and thought for a long time. No one

talked about *Inquiry* anymore. During my training the Explorer program was rarely mentioned, and when it was it was handled in a clinical way. No one talked about the crew. No one said their names.

But since I'd arrived at the *Sundew* I'd thought about them a lot. They were with me as I floated through the station's modules and airlocks, hauled crates and sacks from one hold to another, and ate breakfast with Amelia or Simon in the galley. When I strapped myself into a jump seat, the restraints tight against my chest, I pictured Anu secured in an identical seat. When I squeezed behind a panel with a tool in my hand, I wondered how many times she'd done the same on *Inquiry*.

It was a wild thought that they could still be alive, five years later. I pressed the notebook to my chest and swam to the SM.

Simon was there, strapped into a seat, doing a systems check. One of the gyroscopes is trying to die, he said. For real this time.

I hung in the air in front of him. I need to listen to something.

What?

The *Inquiry* feed.

He looked at me steadily and I remembered the day he sat next to me on the bus to Peter Reed, the picture of Anu he'd tucked inside his book. Why?

I'm just . . . curious about something.

Okay. He pressed buttons, and the screen lit up with the familiar communications log, the one-way conversation between mission control and the *Inquiry* explorer. Only now it was a no-way conversation because control had stopped sending status checks two years ago.

I belted myself into the seat next to him, opened my log, and pointed at the list of channels. That one. AUX27. Start it from a week ago, I said.

But he was unstrapping himself from his seat. I'll leave you to it.

Stay. I started pressing buttons and turned the channel up loud.

His face was grim. I don't want to.

But he didn't leave—he hung on to the back of his seat, his feet waving in the air behind him.

The channel was a long unbroken fizz. I waited and nothing happened. I checked its designation again. AUX27. I skipped ahead several hours. And then a full day. Still nothing. No hums, no pops.

I let out the breath I'd been holding. That was it then. I turned the channel down.

What were you listening for? Simon asked.

It was stupid. I thought—

A low hum filled the room, broken by seven snapping pops. G1 and H2, just the same as I remembered them. Just the same as the sound I'd heard inside our own urine processing tank.

I pulled myself to the screen, skipped ahead three days. Again, a low hum and seven snapping pops.

Tell me what that is, Simon said.

It's going to sound crazy.

Say it. He held the back of his seat with two hands.

Proof the *Inquiry* crew are still alive.

His mouth was a thin line. It seemed for a minute he might turn and swim out of the module. But he didn't; he pulled himself into his seat, strapped himself in. Start from the beginning, he said.

The *Sundew* and *Inquiry* are the same age, I said. They have a lot of the same equipment.

Right.

They have the same urine processor. Same manufacturer, same model, installed within months of each other. Its brine reservoir has to be vented manually.

I played back G1 and H2. The vent makes a distinctive sound. Exactly like this—

NSP has been listening to the feed all along, he interrupted. There's nothing there.

There's static.

Interference that could be a million different things.

This channel— I pointed at AUX27. It runs through an antenna on the underside of the explorer. I looked it up. It was installed for a waveform communication experiment, and is right next to the urine processor's vent.

If they were alive NSP would know it. They would have figured it out.

It's not impossible they missed this.

Or they do know it, he said slowly. And haven't said anything because there's nothing they can do about it.

A fan near my right ear began to whir; cold air filled the module. Don't say that.

They want to forget them June.

Something in the fan began to flap—a cargo tag stuck in its filter—and I unstrapped myself and swam to pull it out.

Simon's hands floated. I told Anu she shouldn't go, he said. I said the explorer wasn't ready. The fuel cell needed more testing, a longer study. She said that if NSP did all those tests she might be too old to go by the time they were done.

She was probably right.

I said there was more to life than one mission. There was me. Her friends. Her family—

You couldn't convince her, I said.

She convinced me. There are risks in every mission. If something does go wrong, who should NSP trust to make it right? Who would I trust? Anu.

That's true.

But that stupid speech I gave got in her head, he said. The day of the launch I stood at the bottom of the elevator and waited to wave goodbye. When Anu walked toward us in her jumpsuit she looked so capable and strong. But when she got closer I saw doubt in her expression. Maybe fear.

I folded the cargo tag in my hands. What would she say if she were here right now?

She'd say— Oh I don't know. She'd say we have to replicate it, Simon said. The static. But we don't have an antenna anywhere near that vent.

You and Amelia could install one during your spacewalk. It would take ten minutes. Fifteen tops.

He didn't say anything. He unstrapped himself from his seat. Amelia won't do it, he said.

Why?

She wants to forget too.

I waited until the next day when Amelia was in the gym, strapped into the stationary bike and pedaling hard. I hung on to a handrail and told her what I'd discovered and what I thought it meant. I spoke over the circular whine of the bike.

As I talked she didn't react. Her feet didn't slow; she stared straight ahead out the porthole, sweat darkening her T-shirt.

I got to the part about the antenna before she said anything.

You think the *Inquiry* crew are alive. Despite her physical exertion, her tone was even. Unemotional.

Yes.

And you want us to install an antenna during our spacewalk so you can prove it.

It won't take long—

Dimitri, Lee, Missy, and Anu are dead.

That's what everyone thinks.

They're right. Because the alternative is— Her pace slowed by a little, and she shook her head slightly. Unthinkable.

She sped up again.

I kicked my body forward in the air and put my hand over the porthole in front of her. If they're alive we can save them.

She looked at me. She was so thin. Sweat had pooled in the sharp notch of her clavicle.

Did you talk to Simon about this?

My feet waved in the air below me. Yes.

She sat back in her seat and the pedals of the bike drifted slowly forward. That was a cruel thing to do.

Can we install the antenna or not?

It's a waste of time.

You're wrong.

I waited for her to round on me then, to tell me off. She'd done it before, when we disagreed about the fastest method to unload a shipment or the best way to fix a piece of equipment.

But she didn't. She turned back to the porthole, gripped the handlebars of the bike tighter, and sped up. The only fuel cells that could carry an explorer that far failed, she said. And we don't know why.

We could find out—

We tried. We were all on the Pink Planet for months—me, Simon, James, and Theresa. Taking the fuel cell apart and putting it back together, hoping the rescue mission could be salvaged. James and Theresa are still there. It's driven them half mad and they still don't have an answer.

My stomach pressed against my skin. I didn't know that.

There's no way to reach the *Inquiry* crew. If they're alive— a little shudder moved through her body—all we can hope for is that they figure out how to save themselves.

30

Amelia wouldn't talk to me about it anymore that day. But I didn't care. They were alive. I couldn't know that and do nothing; I couldn't know that and sit still. The sound—the rush of air, the high pops—was always with me now, which meant the *Inquiry* crew were always with me too. When the question of how we would get to them—and whether we could do it in time—came into my mind, I told myself, One thing at a time.

Then Simon discovered a leak in his suit, and the plan for the spacewalk changed. We couldn't wait to repair the gyroscope because it was essential to keeping the station from slipping out of orbit. Rachel had to operate the robotic arm to deliver the new rotor for the failing gyroscope. So the spacewalk would have to be performed by Amelia and me.

In the airlock Amelia and I got into our suits. It had been weeks since I'd been in a suit and I struggled to push my limbs inside. My body was different inside its white layers, had expanded in some places and shrunk in others. My torso felt wobbly, but that was nerves. I'd already stowed an antenna in an outer compartment of my suit. I planned to install it next to the urine processing vent if given the opportunity. I hadn't told anyone; I had hidden it that morning when I was doing systems checks alone.

I locked my helmet. Amelia tested the seals on our suits by raising the pressure inside the airlock, and we checked and rechecked our oxygen tanks. Together we opened the egress hatch and sparkling dust burst from the station. Small bolts and screws and a pencil bumped along the lock's walls and wafted away. We blinked in the blinding sunlight.

Amelia pulled out a platform with foot restraints attached to it, and we transferred our tether cord clips from inside to outside and secured our boots. Then we let go and our arms floated and our tethers waved behind us like long tails. It felt as if we weren't moving, as if the station stood still, even though we were speeding at eighteen thousand miles per hour around the Earth. There was complete silence. No wind. No vibration, despite everything going on inside the station's walls, all its fans and pipes and wires.

Amelia talked into her radio, We're proceeding aftward to the gyroscope panel.

Rachel's voice sounded in our helmets, Roger that.

We pulled ourselves along on the handrails and navigated over and around jutting trusses, equipment, and antennae to the gyroscope compartment at the stern side of the station. When we reached the gray box we strapped our feet to the restraints below it. The Earth was gigantic ahead of us and its blues and greens and whites pressed hard against my eyes.

Amelia retrieved a screwdriver from her tool belt and began to slowly unscrew the compartment's outer panel, and then its inner panel. Each screw she carefully placed inside her belt. We're going to rotate the interior tray to access the R3 gyroscope, she told Rachel.

Okay. I'm going to start moving the arm into position.

Amelia positioned herself on one side of the tray, and I did on the other. The sun was behind us now and the station shined brilliantly like sun on water. Through my gloves I felt the heat of my handrail, like the handle of a pot left on the stove too long. We turned the tray, and then pulled it halfway out of its compartment. I pushed my body inside, opened the R3 gyroscope, and began to unscrew the malfunctioning rotor. Above Amelia's head the arm inched toward us.

We had practiced the steps of the repair two times inside, but in our bulky suits each action took three times as long and the job was less a series of steps than a kind of halting slow-motion dance. We usually worked well together. But today was different. Amelia handed me tools before I was ready; our helmets knocked against each other as we reached into the compartment at the same time.

I'm in position, Rachel said. Are you ready?

Not even close, Amelia said. Our shoulders bumped and her wrench slipped from her hand and wobbled away—and then snapped back on its tether. Would you move? she said to me.

I'm doing exactly what we did inside, I said.

No, you're not. You're off.

So are you.

Whose fault is that?

How is it my fault—

Amelia switched her radio to the two-way channel so only I could hear.

I don't want to think about them, she said. If I'm thinking about them, I can't do my job.

The *Inquiry* crew.

Yes.

The Earth slid past us; a storm swirled off the coast of Africa.

If they're alive don't you want to know? I asked.

Your bed was next to Carla's your first year at Peter Reed, she said.

Yes.

Anu's was next to mine.

The array behind her helmet sparked and flared.

She was so smart, Amelia said. And strong. She built the communications system on *Inquiry*. If she were alive we'd know it.

She switched back to the three-way channel. We worked silently: detached the new rotor from the robotic arm, slid it into place, and slowly tightened it. The angle was awkward and Amelia's wrench could move only a quarter rotation at a time. I took a turn; we went back and forth until it was finally secure.

We're nearing the two-hour mark, Rachel said.

I want to look at the other gyroscopes, Amelia said. If their rotors are degrading like R3's did—

Save it for the next spacewalk.

If we need to ask for another rotor in the next packet I want to know now.

Fine. But do it fast.

We entered the Earth's shadow and turned on our head-lamps. The irregular shapes of the station shined darkly in the cool light of the moon, its arrays glinting silver in the deep black. From where we were I could see the length of its starboard and the panel that contained the urine processor vent.

June. Rachel's voice came through my radio. There's a loose panel near the hatch. If you're staying out there I want you to take a look.

Amelia motioned. Go ahead. I can do this myself.

The urine processor vent was only a yard farther starboard than the loose panel, and I thought, I can do both. It would be the work of only a few minutes. I pulled myself from handrail to handrail, navigating around equipment, fighting the drift of my legs and feet. I began to sweat. I halved the distance to the panel and then my tether pulled taut. It wasn't going to reach. I turned, crawled back, and hastily moved my tether clip.

The vent was inconspicuous among all the other jutting and shining equipment on the starboard side of the station. But I knew exactly what to look for.

You've gone too far, Rachel said. Turn around.

I didn't answer. I reached the vent, took out the antenna, and quickly began to screw it into an unused port next to the vent. I was sweating hard; my hands were slippery inside my gloves and my visor fogged.

Rachel's voice came through my helmet again. The loose panel's behind you—

I looked back the way I came. Amelia was still inside the gyroscope compartment.

I had six screws left.

Tell me what you're doing, Rachel said.

I'm attaching an antenna.

Amelia's voice: What antenna?

I turned and we looked at each other across the station's shining starboard. The sun reappeared and its reflection moved across Amelia's helmet, made it opaque. I couldn't see her face but I could hear her breathing.

They're dead, she said.

I tightened my grip on the handrail and turned back to the antenna. They're not.

Rachel's voice was stern inside my helmet. I don't know what this is about but I want you both to move back to the hatch.

I felt movement behind me. Amelia was pulling herself toward me.

I had one screw left. It was done.

I faced her. They're out there, I said. They're alive, and I'm going to prove it.

My tether cord was looped around my left arm and I let go of the handrail to shrug it off. My legs floated out from under me, but my tether caught me. I felt its clip catch. I began to reel myself in.

But Amelia was looking at something. She was moving fast— My tether went slack and I had a sickening feeling of being let go. I looked—my clip floated free. Amelia had seen it before I had, and she scrambled for it. I drifted despite my hands grabbing. My breath was a roar inside my helmet. I was one foot away from the station, three. Four.

The station got smaller. The stars brighter. I saw white feet in front of my eyes. My white feet.

Amelia! Rachel's voice came through the radio. And Simon's too. Port side! There, there!

The station slid from my sight as I rotated backward in the air, boots over head, slowly at first, and then faster. My organs swayed; vomit stole up my throat. I waved my arms as the Earth flashed blue and green and white, and the station black and gray.

Then—a strong tug at my back. Amelia had grabbed the loose tether, was pulling me back in. I heard the rush of her breathing, and my breathing. We bounced and our helmets cracked together. I held on and she held on. We spun into open air and the station was upside down, sideways. Amelia's tether snapped us back. We slid down the starboard and I scrambled for a handrail, an antenna, anything to slow us down. Amelia reached for the loose panel just as both our bodies slammed into it hard.

The panel pinned her hand and she cursed, pulled it free. Our trajectory slowed. Our eyes met through our visors and hers were twisted in pain. She gripped the tethers with one hand, her left. She dragged us to the hatch door, and through it. It shut behind us with a hiss and a thunk, and we collapsed against the wall. She held her right hand to her chest. Her glove was the wrong shape.

How bad is it? I reached for her glove. How bad—

She pulled away. Wait. Her face was gray. Wait for the lock—

Pressurized air rushed around us as we waited for the green light to flash.

31

Earth's gravity pressed at my hips as I swung my legs from the Candidate dormitory cot to the floor. Two points of cottony pain throbbed in my ears but every other sensation was muffled. I'd been back on Earth for five days but my vision was still fuzzy, my fingertips dull. My tongue lay flat inside my mouth, dry and inert.

I set my feet flat on the floor. They were swollen three times their normal size with edema and seemed to squish. I stood, swayed slightly, and saw sparks at the corners of my eyes—but I was used to that. It happened every time I stood up and I was beginning to wonder if it would ever go away. I took a tentative step and squirmed at the sensation of my fluid-filled toes against the hard ground. My oversize compression slippers were tucked under the bed and I inched my feet inside.

I had been staying in the Candidate dormitory since I got back, making slow circuits between my room, the cafeteria, and the rehab gym. I heard about Amelia only from Rachel or Simon. I hadn't seen her since she'd been evacuated from the *Sundew* almost three weeks ago. I knew she had lost her hand, and I knew she wouldn't want to see me. So I didn't go visit her, even though Rachel kept asking me to.

I'd lived at the Candidate dormitory before, the year between Peter Reed and being posted to the *Sundew*—when I'd walked through the halls knowing I was one of the few in the Candidate program who could expect a job in space, rather than in a control room or lab or training facility on Earth. Back then I'd felt larger than life and prepared for anything. Now everything looked the same but felt different. The colors of the furniture and walls seemed brighter; I felt small inside rooms that appeared taller, or wider.

In the cafeteria I toasted a waffle and put peanut butter on it. I had a vague sense of the noise in the room behind me, but the pressure in my ears made it impossible to distinguish individual sounds, and when I moved my knife across the waffle it made no sound.

I felt a hand on my shoulder and turned. Lion was standing in front of me. He looked tall and healthy; his hair was a brown halo around his head.

His mouth was moving but I shook my head, tapped at my ear.

I can't hear you, I said, and he leaned closer.

I was able to make out one word. Amelia.

I shook my head and opened my mouth wide, and the pressure released slightly.

Sit with me, he said, and pointed to an empty table.

We sat down and I cut up my waffle into small pieces, the knife and fork cold and strange in my swollen fingers. What were you trying to say before? I asked, probably too loudly, because the people one table over turned and looked at me.

He leaned across the table. Amelia's being fitted for her prosthetic this week.

I put a piece of waffle into my mouth and chewed it on the left side—the descent to Earth had loosened some fillings in my molars and my right jaw was tender.

You should go see her, Lion said. I was there with Carla.

My throat was dry and I tried to swallow the piece of waffle.

She's been asking for you, he said. She wants to know why you haven't come.

Do you know what happened?

I heard.

She doesn't want to see me. Not really.

Listen. I just told you she does.

Every sound was muted as the shuttle bus lurched through campus. Outside it was early fall and the sunshine made yellow spots on the floor. I watched the spots shift left and then right as we passed flat green fields and squat gray buildings. But when the bus paused in front of the veterans' hospital I didn't get up. My body felt anchored to the blue carpeted seat. I hadn't been there since my uncle was sick and I didn't want to go back.

The bus moved on and I rode it through its whole hour-long loop. When it reached the hospital stop for the second time I got out. I'd barely been outside since I'd arrived back on Earth, had been existing inside the chilly and still air of the Candidate dormitory for days. A tree stood a few yards away, a maple. Its large yellow leaves trembled in the breeze. The air was warm and humid and lifted my hair from my face.

On the rehabilitation floor a nurse pointed me in the right direction, along a dimly lit corridor that smelled like bleach. I walked slowly, my ears full of woolly pain. The door the nurse had pointed to had a window, and through it I saw a room full of equipment and machines. Amelia was sitting at a table. A metal prosthetic was fitted to her wrist and a woman was adjusting something on its thumb.

I opened the door. Amelia's limbs were long and still. Her hair lay flat against her ears instead of floating away from her face. She turned toward me; her cheeks were pink. She said something I could barely hear. I think it was, Took you long enough.

I didn't think you'd want to see me. My voice seemed wrapped in cotton.

She smiled at the woman and asked her if she could have a minute, and the woman stood and said, Just the thumb, okay?

Got it, Amelia said, and waited until she left the room.

I sat down across from her. Up close I saw that the prosthetic had a cupped and glossy palm and slender articulated fingers. I didn't want to look at it. Out the window a large yellow leaf fell from a tree.

Amelia pulled both hands into her lap and began speaking. Her voice was fuzzy. She was talking about *Inquiry*. I didn't want to listen to you, she said, but I should have.

I pressed my swollen foot hard into the floor. Amelia—

She held up her good hand. I just want to talk about what we need to do.

Even if they're alive, we can't get to them, I said. That's what you told me.

James says they're close to a solution with the fuel cell.

How close?

NSP is sending you to the Pink Planet to find out.

I don't want to go anywhere. The pressure in my ears was worse and I shook my head and opened my mouth, pulled at my ears. I want to stay here.

What's the matter with you?

My ears are stopped up.

Her face was exasperated. She said something. I think it was, Have you tried— But I didn't catch the rest. She stood up from the table, hugged her prosthetic to her chest, and hung her head upside down. She pulled at her earlobes.

I got up slowly, bent over, hung my head the way she had. The pressure in my ears stayed the same. I pulled at my earlobes and the two points of pain seemed to bore into my skull, until—

There was the faintest pop and my earache evaporated. I tentatively released my ears. I slowly raised my head and the air was full of sound. A high whistle from a vent, sharp clicking from a nearby breathing-therapy machine, the crunching rumble of a truck on the road outside.

Thank you, I said, and my voice was loud and brittle.

You're welcome.

She sat back down, still hugging her hands to her chest.

I looked at her prosthetic. Really looked at it. In the background the breathing-therapy machine clicked and clicked and clicked. Does it hurt? I asked softly.

She didn't answer. In her lap she worked the thumb of her prosthetic back and forth with a popping motion. Sometimes, she said finally. It's weird. Sometimes it feels like it's still there.

I'm sorry Amelia, I said.

I know you are.

A man wearing shorts and a Candidate Group sweatshirt came into the room. He sat down in front of a machine and began doing leg exercises. I watched him push the heavy pedal with his feet.

There's no official rescue plan, Amelia said. Not yet. But that's what we're working toward.

I'll mess it up, I said.

No you won't.

I'm not ready.

She scrutinized me. You look puffy. Have you been taking the pills they gave you?

They don't work.

It'll get better. In a week or two you'll be ready to go back up.

I started to protest again but she interrupted me. What else are you going to do?

32

When I was a little girl I had night terrors, or that's what my uncle and aunt called them. I'd wake in the night standing in the front yard. The icy air prickling my bare arms, and my uncle's warm hands on my shoulders. It was the only way he could wake me up—to take me out in the cold. I remember the feeling of the sharp gravel against my soft bare feet and the flat black of the night sky above my head.

In the morning my aunt would tell me about the screams that woke them and what I looked like when they went into my room. Red faced and sweaty, my hair a dark nest on top of my head. But I had no memory of those things. I remembered only the cold air against my skin and my uncle's soft and precise voice in my ear. He said my name, June, June, June, until I came to.

Then he took me back upstairs and sat with me. I remember how quiet it was, my aunt and cousin asleep in their own rooms, the curtains in my bedroom drawn. I lay in my bed, and he sat in a chair next to it. Sometimes he read to me or we drew together. But mostly he just talked, about what he was working on, his students, or the astronauts who trained in the buildings next to his lab.

He talked a lot about the Pink Planet. My moon. He described its surface, rocky and rose tinged, and the silt that blew through the air. From memory he drew the structures NSP had built there. He had developed the solar grid that powered its three outposts, so he knew all the minute details. The first two buildings were tiny, a satellite station with an adjacent landing site, and a remote agricultural outpost. The third was the Gateway, a sprawling complex intended to be the home base of the Explorer program, starting with the second mission, because of the favorable launch windows created by the Pink Planet's orbit. Each structure had started as a single mobile habitation unit and had been expanded over time, but the Gateway was by far the largest, with living quarters and labs and control rooms and launch pads growing like limbs from its first and central module.

I remember falling asleep to the soft scratch of his pen, with pictures of pink rocks and white modules and shining panels shuttling through my mind.

When my lander touched down on the Pink Planet with a grinding *thnnnk*, it was night. The landing site was a semicircle of light swimming in an expanse of black, and it felt as if I could be anywhere: the top of a mountain, the middle of the ocean. The moon. Mars. I extricated myself from my jump seat, my limbs stiff with sitting in one position for so long. My right eye twitched and a dull ache vibrated at the base of my jaw. I rubbed my face three times and put my helmet on, secured it, and grabbed my locker.

I stepped onto the surface. I was glad to move. The trip to the Pink Planet had meant too much sitting, too much doing nothing. I turned slowly in place, tried to discern shapes in the darkness. Topography. Anything. There was nothing but an unfamiliar rushing wind. I took a step and my boots sank into the silty soil. And another unsteady step. I reached down and ran my glove through the silt and waited for something. I think I hoped the feeling of sitting with my uncle in the night would come back. The sound of his voice telling me about this place, the feeling of him sitting close.

But my old bedroom at my aunt and uncle's house, with its paintings on the walls and bookcase in the corner and bright rug on the floor, had never felt more far away. I was standing on the moon that I'd heard and read and thought so much about as a child, that had always felt like *mine*, and nothing about it was familiar.

I followed the lights, reached an airlock, and went inside. This was the smallest site on the Pink Planet, the satellite station; it housed a staff of scientists and satellite specialists, as well as rotating maintenance crews. There were ten people inside the five domed modules, but two of them were headed back to Earth. NSP had just shut down the planet's agricultural outpost and they were the last to leave. I was headed to the only other site in operation—the operations station to the north called the Gateway.

I drank water and took a pain pill. I forced myself to choke down an oatmeal bar. Then I helped unload the supplies that had been delivered with me. By the time someone could drive me to the Gateway my eyes were scratchy with exhaustion.

Pink silt swirled in the rover's headlights as it approached the complex, a jumble of gray modules in an expanse of uneven ground. A door opened in one of the modules, and my driver slowly pulled the rover into a dark cargo bay. I put my helmet on and climbed out.

Bits of rose-colored dust blew against my legs and tapped on my helmet as the rover pulled away. The door closed behind it and the dust fell to the ground. I turned on my headlamp and shadows rose up. Except for two parked rovers on one side and a heap of disassembled parts at the back, the bay was nearly empty. It reminded me of the cargo holds on the *Sundew* before a shipment arrived, when they were vast and echoing.

Ahead of me was an airlock and I stepped inside. A small circle of white light appeared in its porthole. It got larger—someone with a flashlight approached along a corridor. The light grew nearer and then stopped. I waved through the window. Behind the flashlight was a dark shape.

Finally I heard the click of the locking mechanism and the air pressurized around me. When the door opened the light was in my eyes; I raised my hand in front of my face. Then the flashlight lowered and revealed a young man in a dirty gray jumpsuit. A lean body and an angular face, keen eyes. Hair that curled over his ears. James.

Memories rose up in my mind of James and my uncle, their

heads bent together over a table littered with metal shapes. James in a blue Candidate's uniform running on the track at Peter Reed. In the office he shared with Theresa, his hair wild and his eyes tired, my pneumatic hand drawings spread out before him on his desk.

I took off my helmet and the air was salty, and also sweet.

It's June, I said.

He ran a hand over a dark patch of stubble on his cheek.

Peter Reed's niece, I said.

Right.

Where is everyone? I squinted down the dark corridor. Sleeping?

Last maintenance crew left and the next hasn't arrived yet.

You're here by yourself?

A beeping sound came from above us. For a couple of days, he said, speaking over the sound.

What about Theresa—

A wailing alarm joined the beeping; behind us the airlock slid shut with a thunk.

Damn it. He started to stalk away.

I followed him. What is it?

We're on low power. It keeps tripping the life support alarm.

Why?

The system thinks we're running out of oxygen—

No why are you on low power?

Busted solar panels.

I can help fix them.

He turned around and didn't say anything. He just looked at me from behind his flashlight, and I had a strange sensation that the light was holding me, pinning me in place.

He lowered the flashlight finally. No need. He gestured down an open airlock. Bunks are that way. Then he turned to walk in the other direction and the light went with him.

Soon the corridor was completely dark. On the wall was a switch; it worked. A dim trail of blue lights appeared along the floor.

His voice came from far off: If you want to eat or drink—or breathe—in the morning, I'd shut that off.

I need a light—

Behind you.

I ran my hand along the wall again and found a flashlight, turned it on, and walked in its small circle of light, looking into empty rooms and dark airlocks. The Gateway was sprawling and irregularly laid out. Some sections appeared brand-new. The plastic walls of the modules were bright white, the corridors wider and cooler. My footsteps echoed slightly there. Other parts were clearly older, built in an earlier era. Those corridors were dark and narrow and smelled like old air filters. Their tan walls muffled sound. Rooms were connected at odd angles; there were step-ups and step-downs in unexpected places, and I stumbled several times.

I tried to recall my uncle's drawings to get my bearings but I saw no correlation between the shapes I had in my mind and the snaking corridors in front of me. At a dead end I backtracked and opened airlocks. Behind one was another corridor, even darker than the one I'd been in. The portholes were smaller and thicker here, and the air was hot and close. I bumped along until I found a room with beds inside.

It was empty of anything except four beds, four storage cabinets, and a sink with a mirror above it. I dropped my bag on the floor and slowly pulled my arms out of my suit with a feeling of relief. My limbs ached from its weight, and my elbows and knees were slow to bend. I leaned onto the bed to extricate my legs. The pain in my molars had settled into a diffuse ache at the back of my jaw.

The mattress on the bed was wider than any I'd slept in for a long time. I wanted to lie down but worried if I did I wouldn't be able to get back up again. I grabbed a fresh T-shirt, pushed my locker under the bed, and went back into the corridor. With my flashlight I found what appeared to be a central module, with a small galley and a laundry. The portholes were larger here and the sky a dark blank outside. It was oddly quiet. The *Sundew* was always full of sound, whirring and blowing and beeping. The vents here were nearly silent. Cool, moist air drifted from them without a sound.

In the corridor next to the galley I opened doors. All the modules behind them were empty, except for one, a workshop that contained a large table and shelves full of tools. Strewn across the table were pieces of something—

The suck and hiss of an airlock came from down the corridor, and I moved quickly in the direction of the sound, back toward the cargo bay where I'd started, at least I thought so. James stood at the end of the corridor. He was climbing into a suit, slimmer and more compact than the one I'd worn here and the ones I was used to on the *Sundew*.

Where are you going? I asked.

South solar field.

There were more suits hanging on the wall. One was smaller than the others and I grabbed it from its hook. I'll come.

I'm fine on my own. Stay here.

I'd rather work.

He held his helmet against his broad chest and looked at me, and again I had the strange feeling of being pinned in place.

I'll be handier than you think, I said.

He pulled on his gloves, secured them at his wrists. I see you haven't changed.

So you do remember me.

I remember a scrawny girl who used to sit reading books she didn't understand in Peter's lab.

I remember a man with short hair and clean clothes.

He smiled slightly and put on his helmet. I did the same. He opened the airlock and I followed.

I understood those books, I said, my voice tinny inside my helmet.

33

Inside the rover James pressed some buttons and the cargo bay door opened onto darkness. He turned on the headlights—they made the ground outside sparkle—and the rover rolled forward onto the pink silt. Our seats were close and as the rover bumped over the uneven ground I held my body straight, my helmet in my lap.

He accelerated toward a ridge and the wind picked up. There was complete darkness in every direction except for the one the headlights were pointed in, and it seemed as if we were climbing up and down the hills of silt nearly blind. How did he know we weren't about to fall off a ridge or drive into another? I looked at him. His beard was patchy and uneven; there were dark circles under his eyes. Amelia had thought it was a good idea for me to come here, but now I wasn't so sure.

Silt hit the windows in waves, buffeting the rover to the left and then the right. I secured my restraints. He left his off. The sound of the wind was low and loud, *SHOWWW, SHOWWW.*

How far is the field? I asked over the muffled roar.

About thirty minutes.

What else does it power? I held on to the side of the rover as we skidded across a rocky plateau. In the distance was a dark shape.

Gateway, satellite station.

That's it?

Agricultural outpost's shut down.

The headlights reached the shape—it was a disintegrating lander, its portholes like dark eyes in its dented white sides. More shapes appeared. Two wind-battered rovers, their legs splayed like injured spiders. A rocket engine half-buried in the silt, its insides exposed.

What happened to all the testing facilities, the labs?

Gone. Shut down.

Why are you still here?

Because I don't want to study anything or test anything.

We accelerated over the crest of a ridge and I held on tightly as the rover skidded forward. For a split second we were airborne and then hit the ground with a crushing thunk that made my back molars ring with pain. I blinked, moved my body in my suit. He kept driving.

Then what's all the stuff on the table in the workshop? I asked.

He didn't answer. We were climbing an even steeper hill now and the rover's tires bumped and slipped over the uneven ground. When we got to the top the wind was one long roar. It seemed we would tip over; the rover started beeping. I held on.

I tried again. Amelia said you've been working on the fuel cell. She said you were close to a solution.

He shifted his body opposite to the wind, and his elbow bumped my side. Not anymore.

Because Theresa left?

He looked at me. No.

Why did she leave?

He veered around a wedge of rock. Ahead there were more shapes: a huddle of wind-battered satellites, the metal spine of a probe. A faint rosy glow came from the horizon and they glinted in the light.

She hates this place.

So you've been working alone—

This is what I've been doing. He gestured ahead to an expanse of glass that mirrored the brightening sky. Clearing silt from panels, hauling water tanks, flushing water pumps. That's all.

The rover lunged and skated toward the field and when we bumped to a halt he put his helmet on and locked it in place. I did the same. He opened his door and stepped onto the pink rocks, but when I followed I stumbled. The ground was soft in some places and hard in others, and my boots sank immediately into the hollows. I squinted at the ground, my breath loud inside my helmet, held my gloved hands out in front of me, and tried to stay upright.

Up ahead he had already gone into a small outbuilding and pulled out two brooms. He handed one to me and then walked to the nearest solar panel and began to brush pink silt from its tilted surface.

It was something to see it up close, the solar field I'd heard so much about as a child. But I was confused. Why do we have to do this? I asked. With some effort I swung my broom onto a panel. What's wrong with the cleaning mechanism?

Broken, and they don't make the parts for it anymore. His voice came through inside my helmet.

The sun was brilliant now and turned the cleared panels into mirrors. I tried to keep pace with James and began to sweat, felt my underclothes cling to my skin inside my suit. He moved on to the next panel, and I did too. We kept working, moving from panel to panel, row to row. He gained on me and was soon several panels ahead.

Found the row that's out, he called.

I kept going and finished three more panels. My arms ached and my eyes stung with sweat.

The wind picked up again. Grains of silt hit my helmet like a hundred tiny pinpricks. I watched with a feeling of desperation as the panels we'd just cleared were slowly being covered again.

This is pointless in this wind, I said.

It'll stop, he said.

The ground thickened and swelled. Silt covered the tops of my boots. I set my broom down and walked to the next row, bending my body into the wind as the dust tapped furiously against my visor.

What are you doing? I called.

Whole row's out because of one panel. We'll take it back with us.

Wait, I said. Let me help you.

There was a pause and a crackle inside my helmet. Then, God damn it! And a groan.

I wove through the panels, around their sharp corners, my boots clumsy on the uneven ground. The thickening clouds of pink dust made it impossible to see more than a few inches in front of me. Then, the glint of his visor—maybe.

I kept moving and finally my foot hit something. It was him, on the ground, nearly buried in silt. His leg was pinned beneath a panel, he was trying to push it off but couldn't get enough leverage. I got down on the ground next to him.

Why didn't you wait?

You think you know what you're doing, but you don't. He shifted his body on the ground and winced.

Well now you'll have to let me help you, I said.

He leaned on his elbows. I guess so.

The panel was like a slab of concrete and after straining against it for several minutes, I could move it only a fraction of an inch. I sat back on my heels and the wind buffeted my helmet. Are you hurt?

It was hard to see his face clearly through the swirling silt. I bent my head closer and our visors touched. Sweat had pressed his dark curls flat at his temples; his mouth was a thin pink line.

I'll live.

I got up and slowly found my way to the rover, found a cable in the back, and tied it to the hitch. Then I returned to James and looped the cable around the panel.

Ready? I asked.

The angle's wrong, he said.

The angle's fine.

I got in the rover and took a minute to figure out the controls. Then I inched forward, its tires crunching slowly over the silty ground, until I heard a deep groan.

Outside I bent into the wind. A big gust of silt nearly tipped me backward, and then—all at once the wind stopped. The swirling silt fell to the ground. The sky was almost instantly, eerily clear.

Told you it would stop, he said. The ground sparkled in the sunlight.

I unhooked the cable from the panel and returned it to the rover. Then I crawled under the malfunctioning solar panel, unscrewed its back cover, and powered it down. In my mind I saw my uncle's drawings of the solar field. His detailed pictures of each panel, stacks of circuits and twists of wires inside. I pulled out two connections and reconfigured them.

What are you doing? Don't mess with that. He held his injured leg in both hands.

I turned the panel back on. The other panels in the row clicked twice and then hummed.

At the sound he turned his head. What did you do?

I bypassed the panel and fixed the row.

34

I half walked, half dragged him to the rover, his arm a bulky weight around my shoulder. The landscape had transformed. Now that the wind wasn't blowing, everything was so still. So uniformly rose colored. Our labored breaths were loud in the quiet.

Hold up, he said. He turned and we nearly fell. Can't leave it like that. He gestured to the panel that had pinned his foot. It was on top of a cable.

I walked back and tugged at the cable but it didn't budge. I squatted and leaned back. It still didn't move.

Is this something important?

Yes.

I sighed and pulled harder, and without warning it suddenly gave way, its metal connector hitting my head hard—so hard it knocked my helmet off. I closed my mouth, shut my eyes, and scrambled for my helmet with my bulky gloves. Salt stung the inside of my nose, the creases of my eyelids. Help me, I croaked. I crawled my hands through the loose silt and I found the smooth dome of the helmet and tried to put it on. But my hands slipped around the seal.

Calm down. I heard him crawling toward me, dragging his leg behind him. The air's not going to kill you. Not that fast—

I cracked open my eyes. My throat was on fire; tears ran down my face.

Then the sensation changed. My lips went numb and my cheeks tingled. My vision wavered and the light shifted and turned strange. My hands fell away from my helmet. I watched James crawl along the ground, a refracted pink glow surrounding him. I watched him without emotion. My head felt hard and dense, a solid object. But my hands and feet tingled, and my aching molars were light as air.

Then he was right in front of me, his face huge behind his visor. His features were wrong. His nose, forehead, eyes. Like they weren't in the right places. Like they'd migrated around his face.

He took hold of my helmet, pressed it down hard, and locked it into place, and I felt a rush of oxygen from my suit. I took big breaths and the numbness in my face faded. My eyes and nose watered and my throat ached.

I don't understand. I struggled to form words. My tongue was gritty and raw; it kept sticking to the roof of my mouth.

It won't kill you to take off your helmet for thirty seconds, or longer even.

His features had reoriented. His nose and eyes were in the right places. He pushed himself to standing and shifted his weight onto his good foot. With effort I stood up too and offered my shoulder for him to lean on.

I think you need me to help you more than the other way around, he said.

I blinked my burning eyes. I'm fine.

We walked to the rover. Slowly, haltingly. It seemed to take us hours. I scrubbed my tongue on the roof of my mouth, over and over, but it didn't help. Tiny grains of salt rubbed at the corners of my eyes. When we finally got there he pulled himself inside, and I collapsed into the driver's seat. We waited for the rover to pressurize, then took off our helmets and gloves, and the silt fell 'from our suits. I scratched at my neck and wrists, rubbed my nose and eyes with the back of my hand.

I feel awful, I croaked. I touched my lips. They weren't numb anymore. They were on fire.

You'll be all right.

He handed me a container of water. I unstuck my tongue from the roof of my mouth and drank it fast, splashing water on my raw cheeks. All I could taste was salt no matter how much I drank.

He took off his boot and pulled up his suit to inspect his leg. He tried moving his foot and made a low, uneven sound.

Broken?

Maybe.

It was stuffy inside the rover. I turned on the air, pointed the vents at my burning face.

Why's it so hot—

Give it a minute. He unzipped the top of his suit and pulled the sleeves off. A mottled scar marked the side of his neck, white at the edges and pink in the middle.

I unzipped my suit too but kept the sleeves on, turned on the navigation, and buckled myself in. James leaned back in his seat. The interior of the rover began to cool and my eyes strayed to the scar on his neck. I wanted to ask how he'd gotten it, but instead I put the rover in gear.

When I hit the gas it jumped backward.

You're in reverse, he said.

I changed gears and the rover jerked forward and the wheels spun.

Slower.

I tried again and we rolled slowly forward. According to the navigation screen we were headed in the right direction, north. We crested a ridge, crunching over the rocky surface, and the sunlight was bright. The controls were sensitive and I kept over-steering and then having to correct.

You're not very good at this.

The rover veered right and I gripped the wheel.

What would have happened out there if you'd been alone? I asked.

I would have figured it out.

You were pinned.

Yeah. Maybe I wouldn't have figured it out. He grimaced and shifted his foot.

We were nose down on a steep hill and the rover started to tilt to the left. I bent my body to the right and he did too, and I felt the solid bulk of his arm against mine. The silt-covered shape of something that might have once been a satellite or a probe rose up and I steered around it.

Can't do it without you now, he said.

Do what?

Everything probably.

The rover slid down the hill in a slow zigzag, the wheel fighting me the whole way. But I got us to the bottom.

The air did something to me, I said. It was like I was drugged. Why?

He shifted his foot again. I don't know.

What have you done to find out? I rubbed my eyes with the back of my hand. Have you reported it to NSP?

He tapped the window. His hand also had small scars, across his knuckles and in the crease of his thumb. We need to turn right, he said.

Navigation says the Gateway's straight ahead.

It's busted. You have to input your location before you get going for it to work.

Why didn't we take the other rover?

Because it needs new shocks.

I turned sharply.

If you're not studying the atmosphere, how did you find out about it in the first place?

Same as you. By accident. He pointed. That way.

We passed a clump of broken equipment too covered in dust to know what it was. The sun was high in the sky now.

Your foot will need to be splinted, I said.

He made a noncommittal sound, rubbed a hand over the stubble on his cheeks.

It's not complicated. I can do it when we get back.

He was quiet for a minute, and then he said, All right.

Once I'm done you can show me what you're working on.

I already told you there's nothing to show. He leaned his head back on the seat and closed his eyes.

35

In the blue-lit medical bay we moved to separate sides of the room and climbed out of our suits, making two piles of pink silt on the floor. In a T-shirt and tights I splashed water over my face at the sink and scrubbed my itching eyes with a wet towel. Across the room James leaned against the wall and slowly extracted his legs from the bottom half of his suit. Then he sat down on a bench and stretched his injured leg straight.

This module must have been a more recent addition to the station because everything was clean and shining. The air was cold and still, and I was conscious of my sweat-dampened clothes, my burning lips. I poured some water into a plastic cup, lifted it to my mouth—it was so cool on my raw tongue—and drank it quickly, my swallows loud in the silent room.

A task light hung above the metal table in the center of the room; I turned it on and opened drawers and gathered what I thought I'd need. Surgical scissors, antiseptic, plaster, bandages.

You've got to lie down, I said.

He eyed the table and the circle of light in its center, then rose and hopped across the room. He pulled himself up but stayed seated.

I waited.

He looked at me sideways and slowly lowered himself to his elbows, making the table creak, and then onto his back. He smelled like salt and sweat and coffee. His helmet had pressed dark curls around his temples, and his face was softer with his hair pushed forward. More boyish. More like the kid I remembered from the doorway of my aunt and uncle's house, a stack of papers in his hands.

He raised his eyebrows.

I'll get started, I said.

There was the hint of a smile at the corners of his mouth.

I moved the task light above his foot as if I'd done this a hundred times.

Under his jumpsuit his leg was lean and covered in dark wiry hairs, except for a small patch below his kneecap where he had a scar, a small half circle of mottled skin. The tight fabric of his right sock was damp and clinging. I worked it over the jut of his ankle bone—his skin was slightly tacky—and around his heel.

When I reached his toes his leg stiffened.

I'll cut the sock off, I said, and carefully slid the surgical scissors between the fabric and his skin, cutting toward the sock's toe. I peeled the material away to reveal the bent angle of two of his toes.

Broken toes, I said, and ran my hand along the top of his foot, felt the wiggle of his veins, the splay of the thin bones underneath. Then I took hold of the whole foot and gently squeezed the metatarsal bone, and he made a sound, a cross between a groan and a squeak.

I let go. And a hairline fracture, I said.

I ran the plaster under some water, spread it over the top of his foot and across the two broken toes, and let it set for a minute. Then I wound a stretchy bandage tightly around it, cut off the excess, and secured the end with tape.

He watched me intently. He motioned to his face. You look a little like your uncle, he said. The set of your mouth—

I waited for him to say more, but he didn't.

How did you get the scars? I pointed to his neck and his knee.

Probably the same as you. He nodded at the spray of pink spots around my right eye.

Getting hit in the face with debris in a depressurized cargo hold?

Something like that. He sat up, slowly swung his legs over the side of the table.

A pair of crutches rested against one of the walls and I handed them to him.

Thanks. His slight smile was back.

You're welcome.

He leaned on his crutches; the curls at his temples had dried and they fell across his face. We stood there looking at each other for a minute. The room was very quiet, very still. We were the only two people here. The only two people for miles and miles.

I need to tell you something, I said.

Okay.

The *Sundew* and *Inquiry* use the same liquid waste disposal system.

Wait. He frowned. What?

It has to be vented manually. With four people using it, about every three days.

He leaned away from me on his crutches. Why are you telling me this?

They're alive, I said. The *Inquiry* crew. I came here to tell you.

His lip twitched. The patter of silt came from the roof above us.

When the fuel cell is ready we can go get them, I said, and felt a soaring lightness in my chest.

It's not going to be ready.

You told NSP you were close to a solution.

The expression on his face was strange. I lied.

Why would you do that?

So they wouldn't send us home.

You and Theresa.

Yes.

But Amelia and Simon said—

Amelia and Simon. His voice was bitter; his bandaged foot swung slightly in the air. What do they know about it?

They helped invent it—

The fuel cell can't be fixed, he interrupted. I know because I've spent the last six years trying.

36

The next morning I woke with a leaden ache behind my eyes. My mouth was dry and still tasted of salt; my back molars smarted. I wanted water but my body was heavy in the bed. My thoughts were heavy too, slow moving, gloomy. I missed the *Sundew*, and Amelia and Simon and Rachel, and maybe more than anything else, the work. I knew how to do those jobs, fix that equipment, load and unload those crates, but I didn't know how to do what I needed to do here.

I hadn't seen James since we were together in the medical bay; once I returned to my bunk I slept through the afternoon and night. Now I recalled his face when I told him about *Inquiry*, the way it seemed to close in on itself. Maybe I'd made a mistake coming here. He wasn't the person I remembered from Peter Reed; something had happened to him in the meantime.

I roused myself from the bed and dressed slowly. Tights, T-shirt, socks, sneakers. At the sink I washed my face and my skin was dull and rubbery under my fingers. Outside my room my body was like a stone I had to push forward with each step. The path was dark and narrow and the blue runner lights glowed faintly. I hit a dead end. I was lost again and I kicked the wall.

Doubling back I went from one corridor to the next, in and out of faint blue light and smudgy darkness, into air that was cool and then hot, and then cool again. Then a sound broke the silence. A moan? I blinked, rubbed my face. I called out, tentatively, James?

The corridor was a gray-blue cave of panels and cabinets. No doors. The largest cabinet was at the dead end and it looked like it was for storing suits. I tried its latch—it was locked. I ran my hand over the cabinet door, felt a slight vibration, pressed my ear to it, and heard a hum. Then—a movement of air, a slight draft against my skin. But the crack between the door and the wall revealed nothing but darkness.

When I finally found the galley, a room with a low ceiling and dusty yellow lights, James was there, drinking coffee and writing in a notebook. His hair appeared freshly washed and instead of his jumpsuit he wore a clean white T-shirt and sweats. One shoe on his uninjured foot.

He watched me slowly open cabinets and drawers packed with food and supplies. I discovered enough oatmeal, egg powder, and dried beans in one cabinet to feed a crew of twenty for a year. In another, at least a hundred pounds of vacuum-packed beef and fish jerky. Also huge sacks of sugar and coffee, and packages of dried vegetables and fruit—apples, bananas, raisins, carrots, peas, yams.

After the thin provisions on the *Sundew* I was dazed by the quantity and variety of the food. I found a glass and drank some water, still staring at the cans and containers of food. Then I reconstituted a packet of dried milk, scooped some cereal into a bowl, and sat down across from James.

But when I looked at my food my stomach turned.

It's the silt, he said. The next morning it's rough. His voice was easier than it had been the night before. He got up, balanced on his good foot, and poured coffee into another mug.

I raised my spoon and lowered it without taking a bite.

He held himself steady with the back of my chair. Drink this. He handed me the mug and his skin had a soapy smell.

I don't drink coffee.

Today you should.

I took a sip. It tasted terrible.

He grabbed his notebook and his crutches and hopped to the

door. I thought he was going to leave but he didn't. He leaned in the doorway, his bandaged foot hovering an inch above the floor.

Keep drinking, he said.

After more sips from the mug my limbs started to feel lighter, my head clearer. I managed a bite of cereal. The pain in my back molars had returned so I chewed on the left side.

So what's the plan? I asked. Are there daily checklists or what?

I've got to haul water tanks.

I gestured to his foot. How are you going to do that?

You're going to help me I guess.

Good. I spooned cereal into my mouth until my bowl was empty. What did you do to life support? I asked. It's a system I know, but when I opened up the box it's completely rewired. And the ducts are silent—

I made it better.

How?

You're not actually interested in that.

I am.

He showed me the modifications he'd made to the life support system, moving down the corridors slowly with his crutches, and how the station's power supply worked—a snaking system of conduits that drew power from the solar fields. And a smaller-scale molten salt battery system that had been a pilot project when the Gateway was established. I'd worked on a similar project at Peter Reed and I wanted to see how he'd dealt with the heat transfer issues we'd experienced in the lab.

But something simpler demanded our attention—the sink in the laundry module had a leak. We gathered the tools we needed and spread some towels on the floor. It was a tight squeeze to get at the pipes because they were installed behind a filtration unit, and the smell of laundry detergent and plastic piping filled my nose as I wriggled behind the drum filter. James leaned over the top of the sink, his weight on his good foot.

I tightened the valves first and they squeaked as I turned my wrench. The last time I'd done a job like this I had zero gravity to contend with. This was much easier, although more than once I absentmindedly tried to press the wrench to my pant leg where a strip of Velcro would have been.

I asked him to run the water and the leak lessened but didn't stop. Do you have a basin wrench?

Hold on. I heard the rattle of him digging in the tool kit.

But tightening the base nut did nothing.

James unscrewed the faucet and pointed a flashlight into the cabinet below. I blinked in the bright light. I know the leak isn't in my eye.

He moved the flashlight to the pipes above my head.

Tighten the valves? he asked.

I did that already. I think there's more than one thing going on—

I squinted at the plastic joints above my head and then loosened the nuts that connected them. I need a bucket, I said, and reached out my hand.

I wedged the bucket under the joints and eased off the P trap. Salty water splashed into the bucket and onto my face.

Damn. Water falls downward here.

He laughed. It does.

I dried my face with my T-shirt and peered into the P trap. Do you have extra joints? This pipe is corroded with sediment.

No, but we can scavenge.

We walked together to the north corridor, James slow on his crutches, and passed through a series of modules I hadn't seen yet. There were more bunks, with four or six beds to a room. And then the corridor unexpectedly opened up and we were in a large, dim room. Rows and rows of blank computer faces looked back at me.

The control room, I said. I switched on the light and nothing happened.

I've got the power shut off, he said.

I took out the flashlight I had in my pocket and pointed it into the large, dusty room. I remembered my uncle's drawing of this module, the new and gleaming equipment, and the excitement in his voice when he talked about it. They were going to run the Explorer program out of this outpost, I said. I swept my flashlight beam over the tops of dark computers, straight-backed chairs, and a wall of screens at the front of the room. Starting with the second mission.

Yes.

The one you were supposed to command.

Right. Come on.

Is it still here?

Endurance? Yes, it's still here. He gestured out a porthole. Quarter of a mile that way.

I felt a ripple of excitement. NSP's second explorer, the exact replica of *Inquiry*, was steps from where I stood. Can I see it?

The hangar's sealed up, he said.

Why?

He waved me out of the control room with his crutch. Honestly I think NSP's forgotten it's here.

He led me to a large bathroom with rows of sinks and toilet compartments. We can grab what we need from here, he said, and we set to work dismantling the piping from the first sink in the row.

37

Every morning was the same. Me eating cereal, him leaning in the doorway. He was in the galley when I got there, no matter how early I rose. I would pour myself cereal and we would talk about the work there was to do that day. The maintenance crew had arrived—a group of four men who spoke to one another in Russian and split their time between the satellite station and the Gateway. They took care of the solar fields and power and life support at both locations. But the Gateway had hundreds of systems and rooms upon rooms of equipment. Most of it was unused or off-line but still routinely checked, as if a full crew might arrive at any moment and the Gateway would again become a fully operational research and control station. Keeping up with all those checklists was up to James and me.

We worked long days, twelve, sometimes fourteen hours, almost always together because of James's injured foot. Then one morning he wasn't in the galley. I ate my breakfast alone, and aside from the buzz of the yellow overhead light, the only sound was the scrape of my spoon against the bottom of my bowl. It was odd to sit there without his frowning face in the doorway. The airlock was open to the dim corridor outside, to the lumbering expanse of connecting corridors and modules. A labyrinth of dark and empty space.

We had planned to spend the morning checking all the fire alarms and extinguishers. I waited a few minutes longer in the galley and then got a ladder and started the job alone. It was tedious: I set up the ladder, climbed it, tested the first alarm, and then climbed back down. There were over a hundred alarms and at least twenty-five extinguishers (these were installed in the walls of all the bunks and at intervals in the corridors). Each alarm needed to be partially dismantled and cleaned of dust and then manually set off. After each shrill beep I thought James would appear, but he didn't.

My neck was stiff and my ears rang. I took a break and hauled water tanks. After that I was tired and irritated and walked the corridors in search of him. The maintenance crew were gone for forty-eight hours replacing cables near the satellite station, and there was a lot more to do that day. It was taking too long work-ing alone.

James wasn't in the galley or laundry or any of the equip-ment rooms. His bunk was empty and lit only by the blue runner lights. Everything was in shadow, his rumpled unmade bed, a mess of papers and mugs on the floor. The air smelled of sleep and stale coffee and laundry detergent—and something else, something unidentifiable. A sharp and sweet and slightly feral smell.

In the east corridor his suit was hanging on its hook, and through the porthole the rovers were parked in their usual spots in the cargo bay. He was here, somewhere. Maybe he didn't want to be found. I stopped looking and walked to my room through the dark and narrow south corridor. The air there was close and humid. As I turned a corner a flash of light appeared about thirty feet away, and I called out. But no one answered, and the light disappeared.

I reached a dead end, and in front of me was the cabinet I'd noticed days before. I tried the latch and this time it opened. It wasn't a cabinet at all, as I'd thought, but a door to another room. Or rather, a short corridor. I stepped inside. A vibrating thrum filled the narrow space. There were three doors, two to the left and one to the right. All the doors were shut.

Behind the first was a dark empty module. The noise was louder at the second. Its latch was hot, and I pulled my sweatshirt over my hand and opened it. The room was so full of whirring equipment I couldn't step inside. It wasn't one machine, but rather many machines stacked together. I knew them immediately— they were my uncle's fuel cells. Rectangular, about the size of a bread box, and enclosed in thick metal casing.

They were stacked back to back and top to bottom, just as I'd seen them in my uncle's schematics, but there was something wrong with them. They gave off heat like a furnace. They shuddered and groaned. They weren't supposed to sound like that; they were meant to hum softly. These cells sounded like they were dying.

What are you doing in here? James's voice came from behind me. He grabbed my wrist. He steered me away from the hot room, out the cabinet door, and into the main corridor.

I shook him off. What's wrong with those cells? I asked even as the notes from my uncle's schematics rose up in my mind. Five voices arguing about time and vibration and what they might do to the cells. How the cells might fare over weeks, months, years.

I'll tell you. His eyes were oddly unfocused, as if he'd just woken up, and his speech was slightly slurred. Later.

When?

He leaned on his good foot. In the morning.

I don't want to wait until morning.

Just say yes June. He moved closer to me. Okay?

In my bunk my mind worked at what I'd seen. The heat, the noise. I pictured those cells stacked four to a row inside the walls of *Inquiry*. Connectors snaking to every system on the explorer: its engines, communications systems, life support, grow modules . . .

I wanted to get up, go back to that room with my tools, and look more thoroughly at the cells. Listen more carefully to their vibrating noise. I wanted to disconnect a stack and take it apart. But I didn't. I stayed put. I sat on my bed and the minutes ticked by. It was dark now; my arms ached from hauling water tanks that morning and my eyes grew heavy. Finally I laid my head on the pillow and fell into a dream.

In the dream I was back in my aunt's basement, in front of the old boiler, a box of matches in my hand. Its drawer groaned when I opened it. I dropped lit matches inside and there was a hot metal smell and a bloom of charcoal smoke that singed my skin.

I woke with a start, a dark smell in my nose. I sat up and sniffed the air, and the sweat in the creases of my arms and legs went cold. I jumped from my bed and ran. A black cloud hovered at the end of the corridor, the color of charcoal, the color of char. It choked me; it scorched the hairs inside my nose, and I pulled my shirt over my face. The door to James's room was open and smoke poured from it.

My throat closed. I couldn't keep my eyes open; the air was made of fire. With my eyes squeezed shut I lunged through the door blindly, coughing, spluttering, calling his name. My hand closed around the fire extinguisher attached to the wall. I bit its cap, squeezed its lever and sprayed. I allowed my eyes to open a slit, saw nothing but white. Then, in the corner, red. Fire jumped up the wall; flames leapt at my arms. I batted them away and sprayed again.

In the middle of the bed a curled shape lay covered in white foam. James's shape. A blackened electrical panel above his head. I shook him. He coughed. I shook him again and he opened his eyes. June.

He stood up and coughed and waved his hands through the haze. He pulled the sheets from his bed and threw them on the floor, stamped out cinders with his bare feet and winced.

The electrical panel on the wall was slightly ajar. I picked up a T-shirt from the floor and used it to open the panel all the way and smelled hot metal and melted plastic. Its insides were a mess of burnt wires.

This is weird, I said. Look at this—

I don't need to look at it.

Wires have been cut. I blew air into the panel and bits of charred paper came flying out. Someone's stuffed paper in here.

But he wasn't listening.

Stay here, he said, and he limped to the door. The haze from the fire extinguisher still hung in the air and he moved through it as if it was a thick fog. At the airlock he turned back and pointed to the bed. Don't move. He took a flashlight from the wall and left me alone, closing the airlock behind him.

When he came back he was pale. He stood in the doorway looking at the ruined room and at me. Foam clung to his hair and smoke darkened his skin. Are you all right? he asked.

I felt the cold singe of a burn on my forearm and I shivered. Yes.

He pulled a blanket from a cabinet and wrapped it around my shoulders. He drew the fabric tight below my chin. Our faces were close. The air was cloudy; white dust settled on our skin.

Are you going to tell me what's going on? I asked in a whisper.

He didn't answer, but he didn't move away. Heat came off his body in waves.

You saved my life, he said. Again.

I motioned to the melted electrical panel. Did you do that yourself?

He looked at the panel, and then back at me. I had the feeling, again, of being pinned in place.

You said you know the *Inquiry* crew are alive. How?

I took a step back. I have a recording.

I want to hear it.

Now?

Yes.

Then come with me. I got up and walked to my bunk, and he followed.

38

In my bunk the air was clear and cool but we brought the smell of smoke with us. I sat on one end of my bed, and he on the other. The blanket was still wrapped around my shoulders and the burn on my arm throbbed.

I set a digital recorder between us. On Earth I'd copied several months of feed from both *Inquiry* and the *Sundew.*

They keep the *Inquiry* feed open, I said. Even though nothing comes through. Or, they think nothing comes through. There are hundreds of channels—

I know all this, he said. There were smoke rings around his eyes.

I told him more about the liquid waste processor that the *Sundew* and *Inquiry* shared and about the interference I'd discovered on the *Inquiry* feed.

I pressed play on the recorder and white noise filled the room. Right there, I said, as the channel was broken by a low hum and seven snapping pops. That's G1 and H2.

He frowned.

I named them at school. In between classes I used to listen to the static on the *Inquiry* feed, to record the different sounds I heard.

He smiled slightly.

NSP has always said the inconsistencies in the static are interference, I said. That they're random. But G1 and H2 aren't random. They come every three days.

I switched recordings. Now this is the urine processing unit being vented on the *Sundew,* I said, and pressed play.

When the rush of static and the snapping pops came, he blinked.

If they were dead—

—nothing would be being vented. He finished my sentence.

The patter of silt came from the porthole.

Now it's your turn, I said, and pulled my blanket tighter around my shoulders, moving my burnt arm gingerly. Tell me about the fuel cells.

They shut down, he said. At around three hundred and seventy-five days. They start to sound funny a few days before. Then—like a switch has been flipped—they power down. When I try to start them back up, they only run on quarter power.

Why?

A combination of things. He rubbed the scars on his knuckles. But mostly—vibration, plus time.

But you accounted for those factors.

We did. Or, we were. But when Peter got sick— He was quiet for a minute and I felt the weight of his body at the other end of the bed, a solid mass. I told them we needed more time, he said. But NSP didn't want to postpone the launch timeline.

What have you done since then?

Reduced the heat problem, some.

What about the vibration issue?

He shook his head.

But you've tried—

A strangled sound came from his throat. Tried and failed.

The wind shifted outside and silt hit the portholes in uneven waves.

I picked up the recorder and rewound the feed, played it again, turned it up loud.

Sometimes I imagine where they are in the ship, I said. What they're doing. Eating, sleeping, doing a job.

I used to do that, he said. I pictured Anu working on the cell. I saw the four of them puzzling over it, talking back and forth. Then I stopped.

You were friends at school.

But we were pitted against each other. They said it wasn't a competition but of course it was, between my team and Anu's. They did things like schedule training tests on the same day—

Like the simulated water crash, I said. I watched with my uncle. Your crew did everything right.

I thought so too, but then I stuck around and watched Anu's team.

I didn't see their test—

It was a disaster. Or, it could have been a disaster. The drill supervisor dropped the helicopter into the water at a weird angle. They were upside down and struggling. Anu pushed herself out first, but when she surfaced her face was bloody. Everyone else was still submerged. Missy's leg seemed to be snagged in the helicopter door, and Dimitri was swimming the wrong way, down instead of up. Lee was able to roll himself into a ball and float out of the helicopter, and he was trying to extricate Missy's leg.

The trainer should have hauled the helicopter back up but the tow crank wasn't working. Anu dived back in, grabbed Dimitri—he had hit his head—and pulled him up. Lee came up for air too, and then the two of them dived back in for Missy, who was still stuck. Together they tried to torque the door and release her leg, and at the same time Dimitri set to work on the broken tow crank. But all this was taking too long. Divers went in but Missy still wasn't free. Finally Anu and Lee extracted her leg, and together they dragged her to the surface. She was still conscious, which was incredible.

That's a crazy story—

It was supposed to be us, he said. Everyone said it would be. Amelia, Theresa, Simon, and me. But when I saw that I knew their team would be chosen. They didn't work like individual people under that water but like one body with many limbs. Afterward, on the drill deck, when they were dripping and hugging each other, they seemed huge. Superhuman. Bigger than anything space might throw at them.

He stood up and started pacing the room, his limp making his stride uneven.

I've tried every angle, every possibility, he said. But every change I've made to the cell has been incremental, and *Inquiry* needs something more than incremental. It needs something revolutionary, and I know only one person who could make that kind of leap.

My uncle.

That's right.

I felt the big, empty, sprawling station around me. Its twisting blue-lit corridors, dark airlocks, empty bunks, and dusty control room. There was no one in this place but the two of us. Well he's not here, I said. But we are.

39

We stood across the table from each other in the workshop, where the smell of machine oil and air canisters mixed with the hot plastic smell of a 3D printer. A long metal table had a mess of parts on top of it, and the walls were lined with shelves full of tools, equipment, and materials. James made a space in the middle of the table, put a half-built cell in its center, and told me what he'd done. He spoke slowly, methodically, in a kind of monotone.

He had developed a modified venting system, he said, and a new kind of sealant that protected the cells from temperature fluctuations. He'd reduced the size of the cell by nearly half.

You've done a lot, I said.

But there's still the core problem, he said. These cells have to function as part of a moving object. They have to withstand acceleration, deceleration. And vibration. Always vibration.

I picked up the cell. It was much lighter than my uncle's, but at the same time, I felt the weight of all the hours James had worked on it. When I was younger that would have seemed like some kind of paradise—a problem that needed to be solved, access to a wide range of materials and tools, and almost complete solitude in which to solve it. But I didn't feel that way anymore. Now it just seemed incredibly lonely.

Can we take it apart? I asked.

Yes. Sure. He began to dismantle the cell and lay all the pieces on the table, each plate and board and screw. I watched his scarred hands. They were careful, but there was a finality in the way he set the parts down on the table with a tap or a snap or a *tunk*. Like he didn't want to pick them up again. As he did this he explained the modifications he'd made. What he'd tried. What had worked and what hadn't.

I asked questions and he gave short answers. I picked things up and put them back down and proposed a different configuration for the cell's O2 connectors. He said it wouldn't work. I described how I thought it could succeed, and he explained why it wouldn't. His voice had an edge of irritation, and when I pressed the idea, he pushed the pieces of the cell aside, grabbed a big sheet of paper and a marker, and drew the problem as he saw it.

I took the marker and sketched what was in my mind, or tried to. He leaned over the paper, his head close to mine and I smelled smoke on his skin. He asked me a question. I thought hard and answered. He took the marker back and drew again.

Like this?

Yes. But make it more— I made a shape with my hand, and he crossed out the drawing and began again.

He drew and I talked. Then I drew and he talked. We argued, then agreed, then argued again. We went through four or five sheets of paper and the air seemed to tighten around us. Our hands were moving quick, our minds quicker. We had a hold of something, the start of an idea. It pulled taut between us like a thin, invisible cord.

We drew and talked and worked until our voices became hoarse. Until the room turned stuffy with the heat from our bodies and the 3D printers, until metal shavings and bits of stripped wire casings and discarded bolts and screws grew thick on the table.

We didn't leave the workshop that night. The next day we slept for a few hours, got up, drank coffee, ate cereal, and were back at it again. We let the maintenance crew worry about the solar field and the power and oxygen supplies. Other tasks we delayed or abandoned. Days and nights began to run together. I knew only the hot room, his hands, my hands, the cell in parts, the cell put back together, the cell in parts again. I recalled other things only in outline. Amelia. Simon. The *Sundew*. Carla and Lion and Nico. My aunt. These memories were devoid of color and texture; they seemed to have no claim on me. Not in comparison with the cell—its shiny casing, its delicate boards and intricate wiring, its impossible connectors. And not in comparison with James.

He was still quiet about a lot of things. He wouldn't tell me what it was like at the Gateway before I came and wouldn't talk at all about Theresa. Or my uncle. But we spent so many hours together he became familiar. I knew what his face looked like when he woke up, the dark stubble on his cheek. I knew the rough sound of his voice late at night. He kept things to himself—thoughts about the cell, qualifications, corrections—but I learned how to draw him out. Or ignore him if I could guess what he was worrying about and didn't think it was important. His anxiety would eventually burst forth in some angry way, but I didn't mind. Even when he was grumpy or irritated or angry I felt more at ease with him than any other person, including my uncle.

On the eighth day (I think it was the eighth day) we worked through the night, until the sky through the porthole turned the color of a carnation. The workshop smelled like sweat and adhesive and the table was littered with dozens of drawings and a messy jumble of parts from the old and new cells.

We were long past talking in full sentences but used shorthand, interrupting, talking over each other, our words mixed up, not wholly his or mine, but some amalgamation of the two.

Try this, not that.

What about the other—

Yes, the other.

No.

Yes, yes!

Why didn't I think of that?

You did.

I didn't.

It wasn't me.

You said it.

No, that was you.

It doesn't matter; just hand that cable to me. Let's finish this tonight—

I reached for the cable and he did too and our fingers touched. We were always grabbing at the same tool as we worked across the table, but this time we both held on. We didn't look at each other and we didn't let go. Silt batted against the porthole and a soft ticking came from one of the 3D printers. He let go.

We sat down; he went back to soldering the expanded circuit board and I returned to reconfiguring the O2 connectors. The task wasn't complicated but I did it poorly and had to start again. I was exhausted. My stomach was empty and raw from too much coffee and too little food. I put my head on the table and rested it in the crook of my arm. From this angle, in the rosy early morning light, the detritus on the table looked like the craggy landscape outside, and I thought of my uncle's drawings of the Pink Planet and how I used to imagine myself in them, climbing the planet's ridges in a bright white suit.

James stared at the board in front of him and rubbed his eyes. I can't see straight, he said. He pulled the stool closer to the table and its loud skidding hurt my ears. He laid his head down too. His face was close and his breath warm. He shifted his elbow close to mine and tapped it lightly and I felt a tight shiver run down my back.

We're not done, I said. Not even close.

No. Not done. We'll keep going.

But we'll sleep first.

Yes. Sleep.

We got up and walked down the corridor together until we reached the central module. To the left was his bunk, to the right mine. I didn't want to go to my bunk but I moved that way. His eyes were like two pinpricks on my back but he didn't say anything, didn't follow me, and when I got to the end of the corridor and turned, he was gone.

My room was freezing. We'd been functioning on low power for several days because of windstorms disrupting the solar grid, but I hadn't felt the cold until now. There were rings of frost in the portholes; an icicle hung from the faucet in the sink. My teeth chattered and I grabbed an extra blanket, turned off the light, and lay down. My body was heavy in the bed and my feet ached with relief. But when I shut my eyes I saw James, his tousled hair and dark eyes. His scarred hands. I rubbed my feet together. I turned to my right, to my left. It was impossible. I sat up.

The vents overhead whirred softly; the wind whistled faintly outside. I pulled on an extra pair of socks and left my bunk. In the corridor my heartbeat was loud and thick in my throat and my breath made clouds in the air. Time seemed to spread out and each step took longer than the one before, but I didn't turn back.

The runner lights outside James's bunk glowed blue at my feet, and the button for the airlock was flat and cold under my fingers. The lock opened with a suck and a hiss. His back was a gray hump in the bed; it rose up, down. His face was one shadowy cheek, one closed eye. His breath was a roar. He was sleeping—I couldn't believe he was sleeping. Anger squeezed my body, and the squeezing felt good and bad.

His eye opened. He sat up and his chest was dark with woolly hair. What's the matter?

I felt cold, and hot. My body was trembling but I moved toward the bed. I sat down. My back was to him, my hands flat against my thighs. The room still smelled of smoke and also something else, the slightly feral smell of his skin and hair.

Nothing happened.

Then, the pressure of his warm hand flat against my back. The feeling of his strong fingers inching their way up the notches of my spine, until they reached the base of my neck and he pulled me down.

I held my body stiff and straight and I shut my eyes.

We can just lie next to each other, he said.

I don't want that, I said. I took a breath. I want something else.

Another minute passed and I felt his warm breath on my cheek. He pressed his mouth along my jaw and his beard scratched my skin. He lifted my shirt and my stomach shook and I pushed his hands away. He kissed my ears—softly—and my nose. The crook of my arm. My breath slowed; my limbs relaxed, a little. He went back to my stomach, kissed it. He tugged my tights down, moved his mouth over the sweep of my hip. He held my thigh tight in his hands.

He took hold of my ankle with his teeth and shook it, like it was a bone. I liked it. I didn't like it. My laugh came out like a cry.

When he let go of my ankle, his mouth traveled upward again. But slower, softer, until it was only breath on my thighs. My chest expanded. I shivered but wasn't cold. His breath grew hot again. His tongue parted my legs. I held my hand over my mouth and felt I would laugh or weep or sneeze! My heels pedaled against the sheets. He put his hand flat on my stomach and his tongue was warm and rough and moved slowly, rhythmically, like it was following a silent beat. Then it changed, and oh! My head was so hot, as if my scalp had caught fire—

I fell against the bed, shivering and sweating, and pressed my hand between my legs until the pulsing slowed.

I lay still next to him for a long time. His breath slowed and his arm rested heavy on my chest. He seemed to be dozing. But I didn't feel sleepy at all; my arms and legs were restless, my face too hot. Behind my eyes the fuel cell worked with a buzzing hum. Worked and worked. I pushed his arm off me and opened my eyes.

Are you sleeping? I asked in the darkness.

I see that damn cell when I close my eyes, he said.

I hear its vents in my ears, I said.

He turned and I felt the heat of his limbs next to mine.

His face hovered; his curls brushed my face. You need another sound, he said, and blew in my ear.

I laughed and shivered.

He wrapped his arms around me tightly, pressed his whole body against mine.

40

When I woke he was moving around the room. He was naked, but in the gloom his body was full of shadows. There were distinct shapes: the muscles in his abdomen, shoulders, thighs. But also the softness of his cheeks and the hair on his chest. He seemed natural in this state. He didn't grab a robe or a towel, and I had a strange picture of him like this, unclothed, just skin and hair and bone, not in a room but outside the station on the rocky pink surface. Nothing between him and the salty air. I thought the idea was funny.

Why are you smiling? he asked.

A picture in my head, I said.

Of what?

You.

I'm glad I amuse you.

He came closer, leaned over me. His breath was slightly sour. I didn't care.

He kissed me, gently, tugging at my lips with his.

I want to see that picture, he said.

He kissed me again, harder this time.

I don't know if I want to see what's inside your head, I said, and put my hands in his hair, which smelled like the wool blanket on his bed and also faintly like . . . what? A soldering iron. I wrapped my fingers around his head, felt his skull underneath. What's in it?

A bad temper.

That's all?

He rubbed his beard against my cheek, rough and scratchy, little hairs dragging against my skin. That's all.

I hope there's a picture of a modified cell in there, I said. One that can withstand more than a year of vibration.

He squinted, looked up at the ceiling, and then frowned. No.

He got up, pulled on a pair of shorts. I lay back against the pillow, watched him walk around the room. An image drifted into my mind—black lines waving in an expanse of white, like the painting that used to hang in my bedroom at my aunt's house. Then I saw the fuel cell, just one, outside its stack. No fixed hardware or sealant. Its interior parts floating freely in the air.

I sat up. What we've been working on, I said. It's a good start. But—

I know. It's not enough.

What if we go back to the beginning? I asked. To what a fuel cell is. What it does.

He shrugged and pulled a shirt over his head. It transforms one kind of energy into another. Chemical energy to electrical energy.

So that an explorer can use that electricity to power its engines and systems.

Are we just going to say things we already know to each other?

Yes, I said. I pulled on my tights and T-shirt and started looking for my socks.

Okay. He opened a drawer under the sink and pulled out a toothbrush. The generation of energy creates vibration. Vibration will always be a problem when an object is in a fixed space—

He held his toothbrush in the air.

I looked at him.

Who says it has to be in a fixed space? we said together.

We didn't finish dressing. We went to the workshop, picked up all the parts on the table, and dumped them onto the shelves behind us. He grabbed paper and a marker.

It needs to be— I made a movement with my hands. So it's free to move—

—the way it wants to move, he said.

He drew and I talked and gestured. Then he talked and I drew. We hauled the pieces of the cell back onto the table and took it apart again.

We didn't stop to explain ourselves. We just said what was in our minds—a shape, a movement. A feeling. A sound. We stood close and reached over each other for tools and parts. It was different than before. It didn't feel like we were two bodies, two minds anymore. We had a hold of something, a growing, pulsing idea. It had a charge like electricity. It was like a great sparking cloud above us, a tiny electrical storm.

41

For days nearly every minute was filled with our work on the cell. Thinking and rethinking it. Endlessly taking it apart and putting it back together. Each morning when I woke I heard my uncle's voice in my head—What does it do?—and I would transform the cell in my mind, through all its revisions and permutations, to where we were now. Then I would thrust my mind forward three, four, five, or more steps ahead. I ran through them fast and then slow, trying to gauge their difficulty, how long they would take—and when we'd get to the very last one.

Our jumble of ideas sharpened and made a definite shape—a shape that solved the fatal flaw of the original cell. The new prototype did more than accommodate vibration. It incorporated it into nearly every part of its design. But there was still a gap between the half-built cell and our perfect idea—we couldn't agree whether the cell should be housed in closed or open stacks. It was the old dilemma, the same question James and Theresa had argued about on the pages of the fuel cell schematics. James wanted to use closed stacks, as my uncle had, to retain power. But I wasn't convinced; an open and modular system meant the cells would be easier to fix if something went wrong.

Then one morning I woke up and heard my uncle's voice again—What does it do?—and saw that the perfect idea I'd been carrying around in my mind wasn't the end at all. Even the decision to use closed or open stacks wasn't the end. Of course it wasn't.

I turned over; James wasn't in the bed.

I went looking for him and he was in the workshop, bent over a 3D printer. We haven't thought far enough ahead, I said.

He didn't look up.

We have to stop working in isolation. We need to talk to Amelia and Simon, and we need to unseal *Endurance*.

He wiped his forehead with the back of his hand. We're not ready.

We are.

He was quiet for a minute. I haven't talked to Amelia in a long time.

So what?

And the last time I saw Simon he punched me in the face.

Simon?

A week before *Inquiry*'s launch.

I remembered James's black eye when we stood together at the airfields at *Inquiry*'s takeoff. Why? I asked.

I wanted him to talk to Anu again about the cell. To give her specifics this time, to show her the calculations we had made about vibration and time. If anyone could convince NSP to delay the launch it was her. But Simon wouldn't do it, and Amelia backed him up. I told them if something went wrong, it would be their fault. That's when he hit me.

That was six years ago, I said.

Right.

I think you can forgive him.

He looked at me. I guess that's true.

The fastest way to send them a message is at the satellite station, he said.

So let's go.

He got up from the table slowly. The maintenance crew has one of the rovers. And I took the tires off the other. I'll have to put them back on.

I occupied myself with 3D-printing some sturdier bolts for the cell's exterior base. But when I started installing them I broke my needle driver. I put the pieces of the driver in my pocket and searched for another in the cabinets and drawers in the workshop. I looked in the equipment room and James's bunk too but found nothing. There were tools in the room containing the failing cells, I remembered, and I went into the south corridor, warm and dim as usual, its walls close.

When I reached the door, the heat of the cells behind it, I heard a noise. It sounded like a word. James. It seemed to come not from the module containing the cells but from another door behind me. It was locked; I pressed my ear to it and heard the sound again. James.

I rattled the door but it didn't budge. Hello? I called.

There was no reply. I shook the door again and then wedged the handle of my broken needle driver into the lock until it sprang open. Inside was another short corridor—it had a rubber floor and smelled of bleach—and a doorway draped with two sheets of clear plastic. A glow came behind them.

I drew back the plastic and it squeaked slightly under my fingers. Behind it, a bright room; a white sheet loosely gathered on top of a high bed. A hospital bed like the one my uncle had slept in on Earth. The bed appeared empty but when I stepped closer, tubes snaked out from under the sheet. A face appeared among the folds. My throat closed. A person. A person lay in the bed. A woman, her face so colorless she appeared transparent. An oxygen mask covered her nose and lips, and a machine whirred near her head.

I thought of the dummies we practiced on at Peter Reed, their hollow rubber bodies. They had more human bulk than this woman, more flesh. She looked like she'd never lived upright. Her limbs were flat and unmoving; her head swam in the sheet's folds, as if unmoored from the rest of her body. My mind worked hard. She was real. Where had she come from? How long had she been in this room?

Then a sound, a rattling whisper. There was no mistaking it. James.

I leaned over her face. Her eyes were open and glossy. Her cheeks so pallid they were almost glassine. The machine at the top of the bed clicked, paused, and then began whirring again.

She didn't move her head, just her eyes. They rolled sideways; they met mine.

I felt something, a flicker of recognition. I imagined her small eyes brighter, her cheeks fuller. Her eyebrows sharper. Theresa. Beautiful, commanding Theresa.

She slid her thin arms upward and I drew back. She pushed herself slightly upright. It was startling to watch her move. She gestured to a door across the room and briefly pulled the oxygen mask from her face. Help me to the bathroom, she said with her slight accent.

I hesitated. I didn't want to hurt her.

I won't break, she said, and there was a surprising edge to her voice.

I reached under her arms to help her sit, and I shuddered. Her skin was like paper, the bones underneath sharp as the prongs of a fork.

I know, she said.

I helped her down from the bed and she winced when her socked feet touched the floor. She swayed a little and I held on to her. Then we walked slowly to the bathroom, pulling her oxygen machine with us on its rolling stand.

I'm fine from here, she said.

Are you?

I said I'm fine. Her eyes were clearer now. She seemed to hold her thin body straighter too.

I waited outside the door. When she came out she was able to walk without swaying and moved her legs from the floor to the bed without my help. She laid her head down on the pillow and looked at me.

Theresa, I said.

Yes.

How long have you been here? I asked.

In this room? Her voice was muffled by the oxygen mask. Three months. Maybe more.

Do you know who I am? I asked.

I remember you June.

I sat down next to her.

You're helping him, she said.

My mind moved slowly. With the fuel cell? Yes.

Good. She pressed her hands flat against the sheet. I can't do it anymore.

The oxygen machine clicked and whirred. You've been here the whole time, I said.

Are you going to solve it?

We— We have a new prototype.

Solve it. As quick as you can. I want to go home. I want to smell air, put my toes in grass.

You want to leave—

Sometimes he says he'll let me go. But then he changes his mind.

The room was too bright. The shapes of the bed, the table, the breathing machine—their edges too crisp, too clear. I got up. He isn't keeping you here.

He thinks I'm going to get better. But I'm not going to.

The patter of the silt outside mixed with the whir of the oxygen machine.

I thought of the night of the fire. The charcoal color of the air, the acrid smell of smoke. I imagined her—Theresa—walking through the station, up the dark south corridor. All the way to James's bunk. I pictured her stuffing paper into the electrical box on the wall, lighting a match, and watching the paper smoke and flare. It should have been hard to imagine this skin-and-bones woman doing all those things. But it wasn't.

I sat back down.

He locks the door, I said.

Sometimes I get confused. She moved her hands around the sheet. But I'm not confused about going home.

But that night he forgot, I said.

She turned her head away from me.

He thinks he needs me to fix it, she said softly.

I leaned closer.

The cell, I said.

But it doesn't matter whether we fix it or not.

You think they're dead.

I truly hope they are, she said.

I left her and moved through the corridors in slow motion, my eyes unfocused, my hand trailing the wall. I tripped at the step-downs and bumped through airlocks. When I reached my bunk I sat on my bed and put my hands flat on my knees.

I tried to think but my brain was a dense mass; it wouldn't move past the small bright room, past Theresa's thin, ashen face. It seemed impossible she'd been inside that room this whole time. From the day I arrived at the Gateway, until now. She was in that room when James and I drove out to the solar field and sat in the galley eating breakfast and hauled water tanks. When we worked on the cell in the workshop—and when we lay together in his bed.

A wave of nausea moved through my body and I jumped up and ran to the toilets. My stomach heaved as I leaned over one of the bowls, but only spit came up. I sat down on the floor, rested my cheek against the cool stall door. The vents whirred over my head and a soft drip came from one of the faucets. I tried to put the two things together in my mind. James—my James. The way we were together. The way our minds worked the same and the way we could talk without talking. And Theresa—the brilliant, intimidating woman I knew when I was a girl—trapped alone in a room.

Footsteps came from the corridor outside. Then a sharp tap on the door. I pressed my cheek harder against the stall.

A louder tap, and then James's voice: Are you in there?

I got up slowly; my stomach churned. I swallowed, left the stall, opened the door.

He was wearing his suit and had his helmet in his hands. I'm ready. Let's go.

I pushed words out of my mouth. You lied to me.

About what—

Theresa is here. In this station.

His expression changed.

How could you not tell me that?

He drew himself up and I felt the pent-up energy inside him like a tight spring. She's sick, he said.

What happened to her?

We were testing a new sealant for the cell and there was an explosion. I got burned. He gestured to his neck. But it was worse for her. Her mask got knocked off and the chemicals got into her lungs.

Why wasn't she evacuated?

I've followed all of NSP's medical protocols.

She says she wants to leave.

Sometimes she's not herself. The chemicals affected her brain too—

She seemed pretty lucid to me.

One day she says she wants to leave and the next day she changes her mind—

She tried to burn you in your bed!

He opened his mouth, closed it. When he spoke it was in a strangled whisper. She won't survive the trip home.

I made myself small in the doorway. I wanted to move away from his desperate face, but he drew closer, moved his hand to my wrist, encircled it with his strong fingers.

His suit was warm and rough against my cheek. You two were together, I said. Like us.

No, not like us. He held me tighter, his fingers pulling at the thin fabric of my shirt, his nose sharp and wet behind my ear. Not like us at all.

42

I slept in my bunk that night, and he in his. Days passed and we kept working on the cell but made little progress. He came to the workshop late and left early. Often he wasn't in the galley in the morning and on those days I drank my coffee and ate my cereal alone. When he was there he was different, his eyes unfocused and his movements slow. I asked him more than once if he was all right but he avoided the question, said he hadn't slept well or that his foot had started hurting again. The hours he was absent increased and the workshop was cold and quiet without him, the tools and parts and stripped wires on the table inert. My days unspooled; time didn't speed up and slip away anymore but seemed to spread out, long and loose and seemingly unending. The cell had not materially changed but felt different in my hands, as if the life had gone out of it.

At first I avoided Theresa's room, even going the long way to my bunk. I tried to pretend she didn't exist. But when I was alone her face invaded my thoughts. I would be pulling on a pair of wool socks or pouring a cup of coffee or separating a tangle of connectors in the cell, and she would appear—a white face against white sheets in a white room. At night in my bunk I'd hear the wind rushing outside and the silt rapping at the porthole, and I'd imagine her thin breath among the rustling sounds.

The door that concealed both the failing cells and her room was like a magnet. I started walking past it on my way to breakfast, and then on my way to bed. I hovered near it at odd moments. One day I opened the door—it was unlocked—and stood in the corridor listening. Then I closed it.

But the next day I went in. Theresa was alone and awake, and she asked me to stay. After that I went to see her every day. I asked her about the cell, and the components she and James had worked on together, about her time at Peter Reed, and about what it was like to work with my uncle. But she didn't want to talk about those things. She wanted to talk about Earth. I'd been there less than a month ago, and she wanted to know everything about it, what I'd done, seen, eaten.

It feels like I've forgotten it, she said. Not what it looks like exactly, or sounds like. But what it feels like. When I was growing up the dirt in my backyard had little white spots in it and these green shoots that used to come up in spring. I can see them in my mind but can't remember what they felt like. She held out her hand and rubbed her fingers together.

It was always too cold to dig in the earth at my aunt's house, I said.

In the summer, she said. It wasn't too cold in the summer.

I thought about this, tried to recall the warmer months when I was little, and an image appeared in my mind, of my uncle folding a paper airplane on the back steps. I felt the hot sun against the back of my neck. I saw the way his hands pressed the plane's corners neat and flat.

I didn't like being in the garden in the summer, I said. I was afraid of bees.

When you were home it was fall?

Yes.

Did the air smell like leaves?

I thought of the Candidate dormitory and the clean scent of the hallways. I shrugged. Outside it did—

Can you describe it?

I remembered leaving the chilly veterans' hospital after visiting Amelia and walking into the warm air outside. My body felt loose and uncoordinated, my skin unprotected. My swollen feet were huge inside my shoes. I shuffled rather than walked on a sidewalk strewn with disintegrating yellow leaves, crushed by other people's sneakers and boots.

I don't know. I hesitated. Like decay.

She nodded and looked satisfied.

But the next time I visited her she was different. She barely raised her head when I came in and a sheen of sweat made her forehead shine. Her fingers creeped around on the top of her sheets. She didn't answer when I spoke to her. Finally she asked for James, and I went and got him and left them alone.

The time after that was different too. She was up and out of her bed, pacing the room, her rumpled hair streaming down her back. Her eyes flitted wildly; she seemed to be talking to someone who wasn't there. When she saw me she grabbed my arm and shook it, hard. She opened her mouth, gestured to her throat, and began to weep. I backed away, felt for the plastic in the doorway behind me. Then she picked up one of her slippers and threw it at me.

I didn't understand it. The change in her, day by day. When she was back to her normal, lucid self, she didn't seem to remember what she'd been like the day before. I started to believe what James had said. Maybe she was confused; maybe she didn't really know what she wanted. Then one afternoon I went to see her and she wasn't there.

I went looking for James and couldn't find him either. Not in his bunk or in the workshop. Both rovers were parked in the darkness of the cargo bay. Outside the portholes the wind had picked up and the swirling pink silt created a thick haze.

I walked through the station with a strong sense of unease as the wind beat at the walls. I checked the galley, looked through all the equipment rooms and storage modules. Nothing. I went back to Theresa's room, which was still empty. The wind quieted. Then out of the porthole I saw them, both of them. Their helmets were off. James's eyes were closed against the silt, and Theresa's long hair whipped around her face. They were breathing the air.

43

I made a decision. Every day I went to Theresa's room and helped her out of bed. We practiced standing and walking short distances. Getting in and out of a suit, breathing with a helmet. Each time we did a little more. She got stronger; her voice was clearer and she had more color in her cheeks. She was more alert, able to stay awake for longer stretches. But she grew quieter too. She stopped talking about Earth, stopped asking me about it. Even when I brought it up, asked her what she planned to do when she got there and who she would see, she gave short answers.

Two days before the next scheduled supply capsule, I sent a transcript to NSP, informing them Theresa's health had improved enough for her to make the trip home, and I signed it in James's name. Then, when we were alone in her room, I told her to hold her breath when James took her out into the silt. As long as she could.

He thinks it helps me, she said.

Does it?

She was sitting on the edge of her bed, her bare feet swinging slightly over the side. It helps with the pain. But it's not making me better. She pressed her hands to her eyes. And it messes with my mind.

The silt tapped against the porthole outside and I felt the smallness of the bright room, its sealed-in feeling. Do you want to leave this place or not?

The breathing machine at the top of the bed paused, clicked, and then began whirring again. Finally she said, I do.

* * *

The night before a supply capsule was scheduled to return to Earth I went silently to her room. She was already awake and standing, holding on to the bed to steady herself. Her eyes were clear and focused.

I'm all right, she said in a whisper. I'll be all right.

Outside her room I listened but all was still. We started moving. Through the door and down the corridors, softly, haltingly. Through one airlock, then another, through warm air and then cool. I remembered where all the step-ups and step-downs were, and all the unexpected turns.

We passed James's room in slow motion, our bodies stiff with stillness. The minutes seemed to expand. Theresa stumbled. I caught her noiselessly before she fell, and we paused, our arms around each other, our faces blue tinted in the runner lights. A faint rumble of breath came from James's room, and as we moved away I shivered at the thought of his face in the morning, his cheeks pink with sleep, dark stubble on his chin.

We finally reached the airlock leading to the cargo bay and I helped Theresa into a suit, a painfully slow process. I pulled her fingers from the suit's armholes as she pushed them through, and I thought of Simon, who had done the same for me with my wet suit before my first dive at Peter Reed. Theresa was breathing hard by the time we were done, but her helmet was on now, and oxygen was flowing. She smiled weakly through her visor.

Once Theresa was folded into the driver's seat of a rover and covered with a foil blanket I punched the destination into the navigation.

She held on to the steering wheel. Her face had receded inside her helmet but her voice was clear. Thank you June.

My finger hovered over the button to open the cargo door and my heart quickened at the thought of James hearing it. I pressed it and the rover pulled forward with a low whine into the chalky night.

I went to my room but didn't sleep. I stayed in my clothes and counted down the minutes until the capsule's scheduled departure just after dawn, watched the dull pink glow of morning creep across my floor. Then James's footsteps sounded outside. He was moving up and down the corridors, in and out of airlocks calling, Theresa!

His anxious voice drew closer and strangled the sound of her name.

And then, at my door: June! Theresa's gone!

I didn't answer. He banged on the door. Wake up. Wake up God damn it.

He moved away, toward the north corridor and the cargo bay. My breath was fast. He would find the empty spot. Little piles of silt where the rover used to be.

Soon he was back, his voice a growl outside the door.

My body vibrated; my teeth chattered. I unlocked the door and he pushed his way inside.

Where is she?

She's already gone. I stepped back and braced myself, and his body seemed to change shape, to bend, to distort. But he didn't yell. His voice was low and tight. What did you do?

I'd seen him angry, many times, and had laughed at it. Laughed at his hot temper, his easy irritation with equipment, weather, me. But I couldn't laugh at this.

I backed farther away. He stepped closer.

I did what she wanted, I said. I did what was right.

He kept coming. I turned and tripped. He caught me, pulled me to him; he tucked his head and wrapped his arms tightly around my chest.

You've killed her, he said in my ear. He squeezed me and my breath strained against his chest. Do you know that? He squeezed harder.

I couldn't get enough air. I tried to pull away but his arms were a tightening vise. Stop it, I choked. I can't breathe. I can't—

He let go, and I collapsed onto my bed, coughing.

That's what she'll say. His hair was wild; he moved like his body was broken. That's what she'll say in the end.

* * *

I stayed in my bunk; I sat on my mattress and took big breaths. My lungs inflated and deflated, and I pictured Theresa in the capsule, strapped into a jump seat. Her thin face was tired but happy. Then I heard a horrible noise. It sounded like pieces of metal hitting the walls, the floor. James was breaking something. What?

I ran out of my bunk, my hands pushing against the walls, my feet clumsy. I moved in and out of light and dark, hot and cold. He wouldn't. He wouldn't— But he had. He stood in the workshop in the midst of a pile of glittering debris. Metal panels, wiring, connectors, bolts, screws. Our cell. It was a pile of pieces again, only this time even they were broken—cables torn, soldered connections split, circuit boards cracked.

He stood with his legs wide and panted with the effort of smashing it all. It was ugly. He was ugly. I thought I knew him— that I understood him—but I didn't. I thought we were the same, but we weren't.

I walked away from him; in my bunk I put some clothes in a bag and went to the cargo bay. My hands shook as I pulled on my suit, but I got it on, went through the airlock, and climbed into the remaining rover. The bay door opened into the pink glow of early dawn.

IV

44

I drove straight ahead until I couldn't see the lights of the Gateway behind me. My body vibrated but I kept my hands on the steering wheel and my eyes straight ahead. The visibility was poor. The sun was rising but it was barely a smudge of yellow on the horizon. Mountains of silt stretched out before me, uneven, undulating.

I had admired the Pink Planet my whole life. Read about it, talked about it, dreamed about it. It was June's moon. I thought if I belonged anywhere, it was here. The terrain rumbled through my body as I drove up and down the silty crags, one after the other, and around rusted-out landers and satellites and probes. The rover slid into a valley, its wheels spinning as they hit the ground, and silt-covered shapes rose up all around me. Some were discernible—the flat broken wing of a shuttle, the popped dome of an abandoned mobile habitation unit. Others weren't, and specters seemed to rise from their shapes. The steep-angled roof of my aunt's house. *Inquiry*'s tall, pointed rocket. My uncle's high hospital bed. The sharp slope of James's bare shoulder.

I blinked tears as I swerved away from the shapes, kept driving, on and on, until my body felt shattered. I hadn't set my position before I left the station and now numbers on the navigation controls jumped haphazardly around the screen.

67889.0009 00032.0000 7860.0023
21450.0001 12569.5900
00007.0000 45000.9865
10050.0090 90401.0526

I had thought I was headed toward the satellite station—it was due north from the Gateway. Now I wasn't so sure. A series of plateau-like ridges blocked out the sun ahead. I braked, tried to get my bearings, turned. I drove for a while, second-guessed myself, and turned again. I felt a flutter of panic. I'd been driving for a long time, too long. The rovers didn't keep more than a few hours of charge at a time. Ten minutes later lights flashed on the dashboard, and the rover rolled to a stop.

I found the controls for the solar charger and deployed the panels, but nothing happened. I pressed the button again and there was a grinding sound, and then silence. A fiery heat rose in my body; I grabbed the steering wheel, laid my burning forehead against it, and screamed.

The interior of the rover cooled. My breath fogged the windows and obscured the ridges of silt surrounding me. I pulled my helmet on, and my gloves, grabbed a tool kit, and depressurized the rover. Outside, the pink haze had thinned. I climbed on top of the rover and stood; I could see for a long way and there was nothing. No structure, no solar field, no beacon or cable relay. My breath was loud and singular inside my helmet. I was entirely alone.

It took me more than six hours to fix the solar deploy mechanism. It was an almost impossible job to do alone, and the sun was intense. Tools kept slipping out of my gloves. By the time I was finished only an hour of sunlight remained in the day. I got only a partial charge on the rover, three, four hours max—which meant I wouldn't have heat for at least four hours of the night.

I got back in and shut everything down but life support. I forced myself to think, to make a plan. I had a single bottle of water, no food. I had a compass, but I wasn't certain of my location relative to the Gateway or satellite station, and regardless they were too far to walk to in my suit. My communications system was out of range.

I was going to have to wait until the sun rose again. On a

piece of paper I did the math, trying the numbers three different ways. If I cycled the rover on every fifty minutes, I could stave off hypothermia until dawn. The first heat cycle would be in forty-five minutes, and I set my watch in case I fell asleep.

The sun slid lower on the horizon until it was just a thin slice of rosy yellow and the temperature inside the rover dropped. My fingers turned cold and my breath made clouds. I watched the minutes count down. Finally it was time and I turned on the heat, felt the blast of warmth like pinpricks on my face, neck, fingers. I rubbed my hands together over and over. Too soon it was time to cycle off. I set my watch again. There were still six and a half hours till dawn.

My body quickly cooled. I felt the freezing air seep gradually into my skin, muscles, bones. My neck and wrists and elbows turned stiff; my toes seemed to shrink inside my boots. Tremors moved through my body in waves. It was fully dark now. Outside was an empty expanse of black that seemed to stretch forever. Inside I had only my headlamp's single spot of light. My sense of the rover, its titanium shell, pressure coated windshield, metal alloy tires—the shape and weight of all those parts—fell away, and there seemed to be nothing between me and the deep darkness surrounding me.

I went through three more cycles, my limbs becoming more rigid and my mind more sluggish with each one. I couldn't hold on to thoughts, and the color of things changed. My suit turned gray, the rover's dashboard white. The windows blue. The third cycle of heat seemed to have no effect at all. My body was a block of ice, my mind a flat, cold blank. I slowly crawled into the back of the rover, over the battery pack, which still held some warmth, and I pressed my body against it. The temperature dropped further. Memories skittered through my brain, of frozen trees outside the window at my aunt's house. Icy sheets on my bed in the girls' dormitory at Peter Reed. Crystalized condensate on an equipment panel on the *Sundew*. Then the memories began to shift and blur.

I tried to focus on one image at a time. The book I used to read in the window seat at my aunt's house, *New History of Energy.* Carla's hand reaching out in the darkness between our two beds at Peter Reed. But the pictures got mixed up and fused together strangely. Carla's face appeared on the cover of the book. My dormitory bed floated in the darkness outside the porthole on the *Sundew.*

I pressed my body closer to the battery pack, and it was warm. Warmer than it had been, which made no sense. I felt fear, but I couldn't think. The battery grew warmer still, until I was hot. So hot I had to unzip my suit. I had to. My skin felt like it would burn off and I wanted to pull off my gloves, my boots. But I didn't. My brain wasn't working, wasn't processing, but I didn't do it because the heat wasn't real.

An overwhelming heaviness stole over my body, starting with my fingers and toes, and moving inward. My eyelids lowered, and I snapped them open. The next cycle was soon. I had to stay awake. But my eyelids were like lead. They lowered. They lowered. They lowered again.

45

I became aware of light on my shoulders. I tried to raise my head but it was an incredible immobile weight.

Then the light went away. And came back. I blinked. Someone stood in the window.

James.

But it wasn't James. It was a man wearing a patched suit and a helmet with a discolored visor. He tapped on the window and motioned for me to put my helmet on. I couldn't move my head. My face was numb; my cheek felt like it had adhered to my arm.

He tapped again. You have to move, he said, his voice muffled behind the glass. He tapped over and over.

I raised my head an inch and the sunlight was cruel. My head throbbed; a wave of nausea moved through my body. I forced myself to move my arms, and then my legs. Vomit stole up my throat and I swallowed it. I dragged my body sideways, felt for my helmet. I lifted my head more, two inches, enough to get my helmet on and lock it.

I stared out the window dumbly.

The man—who was it?—gestured to my chest. I looked down; my suit was unzipped, the strip of exposed skin red and raw. I fumbled to secure the zipper, my fingers numb and my grasp clumsy. After a few tries I managed it, and he opened the door and pulled me out. My limbs buckled, and he held me up.

Silt popped loudly on my helmet; sunlight bored into my eye sockets. I tried to see past the milky haze that obscured his visor but could make out only the shape of his head, the curve of his ears.

He helped me around the rover and into the passenger seat. He got in too, repressurized the rover, and helped me take off my helmet. Silt fell to the floor. I shook off my gloves; my fingertips were red and fat, the nails a sickening gray. He held out a bottle of water but when I raised my hands they began to pulse with pain. He brought the bottle to my mouth.

I gulped the water. Slowly, he said and his voice was soft and precise. It was my uncle's voice. He pulled the bottle away.

I leaned back in my seat and the rover began to move smoothly over the ground. It felt as if we were gliding. There were no jolts or bumps, only gentle dips and sways. Light flickered across the windshield. A structure appeared in the distance, domed white modules against the pink sky. We slid toward it.

I ran my scratchy tongue over the roof of my mouth. I wanted to say something.

The man's suit was faded blue and covered with a fine dusting of silt. You're not real, I said.

His hazy visor reflected my face.

I squeezed my stinging eyes shut. I wish you were real but you're not.

When I opened my eyes the rover was still and the light was different. The sun was low in the sky. Shallow pink hills surrounded me. Directly in front of the rover was a module with a round top and an airlock in its side.

I looked at my red fingers in my lap.

I looked at the steering wheel and touched it. I was in the driver's seat. I turned my head sharply and there was no one in the rover but me.

I pulled myself out and stumbled to the domed module. The airlock opened. My body wanted to drop to the floor but I stayed standing; my eyes wanted to close but I kept them open. On the other side of the airlock was a dark corridor followed by a series of modules. I pushed through a plastic-draped door and found a greenhouse full of withered plants. Soybeans, I thought. The next room was full of dried-up wheat. I was in the agricultural outpost that had been recently shut down. I kept going and opened doors until I found the equipment room. I needed to find the oxygenator, and when I did, I sat down on the floor and moved by rote.

When I was done I crawled to a life support monitor, pressed buttons, and took off my helmet. The air was warm and still and full of a sweet, fetid smell. Down the corridor I found a module with beds in it. The one closest to the door had a blue blanket and a single flat pillow. I pushed off my boots and wriggled out of my suit. It seemed to take forever, but when I finally got myself out I sank onto the bed. The pillowcase was smooth against my raw cheek, the mattress soft under my hips, my elbows, my heels. I reached my throbbing fingers out so nothing touched them but air.

I dreamed I was with James in his bunk, the air warm and close, his skin damp against my own. His face loomed, his hair a dark tangle. He made a sound near my ear, low, insistent. His arms wrapped around me—

I woke covered in sweat. I blinked; I threw my covers off, got out of bed. My cot was a damp rumple of gray sheets and blue blanket. I pulled the covers to the top of the bed, smoothed them down, tucked them tightly around the edge of the mattress. Then I shook out the pillow and laid it flat.

I went to the equipment room, my socked feet sore on the rubber floor, my fingertips smarting, and ran a systems check. All the status bars lit up green. Then I checked the water reclaimers, made a tour of all the modules and airlocks. I found toilets, a shower room, and a laundry. Inside the food lockers were enough supplies to last for months.

I picked up a bag of dried fruit and then a packet of instant potatoes and asked myself if I was afraid to be here alone. If something went wrong there would only be me. But I wasn't. I asked myself if I wanted James to come looking for me, and I didn't. The supply capsule Theresa had taken was already gone, and another wasn't due for several weeks. For that span of time there was nothing to do but wait. When I thought of waiting in this place alone—without anyone to answer to, without having to explain—I felt intense relief.

At the end of the corridor was a narrow plastic module with sinks and shower stalls. I went inside and the soft sound of silt, *tppp tpppp tpppp tppped,* came from the ceiling. It was cold; condensation on the sinks had a sheen of ice. But when I turned the knob in one of the shower stalls lukewarm water came out.

I found a stack of thin towels and undressed quickly, stepped into the water, and yelped when it hit my chest. There was a container of soap in the shower and I washed, the sensation of my frostbitten fingers against my skin tender and strange. I dried myself, cautiously patting the skin on my hands, chest, and face.

I didn't want to put my clothes back on—they were stiff with dried sweat—so I just pulled on my underwear and wandered. In the kitchen I filled a mug of water and drank it. In the laundry room I found a pair of sweats—they were a men's large but soft inside—and I put them on. In another room, a T-shirt with a European football insignia on it. It smelled clean and I put it on too.

In one of the greenhouse modules I opened the motorized shades—the room was made almost entirely of transparent glass. I'd seen the Pink Planet only through tiny portholes, the silt-dirtied windshield of a rover, and the tinted visor of my helmet. The color of its surface wasn't uniform like I'd thought—the silt was full of different hues. Rose and peach and coral and fuchsia.

I went to the kitchen. I found plenty of food but no readymade meals like at the Gateway. I found oats, heated some water, and reconstituted some milk. When the oatmeal was done I added a spoonful of sugar, and then since the container was

huge, I added two more. I poured some of the milk into the oatmeal and some into a glass. My mind was a blank as I spooned
the sweet liquid into my mouth. I didn't think or make a plan. I
just moved my spoon and tipped my glass to my lips until the food
and milk were gone.

46

The next day I spent an hour organizing the food stores. I did some systems checks, sent a transcript to the satellite station to let them know where I was, and then because I had nothing else to do I went into one of the greenhouse modules and poked at the wilted plants. I'd never grown anything in my life. My aunt used to keep herbs in containers on our back porch in the summer, to use in cooking. Rosemary, thyme, oregano. Lavender and mint. Watering them every couple of days was the extent of my knowledge of plants. I didn't know if I'd ever even looked at a plant up close.

The day stretched out before me with no list of assigned tasks, no piece of equipment that needed attention, no system to service or replace or check. I experimentally tugged one plant from its tray and liked the satisfying sound of its roots pulling away from the soil.

I pulled out the next plant and the next, until I'd cleared about a quarter of the trays. I found some gloves and broke up the earth. Then I located some seeds, read the directions on the back of the packet, and began planting them. The soil was soft and cool on my fingers as I pushed each seed down, and a sharp and musty smell filled my nose. I got the irrigation system working and then turned on the temperature controls. The room grew warmer, the air more humid. I smoothed my hand over the top of each square of wet soil.

Through the walls the sun warmed my face and filled the room with a rosy glow. I moved without thinking, my body loose.

The pain in my fingers receded. I had a feeling of freedom that made me think, for some reason, of my uncle's paper airplanes. How we would stand at the top of the stairs, the three of us, my uncle, John, and me, and give them the slightest push into the air and watch them drift slowly to the ground.

I returned to the grow rooms every morning. I watered. I fertilized. A schedule for all these things was posted in neat script on the wall and I followed it. I'm not sure I had any thought the seeds I planted would grow, but every day I tended to them and planted more, until all the limp stalks and leaves were cleared away and both grow rooms were filled with neat grids of dark brown earth.

When I was done in the grow rooms I worked out in the gym. At first it was hard to do anything but run on the treadmill or ride the exercise bike because of my hands. But when they started to heal—the fingernails on two of my fingers pulled away from the skin and eventually fell off, revealing new pink nails underneath—I was able to lift weights, following the same routine Lion and I used at Peter Reed.

Only now I took my time with the exercises; I didn't speed through them like I had at school, or squeeze them in between other tasks like I had on the *Sundew.* I did extra reps and stretched in between intervals. I noticed which movements came easy and which were more challenging. Some things depended on the day, or the hour. Squats were harder in the morning, running on the treadmill easier. I tracked my progress from one day to the next and noticed slight changes in my body in the mirror in the shower module. At first my torso had a lopsided look to it—my shoulders were round and strong from hauling water tanks and cleaning solar panels, but my posture was stooped from bending over the fuel cell for hours. My legs were pale and thin, my stomach soft. Now I watched as my arms shrank and the shapes of the muscles under my skin turned sharper. As my legs gained bulk and my stomach flattened.

I'd never paid much attention to my body. Now I slept when I was tired. I drank when I was thirsty and ate when I was hungry. I had time to make real meals. They were simple but were better than anything I'd eaten in months. My skin was healthier looking in the mirror; my nails grew and my hair seemed stronger and shinier. My teeth were the only part of me that wasn't improved. When I pressed my tongue into the holes where my molars used to be my molars throbbed.

At the end of the day, after I'd tended to my plants, worked out, and eaten three meals, I watched the light change through the transparent walls of the grow rooms. I'd thought the weather was almost unchanging on the Pink Planet, but it wasn't. In the mornings the light was soft, almost woolly, and the gusts of wind gentle; in the afternoon the horizon grew sharper and the wind stronger and more continuous. At the end of the day there was a peculiar sort of twilight I hadn't noticed until now, when the landscape grew long shadows and the color of the silt intensified and became almost jewellike. Then I'd shut the blinds before the smudgy gloom of night, when the ridges of silt yawned and the dust-covered junk started to look like things that weren't real.

At night I read in bed. I'd pushed all the other cots to one side of the sleeping module, found a small table, and put it next to my bed. I set a pitcher of water on it, and a stack of books. The books I took from a shelf in the corridor that contained a hodgepodge of novels and poetry and old magazines. They didn't teach literature at Peter Reed, and as a child I'd ignored my cousin's picture and chapter books. Now I read it all, everything on that shelf— a book of Coleridge's poems, *Calvin and Hobbes* comics, a biography of Jane Goodall. I liked the stillness of my room and the weight of a book on my lap. I liked being alone. My body was tired from the physical exertion of the day, my mind quiet and slack, receptive to whatever was on the page; it didn't really matter what.

47

But when I slept I tossed in my cot and dreamed of James. Once I dreamed he stood across from me at the workshop table, his angular face focused, intent on an object in his hands. It looked like the fuel cell but he held it as if it were a living thing. As if it might spring from his hands. A steady hum came from it, like a purr or a growl, and I felt the sound in my body like something was scrabbling under my skin.

It's almost done, he said.

His hands moved forward. He wanted to give it to me, gently, cautiously, as if it might run away. I wasn't ready to take it. But I didn't want it to escape, so I reached out, my palms open—

When I woke cold sweat dampened my forehead and under my arms. A prick of pain pressed inside my jaw. I ignored it and went to the grow rooms and did my jobs. A few sprouts were beginning to poke out of some of the trays in the soybean room, and I felt a deep sense of satisfaction when I looked at them.

But as the day went on my toothache grew, became a hot coal in my cheek. In the mirror in the shower module I pressed my finger against my back molar and the sensation was like an ear-splitting sound. I found a cabinet with medical supplies, swallowed four pain pills, and tried to lie down. But being horizontal made it worse; I tried my left side, my right, back, front. I got up. I paced the room.

I'd had every kind of pain imaginable on the *Sundew*— headaches that pressed like a burn against my eyes, sinus pressure that made my head feel like an overfilled balloon, stomach cramps that twisted my abdomen into knots. But they all dissipated with sleep or water or pills—or time. This pain didn't pass; it stuck around for that day and the next. It kept me from sleeping, from eating. I couldn't seem to sit still with its hot pulse in the back of my mouth. I had to move, to walk, to do anything except sit.

I went to the grow rooms and the shoots that had given me so much gratification the day before looked tiny and feeble. They weren't as big as they should be, and only about a third of the trays had any sprouts at all. I started to look things over—the irrigation, the temperature controls. The modules were heated with metal coils about the size of a dinner plate that lined the fabric walls and the floors, and with two box blowers installed in the ceilings. Some of the coils weren't functioning, and the system wasn't efficient at all.

I roamed the outpost and found a box of replacement heater coils, the pain in my tooth a tender backbeat in my cheek. In the soybean room I pulled the broken coils from the wall and started to replace them with new coils. But the way the whole row was installed made no sense. I could think of a million better ways to do it.

I stood back. I rubbed my jaw and tried to imagine my uncle standing beside me, but I could picture only James.

He rubbed the stubble on his face and looked at the whole of the fabric wall, counted, considered. He held up one of the coils, rotating it in his hands to the left and then the right. Do you see it? he asked.

I looked again, and the right configuration began to form in my mind.

Do you? he asked again.

I set to work as the ache in my jaw began to radiate upward into my cheekbone, my ear, my eye. But even as the pain intensified my mind quickened with each coil snapped into place. Time began to move in a way it hadn't since I left the Gateway, with a sense of urgency. I wanted to figure this problem out, to understand it, to make the grow room better. My mind skipped ahead, from the step I was on to the next, and the next.

I took more pills, pulled more coils. Then when the sun began to recede on the horizon and make the ridges of silt outside sparkle, the greenhouse dimmed and the pain began to dim too. I had the thought that I should finish the job before the pain came back. My arms ached and my body itched with sweat, but I'd already completed the first wall and part of the second. So I turned on the lights and kept going.

When I finished it was early morning. The pain had disappeared. I hit the power button for the heating system and watched the soft glow of the coils move down and down the long room.

I was tired and hungry, but for the first time since I arrived I felt like talking. I felt like showing someone what I'd done. I tried to imagine my uncle standing at one end of the soybean room and nodding with approval, but I couldn't picture his face. I switched the system off and then on again, but I felt very little watching it; the thrill of what I'd done was gone.

The toothache came back—I knew it would—but instead of a pulsing ache it was a single searing knife point of pain. I stumbled back to the medical supplies and swallowed more pain pills and a muscle relaxer. They did nothing.

In one of the tool cabinets I found a pair of pliers, but I had no anesthetic. I thought of the medical bay at the Gateway— pictured myself lying on the table in the shadowy room, the single spotlight over my head. James's face appeared over my own; he smelled like salt and coffee. He held a syringe and his fingers were soft and warm against my smarting cheek. When he pushed the needle into my gum the pain emptied from my jaw like sand from a sieve.

In the mirror in the shower module my cheeks were white and my nose wet. My right eye seemed to bulge. I opened my mouth, held the pliers as firmly as I could, and clamped them around the molar. I tasted metal and vomit and pulled hard.

There was a sickening crunching sound; the room dimmed, went black—

I came to on the hard floor, my mouth full of blood and spit. My tongue found the tooth—it was still there.

I rolled over onto my stomach and crawled. The pain came in rolling waves now and the corridor seemed to tilt with it. Something was wrong with my eyes; the periphery of my vision kept going dark, like the burnt edge of a piece of paper that has gotten too close to the fire. I kept moving and dragged my body forward with only one thought in my mind—a memory of when my helmet got knocked off at the solar field. When I breathed the silt-filled air and all feeling in my head and jaw disappeared.

It took a long time, hours it seemed, but I reached the airlock and pulled myself inside. The wind was blowing hard and silt rapped at the porthole. I shut my eyes, pressed the button. The wind gusted and grains of silt hit my face like a thousand pinpricks. I forced myself to breathe in and my inhale was like an icy burn. I opened my mouth wide, pushed my tongue into the salty air. My lips went numb, my fingers too. Next my throat and tongue. The waves of pain in my tooth calmed, became ripples on the smoothest water. Then they became nothing at all.

My eyes went flat. My body seemed to disappear. Shapes came together in my mind. They formed something. What was it? A picture of Theresa and James, out in the silt. Theresa's long hair was loose in the wind, and James held on to her tightly, as if to keep her body from flying away.

Long enough. A voice was loud and insistent in my ear. My uncle's or James's. Or my own. Long enough, long enough.

My arm wouldn't move. I needed to hit the button to close the lock. In my mind I screamed at it to move. I dragged myself closer. I pulled myself up to the button and hit it with my head—

The door shut; the silt fell to the ground. I leaned against the wall and waited until feeling returned to my legs. Then I pulled myself to standing and felt my way back to the shower module, to the mirror. The pain in my jaw was there but far away, like a speck on the ground seen from a terrific height. I braced my hips against the sink, secured the pliers around my molar, and pulled. Nothing happened. I widened my feet; I felt the weight of gravity on my shoulders, like the weight of someone's hands. I imagined they were James's hands. He held me steady and I pulled again. Hard. There was a crunch and a suck and a pop, and tears streamed down my stinging cheeks. I held up the pliers and my molar was in them, flat and white on the top, long and pointed and bloody on the bottom.

I sat down on the rubber floor. Minutes passed. Feeling began to return to my face and hands. The shapes of the room got sharper. The square of the sink, the rectangle of plastic sheet that separated the showers. The caged light. The colors became more saturated. Gray and black and blue inside, and through the porthole, coral pink. Sensation returned to my eyelids and my lips and the inside of my nose.

The light changed. It was too bright, the outline of things too distinct. The floor was hard against my bottom, my tooth like a sharp rock in my palm. I wished someone was here, someone to help me up, to press a cold cloth to my cheek. I rubbed tears and snot and blood from my face, put my head in my hands, and pushed my tongue into the tender, pulpy spot where my tooth used to be.

Then I heard a voice, a human voice. Someone calling my name. I lifted my head. But it wasn't real. I was alone. I didn't want to be alone but I was.

The voice came again: June, June, June. Footsteps sounded in the corridor. People in suits crowded in the doorway. Amelia, Simon, and Rachel. They held their helmets in their hands and stared.

Were they real?

Rachel moved into the room, bent down beside me, and touched my shoulder. What happened?

Simon pushed in too.

I had to pull my tooth out, I said, and the words came out like a sob.

Amelia reached down with her good hand and pulled me up. She rubbed my head. Look at you. You're a mess.

I wiped my eyes. I'm okay.

Simon pulled me close and hugged me hard. You were right June. His eyes shined.

Inquiry made contact with NSP, Amelia said. They're alive.

All of them? I asked.

Yes, all of them. Simon let me go and started talking fast. Anu figured out how to rebuild the communications system. She sent a message—

Where's James? Amelia interrupted.

I shook my head.

You're supposed to be with him, she said. You're supposed to be working.

I was. We rebuilt the cell. But then it all went . . . bad.

So where is he?

I didn't answer her. I went to the sink and splashed water on my face and wiped the blood from my cheeks. I grabbed my suit from the corridor outside and pulled it on. We'll go find him.

48

The Gateway was an outline of gray in the pink haze. The wind battered the rover as I punched in the code to open the cargo bay door, but it didn't budge. Amelia parked and we put our helmets on and got out. My stomach dropped. Heaps of silt stood against the bay doors; it looked as if no one had opened them in weeks.

Let's try the exterior entry hatch. Simon's voice came through the radio in my helmet.

I led them around the perimeter of the station and the silt popped against our helmets. When we reached the spot where the hatch should be I paused and squinted through the silt. It's here. I felt along the wall. Somewhere. My glove found the hatch's groove. I brought my face close to it, dug silt out of the door's hinges. Then I grabbed its latch and pulled hard, and it swung open with a crunching thunk.

On the other side was complete darkness. We stepped inside. Rachel pressed the button to repressurize the lock. Through the porthole the corridor was an empty black and I felt a deep sense of unease. We took off our helmets, and our flashlights made four spots of light on the floor as we moved forward, through corridors that were like tunnels in the darkness. This route had become familiar over the weeks I'd lived here but now I became disoriented. Walls looked like doors, and doors like walls. In our bulky suits we elbowed one another and tripped on the step-ups and step-downs. The corridor we were following reached a dead end, and when we doubled back, nothing was where I thought it should be. The turn for the central module seemed to have disappeared.

Finally after going in what appeared to be the wrong direction we found it. I shined my flashlight into the galley and stepped inside. Everything was as it had been. Table, chairs. The coffee maker was in its spot, clean and empty. I opened cupboards; plates and bowls and silverware were where they always were.

We kept going. My bunk was also as I left it, and so were the equipment rooms. James's room was empty, the sheets stripped from the bed and the floor cleared of its papers and mugs. Back in the corridor Rachel and Simon went to check the other side of the station, and Amelia and I walked to the workshop, the last place I had seen James. It was completely clean. Empty of everything. The shattered fuel cell was gone from the floor, the table. The shelves were bare of tools. I scanned every surface, looked in drawers and cabinets and under the table. There was nothing. Not even a single loose screw.

I touched the metal worktable. It was clean and shining; even our fingerprints were wiped clean. The spot where James had stood in the rubble of the destroyed fuel cell was empty. I had thought he was so ugly in that moment, his legs wide, his arms crossed. But now I remembered his expression differently, more hurt than defiant. The trapped look of someone who couldn't stop himself from doing harm.

There's one more place to look, I said, and led Amelia to the south corridor, to the door, which was unlocked, and then to the short passageway to Theresa's room. The power was on here—light shined through the plastic that covered the door.

This room wasn't cleaned and stripped like the others. In the cabinet between the two portholes were Theresa's books. Her hairbrush still stood on the table beside the bed, her slippers on the floor nearby.

Amelia walked to the cabinet. This is Theresa's room, she said.

Yes.

I saw her, only once. She was so small. I couldn't believe how small—

She died, I said, and Amelia nodded.

I moved closer to the bed. The sheets were rumpled and twisted, as if someone had slept in them only a day or two ago, and there was a head-shaped indentation in the pillow. I leaned in. A few dark hairs lay curled on the pillowcase; I put my hand in the middle of the shallow hollow and imagined I felt the warmth of James's head there.

Simon and Rachel were at the airlock leading to the cargo bay. The other side of the station's got power, Simon said. But there's no one there.

We headed through the dark corridors to the access hatch and back to the rover. Then I stopped. Silt tapped at my helmet. I know where he is, I said, and my boots sank into pits and hollows as I made my way to the north side of the station. I slid around, held on to the exterior walls, kept going. The wind picked up and it pulled at my suit, buffeted my helmet. Amelia, Simon, and Rachel followed close behind. I rounded the cargo bay and the hangar containing *Endurance* came into view, bright against the pink sky.

I got closer and my heart beat thickly in my throat. The hangar's bay doors were open and *Endurance* stood inside. Massive and shining, lit from within.

The ground was softer here; the silt reached my knees and I had to pick my feet up high. All around were the shapes of silt-covered junk. One looked like a boat. Another like a steep staircase, and I remembered the night I ran away from James, the shapes I'd seen in the silt. I'd thought I was alone out there in the ridges of pink in my broken-down rover. But I hadn't been. Not really. James had been with me all along. Other people were pale shapes compared to him. He was hot, and they were cold. He was sweet and sharp; everyone else was like sand.

I reached the entrance to the hangar. A mobile habitation

unit stood at the explorer's port side and I moved toward its air-lock. My breath was loud inside my helmet as I grabbed the latch, turned it, stepped inside. Amelia and Simon were behind me, but I closed the lock, hit the button to pressurize it. Numbers slowly counted down on a monitor attached to the wall. 10, 9, 8, 7, 6, 5, 4, 3, 2, 1—

I took off my helmet and gloves, pushed the interior lock open. I went through the habitation unit and into the explorer. Inside, the dimensions were familiar because they were the same as *Inquiry*'s, but here the walls were stripped down to almost nothing. Shiny cabinets yawned open and empty; wires hung loose from the ceiling and bits of insulation lay strewn on the floor like gray snow. A burnt plastic smell hung in the air.

At the very end of the cabin a figure was bent over an open panel. James. I said his name and he turned. A bandage criss-crossed his face and covered one eye.

June, he said, and his hoarse voice made my stomach turn over.

I set my helmet and gloves on the floor, moved closer. He was thinner and his patchy beard longer. A mottled red burn marked his right hand.

What happened? I asked.

Got electrocuted.

Can you see?

Out of one eye.

It was hard to look at him. His face was as sharp as it had been, but the hollow of his injured eye was deeply bruised and spidery blood vessels crawled down his cheek. I bent down on one knee, bulky in my suit, and reached to hover my hand over the soft bandage on his eye, but he turned his face away.

I sat back on my heels. I have to tell you something, I said.

His shoulders bent. I know. She's dead.

The ventilation system clicked on and humming air blew against my cheeks. The smell of burnt plastic dissipated. I looked around more thoroughly. A few feet away the control panel appeared to be reconfigured and newly wired, and below it some of the stripped fuselage had been replaced with new panels.

One of the newly installed panels was open, revealing a single fuel cell stack. Our cell, as it had been before James destroyed it.

You put it back together, I said.

I tried.

The sound of the airlock came from behind me. Amelia, Simon, and Rachel stepped into the cabin and I stood up.

They took off their helmets and gloves. James, Amelia said. Damn. Here you are.

He squinted at them. Both of you, he said grimly. Like some kind of reunion.

Simon shook silt from his suit. Have you told him?

Inquiry contacted NSP, I said to James. They're alive.

His face paled.

Are you all right? Rachel asked, and she put her hand to her own eye.

I'm fine, James said with effort.

Is the cell ready? Simon asked him. Can it be done?

The vents turned over and hummed louder. I don't know, James said.

Simon gestured at the stripped panels and loose wires and his voice rose. If you didn't think it could be done, what are you doing out here?

Simon— Amelia said.

I've spent six years trying to figure out what went wrong, James said. What have you been doing?

It was always you and Theresa and Peter, Simon said. Your ideas. You didn't want to listen to anyone else—

I tried to stop that mission, James said. Remember?

I did too, Simon said.

You didn't try hard enough, James said. That's the point.

Simon ran a hand over his buzzed head. I thought Anu could handle it.

Amelia said, I did too—

You were both right, I interrupted. The fuel cells failed, but Anu kept her crew alive.

The vents switched off and we were all quiet for a minute.

The only thing that matters is whether the cell is ready, Amelia said finally. Whether it will keep us alive.

James's face was unreadable, so I spoke for both of us. It will be.

49

James and I stood across from each other at the table in the mobile habitation unit. Or, I stood and he leaned. His dark curls fell across his face, and the bandage crisscrossing his eye glowed bright white under the lights. A completed cell stack, removed from the *Endurance* explorer, lay on the table between us, its metal casing flat and shining.

You decided on a closed system, I said.

You weren't here to argue the other way.

I felt a surge of irritation and let it pass. Okay.

You disagree.

I shook my head. I don't know which way is right, not for sure. So we'll pick one and go with it.

He blinked his good eye. Really—

I don't want to waste time talking about it. It's done. Let's move forward.

All right. He got some paper from a cabinet and we made a list of everything that needed to be done, divided the tasks evenly between us, and set to work.

The interior of the mobile habitation unit was loud and its lights glaring in contrast to the quiet and dimly lit workshop at the Gateway. The space was tight, the table small. All the tools and 3D printers and supplies were crammed onto one shelf. We began our individual tasks and didn't talk. It was strange not to talk. My mind churned with thoughts and ideas and questions but I held back, kept silent. I was aware of the billowing whir from the vents and the clicking hiss from the oxygenator. I was aware of his body near mine, his shoulders tense and his movements awkward. He listed to one side in his seat as he divided a tangle of cables; he squinted and blinked his good eye. When he got up he walked at a diagonal and dropped tools and bumped into things in the narrow space. Sometimes he cursed under his breath.

When he began to count and stack circuit boards, some of them needed new screws, and the hardware was tiny and the screwdriver clumsy in his hands. It was too hard to watch—I got up and started typing specifications into one of the printers. Behind me a screw dropped to the table with a small snap. Then another. *Snap. Snap. Snap.* There was a low growl and the sound of his chair skidding on the floor.

He had pushed himself up from the table and the screwdriver was clenched in his fist. He pulled his arm back like he was going to throw it, but then he let his arm fall. He sat down and laid his hands in his lap.

I'll help you, I said.

I leaned over him, took the screwdriver from his hand, and installed the four tiny screws. His hair was longer—curls brushed the collar of his shirt—and his face thinner, but he smelled exactly the same.

I shouldn't have done it, he said and his hands made a tight ball in his lap.

Pieces of his hair were snagged in the bandage that crisscrossed his eye and I felt a strong impulse to reach over and brush them away.

But you shouldn't have left, he went on, his voice soft and strangled. Do you know what it was like when you were gone?

When Theresa was gone you mean.

He turned in his seat and we were eye to eye. No. You.

You destroyed the cell because of her.

He was quiet for a minute. She said it was hubris. That we weren't meant to be here. Maybe we're not.

I thought of Earth and the people I'd left behind there. My

aunt sitting in her bedroom surrounded by soft and beautiful things. Lion diving into one of the neutral buoyancy tanks in his wet suit, falling fast, surrounded by shining bubbles. Carla and Nico standing together inside a cold hangar, preparing a rocket for a test launch, their breath making clouds in the air.

Just because Theresa didn't belong here doesn't mean we don't. I picked up the next board in the pile. You sort, I'll tighten, I said, and pulled my seat close to his.

50

At the Gateway we took off our suits just inside the cargo bay airlock and I recalled the first time I saw James in this corridor, a dark shape behind a bright light. His broad chest and wild hair. Now his suit bagged around his thin frame. His face was gray with exhaustion, his T-shirt stained with sweat. He limped toward his room and I wanted to follow, to help him change his clothes and rebandage his eye. I wanted to help him into bed. But he gave no indication he wanted company; he moved slowly down the dim corridor and disappeared into the darkness.

In the galley I made coffee and ate a bowl of oatmeal. Then I took my mug and went looking for Amelia in the control room; only Simon was there, typing fast on a computer. I guessed he was writing to Anu so I left him alone. The corridors were familiar again. The runner lights glowed blue at my feet. The temperature fluctuated as I walked through them, from cold to warm to cold. I opened doors to bunks. Amelia and Rachel were in the room opposite to my own. Amelia lay on top of the covers still in her jumpsuit, her good hand hanging off the side of the bed and her prosthetic hugged to her chest. She was already asleep and snoring. Rachel was curled next to her, wrapped in a blanket, her hair spread across the pillow.

I should have been tired but I wasn't. In my bunk my old locker was still under the bed. I rummaged through it for a change of clothes, grabbed a shirt and tights and a pair of wool socks. I shook out my old Candidate Group sweatshirt and a spray of papers fell to the floor—my uncle's fuel cell schematics.

I pulled the sweatshirt over my head and spread the schematics out on the bed. They were curled at the edges and smelled of dust and, ever so faintly, of pen ink. Paging through them, as I had done as a child, I watched the evolution of the cell from inception to near completion. I was taken again by the brilliance and daring of its design. The notes in the margins were faded slightly but still legible—five scripts belonging to my uncle, James, Theresa, Amelia, and Simon.

But when I began reading I saw something I hadn't recognized before, a kind of arrogance in their exchange. I paged ahead and it seemed to me that the people who wrote these words were playing at something. Their dialogue read like a game, but the scenarios they described were real. And the horror the *Inquiry* crew would face if any of these things happened to them was real also. Simon was the only one who seemed to fully grasp how multiple and inscrutable the dangers could be—I could tell because he was the only one of the five who sounded scared.

I got to the part where James and Theresa argued about the benefits of open versus closed stacks. Theresa wanted an open modular casing, James a closed one.

Lose less power this way, he wrote next to a drawing of the proposed case.

What if something goes wrong? Much harder to fix, Theresa answered.

Do you want someone messing with what we've built? he asked.

Simon's neat print joined the other two. Something always goes wrong.

This was where my twelve-year-old handwriting joined theirs. I read my responses, my clumsy attempts to describe what was in my mind. Some of it was intelligible; a lot of it wasn't, and I felt an overwhelming urge to get a pen and correct what I'd written. To answer my uncle's questions again and to make sense of what had only partly made sense before.

When I looked up James stood in the doorway. He appeared to

have slept, although it couldn't have been for more than an hour or two. His hair was flat on one side, and a slight indentation lined his left cheek, below the bandage on his eye.

What are you reading? he asked.

I gathered the papers into a pile. The original schematics for my uncle's cell.

He came closer, his body tilting slightly to the left, and picked up the top page. He squinted at it and smiled. He paged forward and then back and began reading. We thought we knew it all.

It was a revolutionary design, I said.

With a fatal flaw.

It didn't have to be fatal.

He didn't answer; he was engrossed in a particular page. There's something here I don't remember, he said. This is your handwriting. Or very like it.

It is mine.

This is where we argue about open versus closed stacks, he said. Theresa's argument is convincing. He rubbed his good eye. But my case for a closed system is strong too. He pointed to the middle of the page. Here's where I bring her over to my side. He paused for a second, reading.

But I didn't convince you, he said. You disagree. You say Theresa and Simon are right, and you explain why.

Yes.

When did you write this?

I was twelve.

There was a curious expression on his face. He bent his head to the page again. You say, We're humans, not machines. We have to adapt ourselves to space. Not it to us.

That part I wrote just now.

He set the page down. I was wrong, he said. Theresa and Simon were right. You were right—

No. We've decided. We're sticking with closed stacks.

It's just the casing. He began moving to the door. We can change it—

You were adamantly against this, I said. And you convinced me. We give up power in an open system. We give up control—

I'm going to start now.

Stop, I said. A wave of exhaustion moved through my body, and a dull ache began to radiate at the back of my jaw, where my molar used to be. You're injured. You need rest. So do I.

I gathered the schematics into a pile and set them on the floor.

We can make the changes, I said. I stood up and pulled him to the bed. In the morning.

His shoulders loosened.

I took the blanket from the bottom of the bed—it smelled of wool and salt. He laid his head down on the pillow, and I did too, and I drew the blanket around us both.

51

Every day in the workshop James and I sat close and worked and talked, and even laughed. He was more forthcoming than he'd ever been about lots of things. My uncle—what he was like as a teacher and a mentor. His training after Peter Reed. Even Theresa and what the Gateway was like when they first came here to work on the cell. One day we were easy with each other like this all afternoon, but as the sun went down and the workshop filled with a rosy glow, he turned quiet and taciturn. He finished what he was doing and got up from the table and moved at a slight tilt to the door.

I'm going to bed, he said, and waited in the doorway.

I put away what I was working on. Then I looped my arm through his. You don't really want to be alone.

No, he said. I don't.

Every minute I wasn't working with James I spent in the station's gym. My first morning the equipment was covered in dust and I started by wiping everything down, all the machines and weights and mats, and the chlorine smell of the cleaner filled the room. Simon came in, and Rachel too. Eventually Amelia showed up also, and we made a circuit, together, of all the machines.

We went on like this for a week, then two. Supplies arrived, and people. NSP officials took over and the station filled up with workers. In the control room a team of engineers upgraded all the equipment and ran launch sequences and communications models. In consultation with Simon and Amelia, a group of specialists from Earth worked to finish rehabbing *Endurance* and to outfit it for its mission.

Simon and I started working out twice a day, and most of the time Amelia and Rachel joined us. We upped the weight on the machines and added a predawn run in our suits up and down the rocky hills outside. I got stronger; I gained power in my legs and back. I watched my body change in the mirror, as I had at the agricultural outpost. My cheeks grew rounder; my stance was straighter and my shoulders wider.

But these changes made James's condition all the more conspicuous. He was getting better, but slowly. Very slowly. He still limped. His eye was healing—the bandage was now just a single strip of gauze—but his eyesight was largely unchanged.

It was most striking when we were all together in the galley. It didn't happen that often, but every few days the whole group would end up in the same room, eating or drinking coffee under the dusty yellow lights. One day I walked into the room and everyone was sitting at the table. James, Amelia, and Simon were talking and laughing about a drill they'd done in Candidate Group. They'd had to crawl in their suits through a pitch-black module full of obstacles to find and fix an unidentified gas leak, and they'd failed three times. When they finally completed the challenge successfully their drill supervisor had chewed them out for how long it took them. It was only later they'd found out that no team had ever completed the drill successfully, even with unlimited tries.

I made myself coffee and stood at the counter. I had my mission binder with me and I half read, half listened. After a few minutes James stood up. You should go through the launch sequences, he said.

I sat and led the group through the plans in my binder and he made more coffee. After a while he began to shift his weight on his feet and brought two fingers to his eye. Amelia was talking; she was going through the plan for capture when *Endurance* reached *Inquiry*. But James saw me watching him. He let his hand drop from his eye, and he nodded as if to say, I'm okay. I stood up so he could sit back down at the table but he stayed where he was.

At night he was restless in the bed next to me, and sometimes I got up—afraid I was disturbing his sleep—and made my way through the blue-tinted corridors to my own bunk.

One early morning when I slept alone in my bunk, I woke to see him sitting at the foot of the bed. I sat up. The room was still dark; silt pattered at the porthole. What's wrong?

Everything's going well, he said. *Endurance* will be ready sooner than we thought.

I wrapped my arms around him. You'll be ready too.

He touched his head to mine and the wild scent of his skin and hair mixed with the antiseptic smell of his dressed eye. You know I can't go, he said.

You can.

He took my face in his hands and looked at me. June.

I'm not leaving on a two-year mission without you, I said and my voice cracked.

His fingers were warm and firm against my cheeks. Let's say things we already know. The silt tapped harder outside. I'm not going. But you are.

52

Time sped up and I tried to slow it down. In my mind I made bargains with it, asked it, cajoled it. But it didn't stop moving forward. I paid attention to the light outside the porthole, how it changed over the course of each day. Noticed how the woolly light in the morning turned brilliant at midday, attended to the moment when the jewel colors of twilight transformed into the murky, silt-covered shadows of night. I paid attention to my body, its weight and strength, its aches and pains, its hunger, thirst, and fatigue. I noticed my own shifting moods, how I felt different from one day to the next and from morning to afternoon to night.

About one thing I felt the same any time of day—the fuel cell. It was complete; a team of engineers took over to install the stacks inside *Endurance.* But a single cell still sat in the workshop— the prototype that had been built by James and me, destroyed, put back together by James, and then rebuilt again.

The day before the launch I stood at the table in the workshop. The cell's open casing gleamed; its red and white connectors were vivid in the low light. I heard my uncle's voice in my head: What does it do? I laid my hands on top of it, and in my mind I made it work. I slowed time down and watched its chemical reactions and electrical connections in slow motion; I sped time up and watched the effects of heat and cold and air pressure and vibration over the course of days, months, and years.

It wasn't going to degrade with vibration like the original fuel cell had—the flexible internal components James and I had developed had solved that problem. There was always the possibility of factors we hadn't accounted for, a difficulty we hadn't foreseen. But the stacks that housed the cells were open and it would be possible for my crew to respond to unforeseen challenges, to adapt or modify the cell en route if we had to.

I sat there for a while, thinking, pushing my mind forward and backward in time, listening to the tap of silt outside and the click of the 3D printers inside. Then I walked to the airlock leading to the cargo bay and pulled on a suit. At the launch pad workers in suits gathered around the exterior of *Endurance* and its rocket, but the cabin was empty. The space was narrower now that it was packed with equipment but everything in it gleamed. I ran my hand over the control panel and remembered when my uncle had taken all of us—my aunt and cousin and me—to see *Inquiry* when it was being built. He went over the whole explorer with us, explaining every design choice and specification. John was quickly bored and went to go find the vending machine outside my uncle's lab, and when we went into the cabin my aunt sat in one of the jump seats and only half attended to what my uncle said.

I remember the air smelled strongly of rubber sealant and the vents hummed softly. I moved around the cabin slowly and quietly. When my uncle opened up panels to show me the equipment inside, I pushed in close. I touched everything. I tried to memorize every detail.

On the morning of the launch I got up from the warmth of James's bed and the air was cool against my bare skin. The room was filled with a soft gloom and the smell of salt and wool and sleep. I opened the airlock and then stood in the doorway looking at James. He was curled on his side with the covers wrapped around him, his hair a dark tangle on the pillow. His face was boyish, his forehead smooth and his cheeks pink. I tried to memorize the shapes of him. The hump of his back under the blanket, the straight lines of his chin and forehead and hands, and the circles of his hair.

I showered, dressed in my mission jumpsuit, and walked slowly back to my bunk. I felt the minutes before the launch fall away like snow, or silt. I slowed my steps even more because when I reached my bunk it would be time to go. Inside the room my suit was laid out on the bed, bright white against the gray blanket. Its patches were straight and its fabric smooth. James stood at the porthole looking at the growing pink light of dawn.

I checked your seals, he said.

He lifted the suit up and I stepped into it backward, and he held the neck ring straight so I wouldn't scrape my face when I pushed my head through. Next he worked his hands into the sleeves of the suit to pull my arms out and tugged my body left and right as he secured the fabric tight across my stomach and chest, tying the closures at my ankles, elbows, and wrists.

He took his hands away and I put on my gloves, picked up my helmet. Inside my suit there seemed a great barrier between me and the room and the ordinary things in it. The uneven stack of books and papers on the floor near my feet, the soft covers on the bed, the round porthole with silt swirling outside it.

Then his hands were back, flat and firm and still on my shoulders. I flexed my fingers in my gloves. I put my helmet on, locked it, and listened to the pop and suck of its seal.

53

At minus sixty-five minutes I strap myself into my seat. I begin my prelaunch checklist and call off tasks as I complete them to Amelia and Simon and Rachel, who are close enough to touch. Their bodies are large in their suits, their heads small. The fuel and oxidizer turbo pumps begin to whine as I finish my list. There is a strong smell of rocket fuel, mixed with rubber sealant and recycled air. Minus five minutes is announced and I check my helmet's seal. At one minute to launch the whine grows; I feel a shuddering vibration through my chest and jaw.

A roar comes from below us and the rocket sways. My breath is hot and loud inside my helmet but my hands are steady as I flip a switch to check the flow of oxygen. The rocket supports fall away and the roar grows; a second passes, two seconds, and then—we leap into the air. My body slams against my seat; my visor fogs. The second-stage rockets fire and my chest presses hard against my restraints. We separate from the rocket, and as it falls away its reflection passes across my crew's visors, briefly changing them from black to white. The air turns silent, cool. My body lightens in my seat, and things float by: dust, bits of fabric, small bolts.

The communications feed crackles and fizzes and I wait for a human voice on the other end of the line. Outside the porthole the Pink Planet isn't visible; there is only an expanse of deep black and it seems to unfold, and unfold, dark and infinite. More dust floats by, hundreds of white pinpricks that match the explosion of stars outside.

The feed crackles on and on.

And on and on.

Then—a voice in my ear, soft and low, slightly tinny. It's James's voice; he is saying my name, June. With the sound the unfolding expanse collapses. Now it's no more than the width of a thread. I say his name too and undo my restraints and let myself float free.

ACKNOWLEDGMENTS

Books have no life without readers and I'm deeply grateful for the incredible early readers of this novel: My agent Brettne Bloom, who knows how I feel about her, and my wonderful editor Andrea Walker. I am blessed with their intelligence and insight.

Thank you also to my longtime writing partners, Lindsey Lee Johnson, Kevinne Moran, and Rita Michelle Pogue. Nine years running, they are always right. Thanks to Danya Bush, who read more permutations of June and James than anyone else. And to my dad David Johnson, who read early drafts and lent his sharp editorial eye.

In preparation to write this novel I read a lot about living in space and am particularly indebted to two memoirs: *Diary of a Cosmonaut: 211 Days in Space* by Valentin Lebedev and *Endurance: My Year in Space, A Lifetime of Discovery* by Scott Kelly. I could not have written this book without Space Camp and the U.S. Space and Rocket Center, where I gained hands-on experience with the equipment and technology I describe in this book. A special thank you to Erin "Clover" Shay and the members of Pioneer Team.

Thank you also to: Everyone at Random House, most especially Emma Caruso, who is always behind the scenes getting things done. Everyone at Transworld, including my U.K. editor Jane Lawson and Alice Youell. Everyone at The Book Group, with extra gratitude to Hallie Schaeffer, who was a perceptive early reader. Jenny Meyer and Heidi Gall at Jenny Meyer Literary. Jason Richman and Nora Henrie at United Talent Agency.

Corporeal Writing, Lidia Yuknavitch, and Domi Shoemaker. Daniel Torday, Courtney Sullivan, Eowyn Ivey, and Danya Kukafka.

Grass Roots Books and Music, The Book Bin, and the Corvallis Public Library. Everyone at Tried and True Coffee.

Perpetual gratitude to:

My husband, Kevin Day, who always supports me, and who helped me keep writing even in the midst of a pandemic. My children, Bennett and Sullivan. Our talented caregiver Camille Carrington. And of course my amazing mom, Jean Johnson.

ABOUT THE AUTHOR

KATE HOPE DAY is the author of *If, Then*. She holds a BA from Bryn Mawr College and a PhD in English from the University of Pittsburgh. She was an associate producer at HBO. She lives in Oregon with her husband and their two children.

katehopeday.com
Facebook.com/katehopeday
Twitter: @katehopeday

ABOUT THE TYPE

This book was set in Photina, a typeface designed by José Mendoza in 1971. It is a very elegant design with high legibility, and its close character fit has made it a popular choice for use in quality magazines and art gallery publications.